Also by Kris Tualla:

Loving the Norseman
Loving the Knight
In the Norseman's House

A Nordic Knight in Henry's Court
A Nordic Knight of the Golden Fleece
A Nordic Knight and His Spanish Wife

A Discreet Gentleman of Discovery
A Discreet Gentleman of Matrimony
A Discreet Gentleman of Consequence
A Discreet Gentleman of Intrigue
A Discreet Gentleman of Mystery

Leaving Norway
Finding Sovereignty
Kirsten's Journal

A Woman of Choice
A Prince of Norway
A Matter of Principle

An Unexpected Viking
A Restored Viking
A Modern Viking

*****

A Primer for Beginning Authors
Becoming an Authorpreneur

A Restored

VIKING

Kris Tualla

A Restored Viking is a work of fiction. Names, characters, places and incidents are products of the author's imagination or are used fictitiously and are not to be construed as real. Any resemblance to actual events, locales, organizations, or persons, living or dead, is entirely coincidental.

Published in the United States of America.

© 2015 by Kris Tualla

ISBN-13: 978-1517770242
ISBN-10: 1517770246

Dedication

Chapter One

Even though Hollis McKenna's abduction only lasted three hours, and took place more than a week ago, she was still having nightmares.

"Give yourself a break, Hollis," Stevie chided. "That was a truly terrifying experience."

The petite museum Registrar who worked side-by-side with Hollis cataloging the huge Kensington bequest sipped coffee from an over-sized mug, her concerned gaze pinning Hollis's.

"I just wish I knew what was happening with Everett." Hollis felt a too-familiar shiver of fear skate up her spine. "I won't feel safe until he's locked up."

"George is on it. He'll let us know as soon as the judge makes a decision on the plea agreement."

Stevie's suitor George was a God-send. Hollis met him first through an online dating site, but when no chemistry sparked between them she gave Stevie permission to pursue the mild-mannered attorney. Now the two were inseparable.

Hollis turned her back on her friend, both to pour coffee and look at Sveyn Hansen. The Viking ghost gave her a tender smile.

No, not a ghost. *An apparition.* The man was caught between

*Generally great
doing great
recap*

life and death. Ghosts were dead people, and Sveyn hadn't died.

His obviously un-solid presence was the only thing keeping her sane at this time.

Yes, it was an oxymoron.

Deal with it.

Her drug-facilitated abduction would have ended much more critically if Sveyn hadn't reacted as violently as he did to her predicament.

Because he didn't have a physical body, he couldn't stop Everett Sage from duct-taping her within an inch of her life and locking her in the museum's huge storage room. The rage and frustration he expressed, however, proved forceful enough to cross into the three-dimensional world and set off the motion detectors.

He saved her before she was permanently injured.

Physically, at least.

Hollis lifted her steaming cup and turned around to face Stevie again. "Let me know as soon as you hear something."

"I will." Stevie followed her from the employee break room. "Do you need help with the descriptions?"

"No, I'm almost finished. " Hollis dragged one hand through her unruly curls. "We can start ordering the plaques by the end of the day."

"That's good. The opening of the Kensington wing is only three weeks away."

"Don't remind me." *Please.* Hollis ducked into her office.

When long-time Tempe resident Ezra Kensington the Fifth died unmarried and with no progeny at the age of one-hundred-and-five, he willed a house packed with his life's acquisitions to the museum.

Book
do

Though the obsessive-compulsive hoarder's collection was atypical of the disorder and actually contained numerous museum-worthy artifacts, they were European and American in origin. The Arizona History and Cultural Center's mission statement limited its displayed artifacts to historical items from the territory.

However, the mission statement was adapted to state

including significant international contributions from long-time Arizona residents' private collections—because Ezra also willed over twelve million dollars to the museum in order to build a wing for his treasures.

Hollis was hired eight months ago as a temporary Lead Collector to dig through the hoard and categorize what she found.

Her office phone's speaker beeped. "Hollis, are you there?"

"Yep."

"Come see me when you have a minute."

"I can come now."

Hollis left her office and walked down the hallway of the museum's administrative area to Miranda's office. The curator—and her boss—was the opposite of petite blonde Stevie. The attractive brunette was at least five-foot-eleven.

"I just got a call from Mr. Benton." Miranda waved at the chair in front of her. "Have a seat."

As much as she respected the General Manager of the museum, Hollis learned quickly that Benton was a media whore.

"What now?" she asked, lowering herself into the chair and steeling herself for the newest onslaught.

"First of all," Miranda grinned. "He called to tell me that, as part of the plea agreement with Dr. Sage, the museum will demand his half of the Blessing of the Gods, so that it can be displayed along with Ezra Kensington's half."

"NO!" The word burst from Sveyn as powerfully as if her constant apparition had breath. He moved into her line of sight. "Hollis, tell her no!"

Miranda's brow twitched. "What's the Norse name for it?"

"*Velsignelse av Gudene.*"

Hollis only knew how to pronounce the name because Sveyn told her. She shot him a warning glance. "I think that's awesome. And terrifying."

"Terrifying?" Miranda chuckled. "Don't tell me you believe that the reunited halves of the icon really *can* make the owner immortal."

"No, I don't." Hollis sighed and wagged her head. "But look

at Sage: the crazies in this world do. Or they will, once they hear about it."

"Hollis, I beg you. Do not agree to this…" Sveyn growled.

Miranda leaned back in her office chair. "What do you suggest?"

Hollis had actually thought about this scenario. Once the other half of Ezra's icon was found, she knew Mr. Benton wouldn't rest until he acquired it.

"I think we put them in the same bullet-proof display case, side-by-side in the direction they are intended to fit together, but not locked in place."

Sveyn glared at her. "You are playing with fire."

Hollis ignored him. "And I'm serious about the bullet-proof part," she continued. "Otherwise we are just asking for trouble to walk in over and over again and try to take it."

Miranda made a conciliatory gesture. "I agree. And I'll tell Mr. Benton the same thing. After what happened to you, I think he'll go along with that plan."

"Good. Thank you." Hollis laced her fingers together. "And what's the second thing?"

Miranda's expression morphed into an odd combination of delight and apology. "The YouTube video has over eight million views."

"Ugh!" Hollis slapped her hands over her face. "Well that's just crap-tastically crap-alicious."

"You have to admit that the images of whatever was locked in the room with you are intriguing."

"And *you* have to admit that Benton is a media whore."

The museum's general manager had ordered the museum's tech guys to splice together the thermal imaging video before the pitch black storeroom's alarm went off with the security camera tape after the lights came on. Sveyn somehow appeared on both, first as a green shimmer, and then as a brief murky smudge.

Hollis uncovered her face and groaned. "He must be absolutely thrilled."

"He is."

Hollis gave her boss a wary look. "And how does this affect

me?"

"We are fielding dozens of calls a day from mediums, ghost busters, and priests who want to exorcise the storage area. All of them are asking for access." Miranda paused.

Hollis tensed.

Her boss continued tentatively, "Access to the storage area… and to you."

"Tell them no!" Hollis blurted. "If we are expected to have the Kensington display ready for the wing's opening on December first, I can't waste my time talking to whack jobs."

"Mr. Benton doesn't consider the guys from *Ghost Myths, Inc.* to be whack jobs."

"The cable show?" This was getting worse—and fast. "What do they want? Please don't say…"

Miranda eyebrows disappeared in her bangs, and her mouth got very tiny.

Hollis scowled at Sveyn. "Why me?"

"Because you have a guardian angel. You admitted it. In front of witnesses." Miranda looked to her right, following the direction of Hollis's gaze. "Are you looking at him now?"

Hollis jerked her regard back to her boss. "What?"

"You do that a lot. Look to the side like someone's there." Miranda stretched her arm out in Sveyn's direction.

He stepped out of the way. "Just in case."

"No. It's just a habit. Helps me think." Hollis smacked her hands on Miranda's desktop to reclaim the curator's attention. "When, where, and how long?"

"I don't know yet."

"Is it just the TV show?"

Miranda winced. "Probably not. He did mention ghost-hunting overnights…"

"With *me?*"

Miranda made that high-brow tiny-mouth face again.

"Aarrgghhh." Hollis stood and pointed at her beloved boss. "I'm going to my office now to do my real job. Any assignments outside of my contract will require additional compensation. Let Benton think on *that*."

he spun and stalked toward the open door.

"What if he fires you?" Miranda called after her.

"Fine. Let him."

Stevie was in the hallway, unabashedly listening. "He won't you know."

"I know." Hollis continued her march toward her office. "But if I'm supposed to act the trained monkey, I better be very well paid for it."

*****

Hollis dropped the empty wine bottle in the recycle bin and carried the full glass of iced Chardonnay to her living room couch where Sveyn sat, watching a police drama.

"I don't know what to expect when these paranormal specialists start showing up." Hollis sat beside the Viking and tucked her legs under her. "Do you?"

Sveyn pulled his attention from the screen. "Do I what, precisely?"

"Know what to expect." She sipped her wine. When he frowned his confusion and didn't answer her, Hollis restated her question. "In any of your manifestations, did you encounter spiritualists who could see you?"

Sveyn's blue eyes narrowed. "No. None that I am aware of."

"Really?" Hollis found that highly unlikely. "So in your twenty-two previous manifestations, going all the way back to ten-seventy when you became like you are, no one has ever tried to prove you exist? Or tried to get rid of you?"

Sveyn laughed. "Tried to be rid of me? Oh, yes. Six priests have exorcised me."

"Did it work?"

He leaned closer. "I am not a demon, Hollis. You do know this."

She did. "But could they feel your presence?"

Sveyn still looked amused. "Not if I had to judge that by the direction they splashed the holy water."

Hollis took another sip of wine, pondering his answers. She

hadn't thought about it before, but with all the mediums and ghost hunters and other people who claim to be able to commune with the dead, why had none of his other twenty-two 'manifestees' ever sought them out?

"What are you brooding on so heavily, Hollis?"

She looked up into his eyes. "I'm just surprised, I guess."

"Surprised?" Sveyn repositioned himself on the couch so he faced her. "You have asked me four different questions, Hollis. You asked first if I knew what to expect with these people who are contacting the museum. I do not. I have no experience with this."

Another swallow of Chardonnay gave her a moment to think. "And then *you* said that no one has been able to see you, other that the men you manifested to."

"That is correct."

"And they tried to force you away by exorcizing you, which was obviously futile." Hollis tilted her head. "What was the last question?"

"Has anyone tried to prove my existence." The amusement left his expression. "I did tell you that some have spoken of my presence, and that got them into very bad situations."

"Yes, you did."

Hollis knew that the passing centuries hadn't changed things much. If she confessed that she had an apparition tethered to her twenty-four-seven, her friends would definitely urge her to seek professional help. And there was no guarantee that she wouldn't be locked up against her will for observation, even today.

"That's what these people who're asking to come to the museum are going to try to do, I think," she said. "Prove that you exist."

Sveyn folded his arms over his chest. The linen of his shirt sleeves was pulled tight by his medieval-life-honed muscles. Hollis wondered if the tight leather pants and laced leather vest were comfortable for him—back when he could actually feel the physical world. The fur wrapped boots obviously made sense in Norway, and luckily for him he was unable to feel the heat of the Phoenix desert while wearing them here and now.

"Will these people be in danger for doing so?" he asked.

"No. Most people think they're weird, but sane." She shrugged. "Somehow, it's more acceptable to go looking for someone else's ghosts, than to claim you are talking to your own."

Sveyn snorted. "That does not make sense."

"No, it doesn't." Hollis drained her wineglass, stood, and headed for the kitchen. "It's time for bed."

Sveyn pointed at the television. "Will you change to the history channel and turn off the sound?"

Hollis turned around and looked at him. "Why?"

Sveyn stood as well, his six-and-a-half feet towering over her. "It is time, Hollis. You do not need me to lie beside you while you sleep. You are safe here."

Hollis fought her rising panic and tried to think of a rebuttal that made more sense than Sveyn's words. Yes, the abduction was ten days past. Yes, Sage was in jail. Yes, she was safe behind a locked steel door.

Sveyn closed the distance between them. "I will look out for you, as I always do, and awaken you if any disturbances arise."

Hollis nodded reluctantly, and set the glass on the dining table. "All right."

She walked back to the living room with him following her and grabbed the remote. "You said history channel?"

She punched in the number, and hit mute. Sveyn, who never slept in his state of being, would be entertained through the night by reading the captions while he watched the silent screen.

"Thank you, Hollis." The Viking laid his palm beside her cheek, and Hollis felt the familiar electric tingle against her skin. "Sleep well, my love."

Chapter Two

Tuesday
November 10

Hollis awoke several times that night, in spite of the hefty dose of chilled Chard. Each time, the flickering blue glow from the hallway comforted her. Her own personal Viking guard was at his post, ready to alert her if anything, or anyone, threatened.

Consequently, she was a little groggy when her alarm went off, and for a minute she considered calling in sick. But that would only push back the workload that was already piled high, and now complicated by the flood of media attention which the security video was generating.

She threw off her covers, deciding in a rebellious moment not to make her bed, and went into the bathroom.

"Good morning, Hollis."

Sveyn's deep voice washed over her like a warm wave. She did feel so much better with him beside her.

She smiled at his reflection in her mirror while she brushed her unruly curls. "Good morning. Anything good on television last night?"

He shrugged. "I do enjoy the series about odd museum items, for obvious reasons. But I missed some of the stories because I was watching you sleep."

"You were?" The hand holding the hairbrush lowered. "Why?"

The Viking's expression was tender in the reflection. "If your sleep was fitful, I would have laid beside you and comforted you with words."

Hollis turned around to face him. "I did wake up a lot."

He looked down at her, his long, dark-blond hair brushing his scruff-bearded cheeks. "But you went back to sleep each time. I made certain of that."

Hollis felt like her heart could burst—not only with love for Sveyn, but with soul-searing grief that he was only an apparition and not a fully-fleshed man.

"What am I going to do with you?" she lamented.

She turned around again, away from those intense blue eyes, and resumed brushing her hair. "The day you leave me, and manifest forward to some other time and some other person, I will be a total wreck. You know that don't you."

He looked sad. "As will I, Hollis."

A thought occurred to her, and she pointed the hairbrush at the mirror. "You could manifest to someone else while I'm still alive, though, couldn't you?"

Sveyn recoiled a little. "How long do people live in this time?"

"My life expectancy is at least ninety years. And I'm only thirty." She whirled to face him again. "If you jumped ahead anything less than sixty years, I might catch up with you."

"Ninety years?" Sveyn's tone was incredulous. "This does present a possibility that has never existed before."

"Would I still be able to see you?"

Sveyn spread his hands to the side. "I cannot answer that. I would think that yes, you would. And of course I could see you. But there is no way to know this."

"Well, I am going to say yes." Hollis put her hairbrush away and grabbed her toothbrush. "On the day that you disappear, I

will console myself with the belief that I *will* see
before I die."

"This conversation has taken a rather morbid turn, has it
not?" Sveyn moved to sit on the counter beside the sink so he
was face-to-face with her. "I cannot predict what will transpire,
and I have no control over my manifestations as you know."

"I know." Hollis squeezed toothpaste onto her toothbrush.
But I don't want to think about that.

"And yet, I will say this once more, Hollis." He leaned
toward her. "I have never felt so strongly tethered to anyone
before. You are very, very different."

"Because I'm a woman," she deflected.

"And..." His lips curled and his eyes twinkled. "Because
you are the dearest love of my never-ending life."

have become

*****

Miranda appeared at Hollis's office right after lunch. "Mr.
Benton wants to see you."

Hollis snorted. "He won't summon me himself?"

"That's probably because I laid the groundwork for you."
Miranda leaned against the doorframe. "I told him that you
should be compensated for additional tasks not originally in your
contract."

"Thank you, Miranda!" Hollis grinned at her boss. "I
suppose that this is the one time when being a temporary
employee works to my advantage."

Miranda's smile dimmed a little. "I'm going to miss you
after the wing is opened, and all the stuff from the hoard is
processed."

A pang of regret, compounded by her conversation with
Sveyn this morning, threatened to derail Hollis's enthusiastic
attentions to the task at hand.

"And I'll miss you and Stevie." Hollis lifted one shoulder.
"Who knows? Maybe I'll stay in Phoenix. Get a different job."

"And maybe I'll convince Benton to make you permanent."
Miranda's brow smoothed with the happy idea. "That wing and

all those artifacts will require constant attention, and they are not in Tony's wheelhouse."

Though the museum's permanent lead collector was the first person at her side when she was abducted, Tony Samoa resisted anything that had to do with the acceptance of the bequest and the changing of their mission statement.

"No they aren't. Plus he is super pissed about the addition of the wing and all things in it." Hollis locked her computer and stood. "If Benton offers me a permanent job, we would need to have a very clear discussion about who has authority over what."

"Agreed." Miranda turned to leave. "Come see me when you finish. The Jane Austin Tea invitations were just delivered."

*****

Mr. Benton was the General Manager of the Arizona History and Cultural Center, and master of all he surveyed—at least in his own mind. He was the one who championed both the acceptance of Ezra Kensington's bequest before the Board, and wrote the addition to the mission statement which made that acceptance possible.

He was also the one who kept putting Hollis front and center in the media as he promoted the new wing and its opening. She really hated that.

"Good afternoon, Ms. McKenna." Benton waved her into his office. "Please have a seat."

"Thank you." Hollis sat. Sveyn walked to the other side of the massive desk and stood at Benton's side.

"Are you recovered from your ordeal?" he asked gently.

Hollis gave the answer she knew he wanted, true or not. Possible employee lawsuits tended to make things messy. "Yes, sir. I'm doing better."

Sveyn sniffed loudly.

How does he do that with no air?

"I'm glad to hear that." Benton's hand hovered over the office telephone. "Would you like a cup of coffee? A bottle of water?"

Wow. This must be some doozy of a request. "No thanks. I'm good."

"All right, then." The hand retreated to interlock with its counterpart on top of the polished walnut desk. "First, I want to let you know that I'm very pleased with all that you've done."

Hollis gave him a tight-lipped smile of thanks. "With all due respect, sir, I am nowhere near 'done' and the wing's opening is in three weeks."

"Yes." He cleared his throat. "And it's shaping up to be a rousing success, thanks to your efforts."

And your numerous YouTube uploads. Sir.

Hollis waited politely in silence.

"As you know, the museum is receiving dozens of requests a day from interested parties, asking to be allowed to come onto the property and run various scientific tests for paranormal activity."

Scientific?

Hollis bit her tongue and still did not respond. She wanted Benton to squirm if he was about to make the next several months of her life miserable. And it looked like he was about to do exactly that.

The man's demeanor shifted suddenly. "Hollis, what was in the room with you?"

Surprised by the question she glanced at Sveyn, realized the tactical error, and quickly moved her gaze in a zigging arch over Mr. Benton's head before meeting his eyes again.

"Sir, I was in a room with absolutely no light. And when the lights did come on, they blinded me for much longer than the smudge appeared on the camera."

"Did you hear anything?" he probed.

"No," she lied.

"Feel anything?"

"Besides panic and a thick layer of duct tape?" she snapped.

Benton blanched. "I'm sorry. That was insensitive of me."

"You want to know what triggered the motion detectors," she said evenly. "I'm telling you the truth, which is, I have no logical explanation."

Benton pounced like a feral cat. "What about an illogical one?"

"Now you have done it," Sveyn warned. "You have laid your own trap."

Shut up.

"I'm afraid I don't have one of those either," Hollis admitted.

Though his tone was calm, Benton's expression shrieked that knew he was back on solid ground. "In that case, doesn't it make sense to grant some of the more reputable inquirers access?"

Crappers McCrapsalot.

"Like *Ghost Myths, Inc.*?"

Benton shrugged. "The increased publicity would be good for the museum's revenue."

"You're the General Manager. It's totally your call." Hollis placed her hands on the arms of her chair. "Is that all?"

"I'm afraid not. Relax, Hollis." Benton stood, walked to the front of his desk, and assumed the I'm-acting-casual-because-I'm-about-to-screw-up-your-life pose: one leg on the floor, one cheek and thigh resting on the desktop. "I have a proposition for you."

Sveyn settled into the twin of Benton's pose, pushing Hollis dangerously close to succumbing to inappropriate laughter.

"Go on," the Viking said. "But make it good."

Hollis bit her tongue—literally.

Benton smiled. "Every one of the requests mentions you specifically."

"I'm not surprised." She really wasn't.

"They want you to be present when they make their observations. In case you're the trigger."

Let the negotiations begin. "What sort of access are you considering?" she asked.

"After hours, of course," Benton stated. "I don't want any of this to interfere with your preparations for the opening. That is the top priority, after all."

"So then I'm expected to put in overtime hours which are not in my contract?"

This time is was Benton who was caught in his own unintentional trap. Sveyn coughed a laugh.

Benton gave an unconcerned nod. "Yes. I believe that's the best solution."

"How much time?" Hollis pressed.

"How much are you comfortable with?" he countered.

Hollis folded her arms. "How much are you willing to pay for?"

Benton folded his arms as well and narrowed his eyes. "How much do you believe your time to be worth?"

"He's good," Sveyn muttered.

Shut. Up.

"More than the museum can afford."

Benton scowled. "Are you refusing to cooperate?"

"No. Not at all." Hollis smiled. "But I do have a counter proposal."

Benton remained unmoved. "Let's hear it."

Hollis regarded the man. "If anyone wants access to the museum—including the storage room—they'll have it on our terms."

"And what terms are those?"

"Access to the public areas on Mondays only, when the front of the museum is closed," she began. "And access to the collections storeroom only on Monday nights. That way, all of my disruptions are limited to one day a week."

Benton nodded. "I can agree to that."

"And we don't begin scheduling anyone until December after the wing opens. There's just too much to be done before that."

The General Manager nodded again and stood. "That's an acceptable stipulation."

"But I'm not finished." Hollis stood as well. "There is one more condition."

"Your compensation, I assume."

Hollis nodded. "I know the museum is on a tight budget— which is why you want the publicity. But there is no reason for you to take my overtime out of the operating budget."

"Then where—"

"Charge these 'scientific' investigators for after-hours access."

Relief and admiration played across Benton's face. "How much?"

"A hundred dollars an hour." Hollis charged forward, hoping Benton would be caught up in her momentum. "Split fifty-fifty."

"Two hundred," the grinning General Manager counter-offered. "If they're serious, they'll pay it."

Hollis laughed. "I have no problem with that. And the higher price should limit the number of disruptions."

Benton circled his desk and started making notes. "Will this be limited to a certain *number* of hours?"

Hollis said the first number that came to her mind. "Four."

"What if they want to stay overnight?"

She shrugged. "The price doubles for hours five through eight?"

"Yes. That's good." Benton grabbed a pad and scribbled notes on it. "I love it."

"I hope this does not fire back at you," Sveyn said.

"It's only one night a week," she replied to the Viking without thinking.

Benton looked up at her. "Yes. Only on Mondays."

Oh, jeez.

Did it again.

When will you learn?

"If we're done, sir, I do have a lot of time-sensitive tasks to finish today."

"Yes. Go ahead."

Before she reached the office door he called out to her. "This is a very good plan, Hollis. I admire the way you think."

"Thank you, Mr. Benton." She decided to toss the next concept out there while he was feeling so warmly towards her. "Please remember that when my current contract expires."

Chapter Three

Miranda handed Hollis one of the fancy invitations to the Jane Austin tea.

"Of course, once we let the Jane Austen Society people know that we found a signed copy of Mansfield Park in the hoard, the original fifty tickets sold out in thirty minutes! So we added fifty more and they were gone by the end of the day," Miranda said. "These invitations are just part of the promised experience."

"One hundred JASNA members, and all of them in costume," Stevie effused. "It's going to be so much fun!"

Hollis looked at Stevie. "George will dress up, of course."

"What?" Miranda's head swiveled to face Stevie. "George has a costume?"

Stevie's cheeks bloomed red. "George is a man of many interests."

"Did I hear my name?" George Oswald walked through Miranda's office door. "What are we talking about?"

Stevie handed him one of the invitations. "The Regency tea at the end of the month."

George grinned when he saw the parchment-and-calligraphy

card. "This is very well done. Very authentic."

"Hollis told us that you'll be in costume." Miranda was clearly struggling to hold back her amusement.

"Costume is not the correct term." He handed the invitation back to Stevie. "My suit is made from a pattern of the era, and in historically correct fabrics. There are many of us who see this as a viable way to keep the history of the Regency era alive."

Stevie beamed at her suitor. "And the romance of Jane Austin just makes it fun."

Miranda regarded George with a renewed level of respect. "Well, I'm looking forward to the afternoon."

George turned to Hollis. "Will you be there?"

Hollis hadn't planned on it. While she loved Jane Austin, she wasn't the dress-up-and-play-tea type of gal. "I don't think so."

"I've been trying to convince her ever since the idea first came up," Stevie groused.

"I don't have a ticket, and it's sold out." Hollis shrugged. "It's too late."

"Don't be silly." Miranda gave Hollis an invitation. "You can be one of our guest speakers."

Ugh.

Just kill me now.

"What would I speak about?" Hollis waved the parchment card toward Stevie and George. "The JASNA members know way more about Jane Austin and Regency society than I do."

"You could tell us about finding the book in the hoard," George suggested. "What it felt like to hold a book that she once held."

"And how we verified both the signature and the age of the book," Stevie added.

Hollis shifted her gaze to Miranda. She was clearly losing this battle but tossed her last objection anyway. "I don't have a cos—historically accurate dress. So I'd be out-of-place."

"That's an easy fix. We'll find you something, won't we George?" Stevie looked to the lawyer for support.

"Of course." George shifted his gentle brown eyes to Hollis. "Please say yes, Hollis. The Jane Austin Society of North

America would be very honored."

"I'll think about it," was all she was willing to concede. "Is that why you're here?"

"No." George's deportment shifted. "I wanted to talk to you. About Everett Sage."

At the mention of her abductor's name, Sveyn strode into the office. When he wasn't in sight, Hollis knew the Viking was always within a hundred yards of her—his invisible tether prevented him from wandering farther from her side.

He had taken to exploring recently, returning to her when he heard her say anything of interest. In this case, her inquiry as to why the lawyer was visiting must have piqued his curiosity.

"Let's go to my office." Hollis walked out the door without another word to anyone else.

*****

Hollis sat at her desk. George sat in the chair which faced it. Sveyn positioned himself to the side where she could see him.

"What's going on, George?" Why did her voice sound so shaky?

"You know that Sage's lawyers are negotiating a plea agreement with the court and the museum," George began. "It's a logical step, since the man has no previous criminal record."

Hollis understood from the beginning that this was a possibility, no matter how badly she wanted the man to fry. Or hang. Or have his balls cut off and stuffed down his throat. "How does that affect me?"

"It means he admits guilt to a lesser charge, so there is no trial." George's expression was kind. "You won't have to testify in court."

"That's a relief," Hollis and Sveyn said in tandem. She looked at her desk and tilted her face ever so slightly toward the apparition in acknowledgement.

"And there is more." George looked unaccountably pleased. "Once he pleads guilty you can—if you want—file a civil lawsuit against him and ask for damages."

Hollis straightened. "What kind of damages?"

"Financial. To make up for your personal pain and suffering, plus the disruption of your professional life."

"I can do that?"

"You can. And he seems to have money." George looked at her, as if trying to discern her thoughts. "I can put our forensic accountant on the case today, if you're interested."

Hollis wanted so badly to hear what Sveyn thought, but wasn't sure he could understand the legalities. She didn't dare look at him, though. Not with George being the only other person in the room.

"What do you think I should do?"

She was looking at George, but Sveyn answered her. "I believe it is best to leave this be."

George shrugged. "You may have to face him in court if you pursue this."

"Couldn't I testify on camera from a different location?" Hollis probed. "I saw that in a movie."

The lawyer chuckled. "I suppose that's possible. It does reinforce the contention that you were emotionally damaged by Sage's actions."

"Then let's do it." Hollis heaved a sigh. "As long as I never have to be in a room with him again, I'm willing to pursue this."

"Oh, Hollis." Sveyn shook his head. "Why?"

"I may not have a job once the hoard is sorted, logged, and on display," she replied to the Viking, though still looking at George. "Having something in the bank to fall back on would certainly make life easier."

"Great." George stood. "If you have no objections, I'd like to act as your lawyer on the contingency that we win."

"Thank you, George. I really appreciate that and gladly accept." Hollis looked up at him. "So how much damage are we talking about?"

"I can't answer that for certain until forensics digs into his accounts." George walked toward the door. "We'll ask for everything he has, and then offer to take less if he doesn't fight it."

Hollis sucked a breath. "And then no testifying in court then either?"

George pointed at her, grinning. "Exactly. And since he will have already pled guilty, he can't say he didn't do it."

Hollis slumped in her chair, feeling the weight of Everett's betrayal starting to lift. "Thank you *so* much, George."

He gave her a small Austin-esque bow. "I'm glad I can help you, Hollis."

*****

Hollis looked at Sveyn once George closed her office door. "Are you angry with me?"

"I am not pleased," he grumbled. "The man is dangerous. He has been driven mad by his possession of half the icon."

"He'll be in prison, Sveyn."

"For the remainder of his life?" Sveyn challenged. "I do not believe that will be so."

Hollis felt a small blade of fear slide between her ribs. "I'll probably be gone from Phoenix by the time he gets out."

The Viking pointed at her computer. "You will still be there. On the internet."

"I'll get a restraining order," she countered, though the efficacy of those documents had good reason to be doubted. "Maybe I'll even be married and have a new name."

Sveyn stiffened, rising to his full six-and-a-half feet. He stared down at her, his blue eyes darkening along with his expression. "Yes. Perhaps you shall."

Hollis stood slowly. "Sveyn, I didn't mean anything by that."

Someone knocked on the door, and then cracked it open. "Can I come in?"

"Of course, Stevie." Hollis dropped back into her chair and pasted a taut smile across her cheeks.

Sveyn glared at her. She could practically feel the waves of his anger washing over her.

Stevie entered her office, her happy expression probably

sincere. "George says he's going to help you go after Everett's money."

"I shall leave you to your happy plans," Sveyn growled. He strode rigidly past Stevie and out Hollis's office door.

Stevie whirled toward the Viking, her eyes wide. "What was that?"

Hollis's heart thumped. *Negative emotions.* Were they making Sveyn visible to others? That could be really good news, in a terrible sort of way.

"What was what?" she asked.

"Didn't you see it?" Stevie faced her again, her face gone white."

"It?" Hollis stalled. "What did you see?"

Stevie waved a hand in a circle to her side. "A shadow. Here. Sort of like what was on the video."

Hollis scrambled for a response, and came up with nothing. "I'm not sure…"

Stevie practically ran to Hollis's desk, apparently recovering some of her composure. "You can tell me, Hollis I won't think you're crazy."

"Why—why would you think I was?" she stammered.

"Lots of people believe in angels." Stevie leaned on Hollis's desk. "You even said you had one and he was in the storeroom when you were locked in there."

Uh, oh.

"When did I say that?" she deflected.

"When we first watched the security videos. Don't you remember?"

"Um. No," she lied. "Sorry."

Stevie shoulders slumped. "Then how do you explain what just happened?"

"I can't. I didn't see what you saw." That part was true.

Stevie straightened, considering Hollis with narrowed eyes. "What did Benton want?"

Good. A change of subject.

Sort of.

"He wants me to cooperate with ghost hunters and other

crazies who want to try and discover what *was* on that video."

"Cooperate how?"

"He's going to allow them to come run tests or whatever. On Mondays. In December. After the wing is open."

"And you're supposed to be there with them?" Stevie gave Hollis a knowing look. "And what will they find?"

Hollis threw her hands wide and spoke the truth. "I have no freaking idea."

"Well, count me in." Stevie wagged a finger in Hollis's face. "I want to get to the bottom of this, even if you don't."

I am really hooked so far on this book - very intriguing conflict! Jay?

Chapter four

Tuesday
November 17

Hollis swiped a trickle of sweat from her forehead. The climate-control system in the new Kensington wing wasn't operational as yet, so no actual objects were being placed in the displays until it was. In the meantime, she and Stevie were busy directing their three interns and helping them get the cases placed properly.

"That's perfect, Tom." Hollis retracted her measuring tape. "You guys can take a lunch break."

Stevie heaved a sigh. "The tracking number says the signage is on the truck and will arrive today."

Hollis nodded. "Good. We can work on that tomorrow."

"We should be able to get everything in place before Thanksgiving, then." Stevie wiped her own brow. "Assuming they get the air up and running."

Tony Samoa sauntered through the plastic veil, past the large posted *The Kensington Collection ~ Opening December 1st* sign, and walked up to Hollis. "Here you are, Miss YouTube

Sensation."

"Stop it, Tony," Stevie chided. "You know Hollis has no control over that."

He looked around the space as if seeing it for the first time. "I guess if I was younger and had long, curly red hair and blue eyes, I could catch Benton's attention, too." Tony's gaze shifted to Hollis. "Oh. And boobs. I'd need boobs."

Hollis swung her arm, but Tony leaned back and dodged the palm that was aimed at his cheek. "Watch it. I'll press charges."

Sveyn stepped between Hollis and Tony. "He is only jealous. Do not allow him to provoke you."

"Benton has no interest in me as a woman!" she snapped.

"So you say." Tony shrugged. "But I hear he plans to work nights with you. In the storeroom. In the dark."

Stevie shoved Tony backwards with surprising strength for such a petite frame. He stumbled backwards, but caught himself and didn't fall.

"What the hell?" he barked.

"Shut up, Tony!" Stevie's eyes flashed. "Or *I'll* press charges for sexual harassment. You have no right to talk to Hollis like that!"

"I was only teasing," he grumbled. "Jeez. Buy a sense of humor, why don't you?"

Hollis walked away before she said anything else. She was so angry that tears blurred her vision and she almost walked into a display case. She turned a corner so she was out of Tony's line of sight.

"Bastard," she whispered. "He's hated me from the start."

"Men are territorial, Hollis. You know that." Sveyn stood in front of her. "He believes you have come in to take his place of importance."

"I'm temporary!" she shouted. "When will he get that through his thick skull?"

Stevie rounded the corner. "You don't have to shout. He's gone."

Hollis swiped her eyes and pointed a stiff finger at her friend and co-worker. "I don't care *how* nice he was to me when he found me that night! If he says one more thing, or gets in my way one more time, I'll have his balls on a platter!"

"I believe you." Stevie squeezed Hollis's arm. "Don't let him get to you. Do you want me to say something to Miranda?"

"Fight your own battles, Hollis," Sveyn urged.

"*I will!*" With a mental slap to her forehead Hollis realized she was answering Sveyn, not Stevie.

Crap.

"I mean, I will. If he says anything else."

Stevie squeezed her arm again. "Let's go out for lunch. Get away from the stress for an hour."

Hollis looked at Stevie. "That's a great idea."

"Greek?"

"Even better." Hollis smiled tenuously at the petite blonde. "Thank you. I'm afraid this whole situation is making me crazy."

"It would make anyone crazy," Stevie said. "Let's go before someone stops us."

*****

Miranda and Benton each carried a box of plaques when they visited the wing toward the end of the day. Hollis opened the boxes, and she and Stevie placed the signs around the wing on the cases which they were intended for. Tom the intern leaned the signs that would be mounted against their intended walls.

"This looks very good, Hollis," Benton approved. "I wasn't certain about the layout when Miranda showed it to me, but she was adamant that it would flow naturally. And it does."

Hollis felt her cheeks warming at his praise. She always found it hard to accept compliments, even when they were deserved. "Thank you, sir."

Stevie grinned at their bosses. "I particularly love how the two collections, American and European, circle around and are joined in the middle by their shared history."

"Yes. That's impressive." Benton faced Hollis. "I assume the Blessing's case will be the center focal point, since it's the oldest object in the collection?"

She nodded and pointed to the gap in displays. "It'll go there. The bullet-proof case should be delivered on Monday."

"Excellent."

Hollis glanced at Miranda, and back at Benton. "Is there any word on the plea agreement?"

Sveyn leaned down and murmured in her ear. "In other words, will you have both halves of that vile thing to display? God willing, the answer is no."

Hollis wished she could elbow the Viking in the ribs, not just jerk her arm backwards and through his torso.

"The final negotiations were completed yesterday, and the agreement will go before the judge tomorrow." Benton flashed a confident grin. "We'll receive what we asked for."

Sveyn swore softly.

"That's good news, sir." Hollis stepped away from the fuming Viking and looked around the space, evaluating what the general manager could see. "Do you have any other questions?"

*****

"You've done well, Hollis. Mr. Benton was very pleased." Miranda ordered another congratulatory margarita.

"I'm so relieved." Hollis reached for a chip and dipped it in the spicy salsa. "Because it's too late to change anything now."

"Two weeks from today, and a holiday in between," Stevie pointed out once again.

"And a formal Regency tea to host, don't forget." Miranda looked at Hollis. "Do you have your dress?"

"Not yet. I haven't had time to go to the shop and try any on." *And if I postpone long enough, maybe I won't have to.*

Stevie pointed a tortilla chip at her. "Don't think you can just not go get a dress, and then get out of this."

Crap.

Sveyn chuckled. "She has figured out your obvious ploy."

Hollis wrinkled her nose.

"Agreed." Miranda gave Hollis a boss-like look. "Go tomorrow during work."

"I don't have—"

"Yes. You do."

Hollis's shoulder fell. "How do you know what I was going to say?"

"Doesn't matter." Miranda accepted her second margarita and handed the waitress her empty glass. "I want you to be there, and as your superior I have the right to ask you."

"And don't call in sick, either," Stevie said. "Because I'll come to your condo and drag you there if I need to."

Damn.

There went that plan.

"Fine. I'll go tomorrow," Hollis conceded, forestalling Stevie's anticipated suggestion with, "Alone."

"Where's the fun in that?" Stevie grumbled.

Hollis smiled puckishly. "The fun is in surprising you when you see me."

"Hmph." Stevie stuffed a salsa-laden chip into her mouth.

"So what're your Thanksgiving plans?" Miranda asked.

Stevie's mood brightened immediately. "I'm going to Las Vegas with George. We're spending Thanksgiving with his brother's family."

Hollis remembered the surprising story. "The one with the tattoo parlor who makes more money than George?"

Stevie giggled. "That's the one."

Miranda's skeptical expression spoke volumes. "A tattoo artist makes more money than a lawyer?"

"Hey, it's Vegas." Stevie grinned. "Lots of tattoos to do—and lots more to fix."

Miranda turned her attention to Hollis. "What about you?"

"I couldn't take the time off to fly to Milwaukee, obviously, so I'll buy a pre-made dinner and enjoy it in front of the TV."

"No, no, no," Miranda objected.

"It's fine, Miranda. I love watching the Macy's parade and the dog show," Hollis insisted. "And after that I'll watch *Miracle on 34th Street*—"

"The original in black-and-white?" Stevie interrupted.

"Of course." Hollis was a historian, after all. "And maybe

launch the Christmas season with a little *Love Actually*."

Miranda cocked one brow. "All by yourself?"

Hollis's gaze flicked briefly up at Sveyn. He had started standing beside whoever she was speaking to once she realized people noticed when she looked to her side. "I really don't mind. I don't feel lonely if that's what you mean."

Stevie was watching her a bit too closely. "Is he here?"

Hollis recoiled. "What?"

"Your guardian angel." Stevie's head swiveled from side to side. "Is he here."

Miranda looked confused. "What are you talking about?"

Stevie expression turned smug. "I saw him today."

"You saw him?" Miranda's eyes rounded.

"You did not," Hollis huffed.

"Well I saw something. You know I did."

Hollis flipped a hand at Stevie. "You're imagining things, my friend."

"We'll see about that." Stevie turned to Miranda. "I'm assisting Hollis when all those paranormal guys come snooping around."

"She has *volunteered* to be there," Hollis clarified. "She has not been assigned to be there."

Miranda looked at her still-full margarita. "How many of these have I had?"

"That's only your second," Hollis answered. "And yes, this conversation has made a sudden left turn into crazy land." She decided to take the hit, rather than continue down this precarious path. "We were talking about Thanksgiving."

"Right!" Miranda smiled. "You will spend the day at my house." She put up a hand. "And before you say no, I host an annual 'Stragglers' Pot Luck' for any and all of my friends who find themselves alone for the holiday."

Hollis felt a little pitied, and found the idea embarrassing. "That's really sweet, but—"

"The only rule is that whatever you bring must be homemade," Miranda continued, ignoring Hollis. "Absolutely nothing made by an institution is allowed."

had given

"But I don't—"

"Don't be silly." Miranda gave her the same hand flip that Hollis gave Stevie. "Everyone can cook something."

Hollis paused, wondering if Miranda had already anticipated her next objection; her boss seemed clairvoyant at the moment. "I don't—"

"Know anyone? Neither did the others the first year." Miranda beamed at her. "Now we're like family. Only more fun. No lecherous uncles or snotty little cousins."

"Give it up, Hollis. She's a steamroller." Stevie lifted her beer. "Give in before she flattens you."

"Good. That's settled." Miranda sipped her drink. "So, what will you bring?"

Chapter five

"No, Mom. I'm sorry." Hollis tapped her forefinger on her desktop. "Even if everything for the opening was finished—and it's not—there aren't any flights available for next week."

Even from eighteen hundred miles away, her mother's disappointment slammed Hollis with guilt. Not that she couldn't go, but because she didn't want to.

Her live-in boyfriend of a decade was also in Milwaukee, along with the woman he married only four months after breaking up with her. Hollis wasn't interested in running into him while hanging out with any of their mutual friends.

"What will you do, Hollis?"

"My boss Miranda is hosting dinner."

Her mother was silent.

"Oh, and did I tell you about the Jane Austin Tea on that Sunday?" Hollis diverted the conversation. "After we found that signed copy of Mansfield Park in the collection, Miranda invited JASNA members to the museum for a pre-opening showing of the book."

Still nothing.

"I have to wear a dress."

"What kind of dress?"

That did it. Hollis told her mother all about Stevie and George and the historically accurate clothing and never once mentioned the abduction or the rescue of the icon. She may be thirty years old, but in her mother's eyes she was still a single girl who needed her parents' protection.

Explaining that a Viking apparition was constantly at her side and actually ended up saving her life was probably information best held back at this time.

George Oswald appeared in her office doorway. He was smiling.

"Mom, I have to go. Give Dad my love." Hollis hung up the phone. "What?"

"First of all, the plea agreement was accepted by the judge. Doctor Everett Sage will serve three years in prison without parole, in a combined sentence covering the Class Four aggravated assault and the Class Six felony theft."

Hollis frowned and did not look at Sveyn. "That doesn't seem like very long…"

"It's not. It's about a third of the time he could have received." George shrugged and his smile dimmed a little. "But that's what a plea agreement does."

Hollis gave a reluctant nod. "I understand."

"The state also offers up to one hundred and fifty thousand dollars in victim restitution," he said. "But we're not taking that."

Hollis frowned at George. "Because?"

"Because he's loaded."

"You know that already?"

George chuckled. "That's based on preliminary findings. I believe we'll be able to quadruple that amount—at the least."

Hollis went limp. "Really?"

"Really. I'll keep you informed." He turned to leave.

"Hey George?" He faced her again and she asked, "What about the icon?"

"The museum gets it."

"Thanks."

The lawyer turned to leave again, and Hollis called out to him once more. She held up her cell phone. "You can call me, you know. You don't always have to tell me in person."

His face flushed red. "I do enjoy the company in this office. It's no bother."

Hollis laughed. "Stevie's in the new wing."

George saluted and left the office.

"He is deeply smitten," Sveyn observed.

Hollis's smiled faded. "Yes. He is."

Monday
November 23

Benton sent his legal team to retrieve Sage's half of the icon from the Phoenix police only after the bulletproof case was delivered to the museum and installed. Hollis and Stevie cleaned the heavy case and laid their half of the icon in its place, along with the plaque explaining the object's history and legend.

When the team returned with the other half, Sveyn hovered so close to Hollis that if he had a physical body she would have been pinned by his weight.

"Get back," Hollis grumbled.

"Do not connect the two, Hollis," he warned. "Do not even get them too close, in the event they try to join themselves."

As silly as his words sounded to her, Hollis knew that Sveyn was completely serious about his concerns.

He claimed that the icon, impossibly carbon-dated at six thousand years old, was made by the sons of God—beings who, according to the book of Genesis, walked the earth in ancient-even-then Biblical times.

When she expressed her doubts, he challenged her. "Have you not heard of Thor? Apollo? Zeus? The Egyptian sun gods? Where do you believe these stories have come from?"

Hollis couldn't buy into the belief that any of these accounts were specifically true, but she had to admit that cultures all around the world did have very similar elements in their legends and oral histories

Sveyn pushed her further, claiming that structures such as Stonehenge, the Easter Island stone heads, and the Great Pyramids were all built with the help of these creatures' super-human strength.

In the end, she had to admit that she couldn't confidently refute those beliefs. Not when a Viking apparition suddenly appeared in her life, claiming to have been transformed after being run through by a broadsword in the year ten-seventy.

"Don't lay them too close," she said to Stevie who was handling the icon with cotton-gloved hands. "We want to give the impression that the legend is true and they can't touch each other."

Stevie placed Everett's half about eight inches from the one that Ezra owned. "How's this?"

Hollis waited for Sveyn to either approve or object.

"A little farther," he said.

"Hmm..." Hollis tilted her head. "I think they will look better if they are a little further apart."

"And maybe offset a bit?" Stevie adjusted the two similar-looking pieces. Both were made of wood and steel—which pierced the wood in ways that seemed impossible to craft—and both were carved with Nordic runes and other symbols even Sveyn didn't know the meaning of. "How's this?"

Sveyn stared at the display, his brow furrowed. "That will do."

"That looks great, Stevie."

Stevie pulled her hands back and Hollis lowered the heavy acrylic top. The lock required both a key and a combination to open the case—a safety feature which Benton planned to make quite public. Hopefully, that knowledge would discourage would-be thieves.

Hollis looked at her watch. "I have to go. Can you finish up?"

"Sure. Do you have a date?" Stevie's tone was as hopeful as

her expression.

"I have an appointment," Hollis replied. "And that's all I'm going to say."

*****

Hollis stood in the costume shop that George suggested and allowed herself to be buttoned into a high-waisted, scoop-necked, narrow-sleeved, floor length dress made of lightweight, butter-yellow wool.

"It's a bit revealing, isn't it?" she asked as she considered her image in the mirror. The swells of her breasts were distractingly pushed above the décolletage of the dress by the snug bodice.

Hollis looked at the gal helping her and pointed at her own face. "I'm speaking to a group and I do want their eyes up here."

"You'll need a scarf, then." The shop girl disappeared from the changing room, and reappeared with a length of cream-colored silk. "Wrap it behind your neck, and tuck the ends in your cleavage."

That's better.

"Too bad." Sveyn was leaning in the changing room doorway, his arms folded and his attention locked on Hollis. "I liked it better without the drape."

"This is more professional," she said to Sveyn. "I don't want to be distracting."

"I understand," the girl said. "And the color is perfect for you."

Sveyn smiled softly. "I do agree with that. You look very beautiful in that dress."

Hollis tiled her head, still examining her reflection. "How accurate is the style?"

"Very," Sveyn confirmed. "I remember it well."

"It's very accurate. This dress was made from a pattern, which was created from a disassembled dress from that period." The girl smiled. "We have a lot of JASNA members who buy from us."

Hollis met her eyes in the mirror. "But I'm renting this, right?"

"Yes. Of course."

"And how to I dress myself?"

The girl lifted Hollis's left arm. "There's a secret zipper here, for ladies who don't have a companion to help them."

Hollis unzipped the hidden fastener and the bodice fell slack. "And then I pull it off over my head instead of stepping into it?"

"Exactly."

Hollis nodded. "Okay. This'll do."

*****

"You were stunningly beautiful in that gown, Hollis."

Hollis smiled at the Viking riding in her passenger seat. "Thank you, Sveyn." She pulled into a family-owned pizza shop's parking lot. "Are you coming in?"

"Yes."

"Then I'll put this on." Hollis reached in her purse and retrieved the Bluetooth earpiece which allowed her to converse with Sveyn in public without looking like an insane person. She slipped it over her ear. "Let's go. My mouth is already watering."

"Yes. The garlic bread knots." Sveyn grinned. "I know that well."

Hollis got out of her car and locked it as Sveyn moved through the passenger door. When she stepped inside the shop, the warm and pungent aroma of roasted garlic washed over her.

She inhaled deeply. "I wish you could smell this."

Sveyn had an odd look on his face. "What does it smell like?"

How do I describe it?

More to the point, did the Viking have a frame of reference for the little bulb?

"Did you have garlic in Norway?"

His brow furrowed. "I do not believe so."

Hollis shrugged. "Then I really don't know how to describe

it. It's…sharp. Sort of stings your nose. But it doesn't make your eyes water like an onion does."

She stepped up to the counter and ordered a personal pizza and half-a-dozen garlic knots to go. After she paid for her order, she sat at a small table to wait.

Sveyn was walking around the shop, examining the food. He went into the kitchen and stuck his face into the oven.

"What are you doing?" Hollis asked softly. She knew Sveyn always heard her voice, no matter how far he was from her. Just like she couldn't *not* see him, he couldn't *not* hear her.

"Sniffing," he said.

Hollis laughed. "Why? You don't breathe."

"To discover if I am imagining things."

Hollis froze. "Imagining things? What do you mean?"

Sveyn left the kitchen and walked to the table where she sat. His eyes were wide and intense under a lowered brow. His hands were in fists. He lowered himself into the chair opposite her.

Hollis's sense of dread kicked into high gear. "What's wrong, Sveyn?"

The apparition looked like he had seen a ghost of his own. "I believe I can smell it. The garlic."

Whoa! :)

You tend to "go big" early which leaves less room to build.

Chapter Six

Hollis didn't speak again until her number was called. She grabbed her order and hurried out to her car, too stunned to know what to say.

When she first met Sveyn back in September, he told her his existence was like living in a dream. He could see and hear, but he couldn't taste or touch—or *smell*—anything.

In spite of that, both she and he experienced a faint electrical tingle when their hands were close to each other's skin. Hollis would have believed it was her imagination if Everett Sage's electromagnetic sensor hadn't registered a reading when Sveyn was standing near it.

The apparition was definitely real. *1, more real.*

And, it would seem, was now becoming realer.

"Can you smell it now?" Hollis asked. The garlicky aroma had mixed with the yeast of the pizza crust and tang of the tomato sauce and filled the interior of her car with nasal deliciousness.

"I am not certain," he replied. "It is not like it was."

"Maybe it was a temporary thing." Why that possibility made her sad, she wasn't certain. But it did.

Sveyn said nothing.

"Tell me if it happens again." Hollis's eyes were determinedly fixed on the road. "Will you?"

"Yes." It was almost a grunt.

Hollis pulled into the condo complex and parked. Battered briefcase in one hand, and dinner in the other, she still managed to unlock her door and go inside. It would be nice if Sveyn could help, but his hands passed through anything he tried to grab.

"I might recognize certain aromas."

Hollis watched Sveyn as she set her burden on the dining room table. "What do you mean?"

He tilted his head a little. "I mean that I might remember some scents if I experienced them again."

"Like a test?" The idea was fascinating—and rife with the very real possibility of devastating disappointment.

Sveyn nodded.

"What scents do you think you'd recognize?" she asked, considering the earthy smells of medieval Norway versus the industrial scents of modern day Phoenix. Would anything smell the same?

"Horse shit. Smoke. Fish." Sveyn rubbed his brow out of habit, though he told her he couldn't feel his own body. "Ice. Rain. Pine sap."

Hollis unwrapped her food. "Some of those I could manage, maybe." She grabbed a bottle of water from the fridge. "I'll think about it."

She settled on the couch with her supper, as was her habit. Sveyn normally sat beside her, but this evening he was fidgety.

"Tell me about the Regency period," she said on sudden inspiration. "Did you manifest to anyone at the beginning of the nineteenth century?"

He stilled and looked at her. "Yes."

"Where?" She bit into a garlic knot and briefly closed her eyes. *Heaven.*

"London. Well, the outskirts, more accurately." He rubbed his forehead again. "He was a magistrate in a small town called Twickenham."

Fascinating. "How long were you there?"

"Just short of five years."

An abrupt thought made her stop eating. "Did you—I mean he—ever meet Jane Austin?"

Sveyn's brow furrowed. "No. Not that I recall."

Hollis knew it was a long shot but was still disappointed. Sveyn's various manifestations over nearly a millennium made him an eye witness to so much history that she suddenly wanted to quiz him about everything he saw.

Not that I could cite him on anything, of course.

But his observations could be used as a jumping-off point for further research. If only he could write down his experiences.

Another abrupt thought shoved her dinner aside and catapulted her toward her phone. "Can your voice be recorded?"

Sveyn's obvious surprise made her laugh. "I do not know. No one has ever tried."

"Not that they could, of course." Hollis opened a voice recording app. "I mean they could in the nineteen-forties, but only with cumbersome equipment. And not everyone had access to it."

She held up her phone. "Tell me your name."

"You can record me on that?"

"Yes. What is your name?"

"Sveyn Hansen."

"How old are you?"

Sveyn lifted one brow. "Thirty-four? Or should I say nine hundred and ninety, give or take."

"How many years have you spent manifesting overall?" Hollis asked—partly out of curiosity, and partly to keep him talking.

Sveyn shrugged.

Not helpful.

"Will you make a guess?" she prodded.

He looked irritated. "Twenty two times before this, ranging from five hours to twenty-seven years? I cannot be expected to remember."

Good point. "Let's say the average was, what? Five years

each? Ten?" she coaxed.

"Seven, I would think."

"Okay, good." Hollis did the math in her head. "So you have walked the earth about one hundred and seventy-five years altogether."

"Then I am either thirty-four, one-hundred-and-seventy-five, or nine-hundred-and-ninety." He lowered his chin and stared at her. "You choose."

Hollis stopped recording. "Let's see what we have."

When she played back her recording, her voice was clear. And while Sveyn's voice wasn't there, something was.

"I need better options," she said. "I'm emailing this audio file to myself so I can download it onto my laptop and open it in an editing program."

Sveyn huffed a wry chuckle. "And I shall pretend that I understood everything you have just said."

Hollis glanced up at him, smiling. "Don't worry about that. Just pray that it picked up something."

He looked puzzled. "Why?"

Why, indeed.

Because I want to tell people that you exist.

Turn back, Hollis. Not a safe path.

"I don't know," she admitted as she pulled her laptop from her briefcase. "I guess in my heart of hearts I do want people to know about you."

Sveyn stepped closer. "They may very well find that evidence when they come exploring at the museum."

"Do you think that's possible?" Hollis opened her email and downloaded the file.

"I think," Sveyn said slowly. "That if I wish to be found, I will be."

Her head jerked up. "Because of the videos?"

He nodded. "And that machine of Sage's that beeped."

Hollis stared at her Viking apparition. "What will happen if your existence *is* proven?"

A flood of unpleasant images surged through Hollis's mind. She saw herself as an even bigger media commodity. She saw people asking her to ask Sveyn all sorts of things about the past, or anything else for that matter. He might even be tapped to be that proverbial but *invisible* fly on the wall for the FBI or CIA or something—as long as she was close enough for his tether to allow him adequate distance.

She shuddered. "I'm not sure we want you to be found."

"Neither am I."

"But they'll have to find something, or they'll never stop coming." Hollis knew that was true. And Mr. Benton would beat that horse long past its death.

Maybe she could use that as a negotiating tool to be hired permanently, but with a big raise.

Sveyn pointed at her laptop. "Shall we start?"

Hollis nodded and opened the audio file from her phone in the media center program. When it played the file, there was a very slight wiggle in the line when Sveyn was speaking.

"I'll have to cut out the parts when I am speaking, because they are so loud by comparison." She highlighted and deleted a section. "That way, I can make the rest of the recording really loud without blowing out my speakers with my part."

"Hmm." Sveyn watched over her shoulder.

When she was finished, she saved the new file. "Okay. Here we go."

There were five distinct wiggles on the indicator for Sveyn's five sentences, which coincided with an unintelligible hum. Hollis turned up the intensity, and played it again. This time, she heard the deep tone of Sveyn's voice.

She saved changes, reopened the file, and turned it up again. Now she heard the pulse of his words.

"Can you hear that?" she asked the Viking as she saved and reopened the file once more.

"Somewhat."

She repeated the process two more times. "I think I've hit the max. It doesn't seem to get any clearer."

Sveyn nodded. "I can make out the words, because I know what I said. I do not believe I could have otherwise."

"You can hear words?" Hollis turned to face him. "Other

than recognizing your name, all I hear is gibberish."

He frowned. "Is that so?"

"Like this." She played the part where Sveyn said, *thirty-four? Or should I say nine hundred and ninety, give or take.* "I hear tretta feeree, eller skall—blah blah blah—yeller tah."

"Yes. Exactly," he said. "Thirty-four, or should I say nine hundred and ninety, give or take."

Hollis shook her head. "Are we listening to the same thing? How does 'tretta feeree' sound like thirty-four?"

Sveyn looked at her like she just asked how he knew the sky was blue. "How does thirty-four *not* sound like thirty-four? I do not understand your question."

Hollis gasped. Her pulse quickened. "Tretta feeree?"

"Yes. Thirty four."

Her jaw dropped. "Oh my god."

His brow plunged. "What is it?"

Hollis's fingers jerked over her keyboard so stiffly that she had to keep backspacing and retyping to get the address right.

"Google translate. English to Norwegian. Thirty-four, or should I say nine hundred and ninety, give or take."

Enter.

The words that appeared on the right side of her screen made the situation pretty darn clear, but when she asked the program to speak them the result could not be more obvious. *"Trettifire? Eller skal jeg si nittenhundreognitti, gi eller ta."*

"You're speaking Norse." She whirled to face Sveyn. "I hear English, and you hear Norse."

The Viking's eyes widened. "You asked about my language once before. You said I was speaking English."

"I thought you were." Hollis stared at the apparition. "This must be how everyone you manifest to understands you. They hear their own language in their accustomed form."

"And I am speaking my own language?" Sveyn scuttled his hands through his hair. "I had no idea anything like this was possible."

Hollis turned back to her laptop. She saved the final version of the audio file and closed out of the program. When she returned her laptop to her briefcase, her hands were shaking.

"I thought just being able to see you was the weirdest thing I ever experienced," she said softly. "But it just keeps getting weirder."

She stood and walked into her kitchen, selecting a bottle of merlot from the wine rack on her counter. She opened it, poured a generous glass, and trudged back to the living room couch and her cooled supper.

"But I heard you speak Norwegian once—remember?" she reminded him. "When you were trying to prove that I wasn't imagining you?"

Sveyn sat next to her. "Yes. I do."

"Can you do that again? Speak Norwegian to me?"

He tilted his head, his eyes questioning. "*Kanskje jeg trenger å konsentrere. Som når jeg passerer gjennom faste gjenstander.*"

Unexpected and inexplicable relief calmed her. "Yes! What did you say?"

Sveyn's brow twitched. "I said, perhaps I need to concentrate. Like when I pass through solid objects."

"That must be it." Hollis took a hefty gulp of the merlot. "Does it work the other way? Can you hear my English?"

"Ask me again. Slowly."

She pinned her gaze on his. "Can you hear my English?"

He leaned away from her. "Yes. I can. It is similar to Norsk, but different."

A soft smile spread Hollis's cheeks. "We have learned something new tonight, Viking."

"Yes, we have." His smile was more tenuous than hers. "I thought I knew everything about my particular situation that was knowable. It is clear that I was wrong."

"Could your situation be changing?" she wondered aloud. "Now that you have manifested to your first woman, and had the audacity to fall in love with her."

Sveyn seemed to blush. "Obviously, I am the last person born on this earth to claim that anything is impossible."

Hollis ate another garlic knot—which was just as delicious cool—then sipped her wine. Warring thoughts and their ramifications sparred back and forth in her mind while she waited patiently for a winner to triumph.

"I think," she began, once the victor emerged. "That we should allow you to be proven after all."

The Viking's expression thundered his surprise. "Do you?"

Hollis pointed at Sveyn with a slice of still-warm pizza. "Yes. Because I think we—or you, more accurately—can control how much they experience of your presence."

"Because Sage's readings dropped off once I moved away from his machine?" He nodded slowly, stroking his beard-scruffed jawline. "And your plan would be to limit what they find."

"Only give them what we are prepared to deal with," she clarified. "Watch and see how things go."

Sveyn's blue eyes softened. "This proof would make you happy."

Hollis flinched, startled by the kind tone of his words. "You think I'm foolish to want that, don't you."

"My presence in your life has been a greater burden to you than to anyone else over these many centuries," Sveyn said. "I am willing to do what you ask because I care so deeply for you. And if that means allowing these ghost hunters to find me, then that is what we shall do."

? Really? What about the man put in the insane asylum? I think that would be a much greater burden.

Chapter Seven

Hollis wanted so badly to kiss him. "Thank you."

The Viking spread his hands. "The consequences will be yours, not mine. But I shall give you as much assistance as I am able."

Hollis finished the slice of pizza and grabbed another. She had another favor to ask but was suddenly shy about it.

"What is on your mind, Hollis?" Sveyn asked softly.

She felt her cheeks heating. "Is it that obvious?"

"Yes." His lips formed a crooked smile. "Because you are quiet and not talking."

Hollis turned sideways on the couch and crossed her legs. "Remember that night when I asked you to imagine we were um, together, in your home village?"

"Making love on a bed of fur? Yes, I remember it well." Sveyn's smile turned sultry. "Do you want me to do that again?"

"Sort of…" Since their discovery that Sveyn's sexual fantasies became her delightful dreams, Hollis looked forward to his lusty visualizations. The fact that he was able to imagine her in his medieval home had given her a unique view into Viking life. Now… "Would you imagine us in Regency England?"

Sveyn folded his arms. "Because the tea is in six days."

"Yes."

"And you want to see what it was really like, not what these JASNA people *believe* it to be like." One eyebrow twitched. "I am right, am I not?"

"Only a little," Hollis deflected truthfully. "But I am curious. Jane Austin's stories have captured so much collective attention that I want to see how accurate our research is."

"The museum's Lead Collector rises to the top." Sveyn laughed. "Shall we conjoin with our clothes on?"

Hollis's eye rounded. "Is that how they did it?"

Sveyn grinned and winked at her. "I suppose you must wait and see."

*****

Hollis was sitting on a white wooden bench in the shade of an arched trellis which was covered in primrose vines. She didn't know how she knew they were primroses, but she did. Dreams were like that.

She wore the yellow dress from the rental shop with a pair of blue silk-covered slippers. She touched her hair and discovered it was in a loose bun on top of her head. Curling tendrils tickled her cheeks.

A man approached her. He was exceptionally tall. Clean-shaven with his dark blond hair tied back. His deep blue eyes were smiling at her.

"I've never seen you without hair or beard," Hollis said. "Or in different clothing."

"Do you care for it?" he asked. He did a slow turn so Hollis could examine the fitted dark green jacket that reached his waist in front, and dropped to mid-thigh in back. The slim buff-colored trousers which hugged his buttocks were tucked into tall, black, and decidedly non-furry boots.

He faced her again, grinning over a froth of white lace at his throat, and offered his arm. "Will you walk with me, my lady?"

Hollis stood and tucked her arm in his. "What will you show

me?"

"Everything."

Buildings appeared and expanded. Clusters of men and women manifested on sudden street corners. Horses clopped by at brisk trots pulling a variety of carriages. The sky scudded with gray-bottomed clouds.

Hollis concentrated on details: the cut and color of the women's dresses, the stance and behavior of the men, the names of the shops and what was in their windows.

"It's too bad you can't smell or taste anything," she said as they passed a pastry shop. "Those look amazing."

Sveyn leaned over and nuzzled her neck. "I smell you. And soon I shall taste you as well."

Hollis looked up at him, surprised. "Is that true?"

The Viking gave her a look that zinged right to her womb. "I have a *very* good imagination."

They turned a corner and all of the buildings and people disappeared. A few steps farther and they were in a fairy circle—an opening in a grove of young trees. A blanket was spread on the thick grass. A basket rested to one side, with a loaf of bread and bottle of wine visible.

"Are we going to eat first?" *Please say no.*

"No."

In less time than was actually possible, Hollis was stripped of everything but her chemise. Sveyn was naked.

"Why this?" she asked tugging on the thin fabric.

"So I can do this." Sveyn laid his hands on her shoulders and slid the straps down her arms. His lips trailed after the fabric, leaving a searing path down her body.

Hollis gripped his head. She was already aroused beyond believability. She assumed the swiftness was aided by Sveyn's 'very good' imagination as well.

Sveyn straightened and took her in his thickly-muscled arms. His tongue plunged into her mouth and she answered the challenge. He lifted her without effort and she wrapped her legs around his hips.

He was inside her without hesitation, filling her with intense

pleasure, and moving with urgency. Her finish came far too
swiftly.

"Don't wake up," he whispered.

"I don't want to…"

Sveyn lowered her to the blanket. He kissed her neck, her
breasts, her belly, and then—

Hollis moaned as the heat of his mouth covered her still
sensitive mound. Her pleasure surged anew, carrying to even
more dizzying heights.

He tasted her very well, indeed.

Hollis opened her eyes, determined to memorize every detail
of the world Sveyn created. Young trees' leaves were turned to
neon green by the sun behind them. Aromatic grasses formed a
cushioned mattress below. A caressing breeze loosened more
wisps from her unruly hair.

With a gasp, she arched her back and gave in to Sveyn's
delicious attentions.

She awoke after her second shattering orgasm. She was
panting and her sheets were damp. Sveyn was on all fours over
her, as if he actually possessed a body that could love hers.

"My god, Hollis…" he rasped.

She stared at him with wide eyes as her breathing slowed.
"What?"

"I—I cannot say. But when I imagined I was in you—I do
not have words to describe what I imagined that I felt…" He
turned to the side and dropped onto the mattress which, of
course, did not jostle under him. "I truly remembered what it felt
like to be inside a woman. The memory was never so real in all
this time."

Hollis ached to hold him close, to feel his masculine strength
and solidity in this world, not only the nether one. She turned on
her side. "I'm sure that's because I'm a living woman who can
interact with you."

"Yes." He covered his face with his hands and pulled a huge
breathless sigh. "Did you see what you wanted to see?"

"I saw you, Sveyn. No beard. Hair tied back. Different
clothing." Her heart still thrummed in her chest. "You're an

incredibly handsome and desirable man in any era."

"Desirable?" He lifted his hands away from his face and turned to her. "Can men be desirable?"

"Of course they can. We women desire men, like men desire women." Hollis huffed a little chuckle. "Only we're pickier, generally speaking. We don't dock at just *any* port, if you get my meaning."

Sveyn cracked a crooked smile. "As a seasoned sailor I do get your meaning and quite clearly."

Hollis stretched, the last glow of pleasure slowly fading from her depths. "I need to go back to sleep, or I'll be useless tomorrow and without any believable explanation for it."

She turned over to look at the clock. Just past one. *Not bad.*

"Do you want me to change the channel on the TV first?" She yawned as she readjusted her pillow.

"No. It is fine." The Viking made no move toward returning to the living room.

Hollis put up her palm so that Sveyn would place his against it. The familiar tingle snaked up her wrist. "Thank you."

"Sleep well, my love."

When he still didn't move, Hollis asked, "Are you going to watch TV?"

"Later." He smiled softly. "I want to lay with you for a while, if you have no objections."

Hollis sighed happily and closed her eyes. "None at all."

Tuesday
November 24

"I got my dress, Stevie. And I actually like it."

Hollis and the petite registrar walked across the museum lobby toward the new wing. Hollis felt heat tighten her cheeks as the mental image of her wearing the dress in Sveyn's fantasy prompted several erotic recollections.

Stevie stopped walking. "You're blushing. Why?"

Crap.

Say something true. "I feel pretty in it."

"You are stunning in it, Hollis," Sveyn murmured in her ear. "Wait until they see."

His words were not helping the blushing situation one bit.

Stevie's resultant smile displayed a very clear I-told-you-so. "Now you'll understand why this is so much fun." She started walking again. "In the twenty-first century we don't get the chance to be elegant and formal the way Jane Austin did."

"No, we don't," Hollis admitted. "I'll give you that."

They were one week from opening of the Kensington wing and things were coming together slowly—but at least they were coming together. Hollis stopped inside the plastic-sheet barrier. "The air-conditioning is on!"

Stevie looked relieved. "Today we need it, but there's a storm on the way. We might end up using the heat next week."

"Either way, we'll be comfortable at last." Hollis walked around the center wall toward the case in the back holding the Blessing.

Sveyn held back. Though the legend that owning one half drove the owner insane, but owning both halves bestowed immortality was ridiculous to Hollis, she knew the Viking believed it.

So did Everett Sage, apparently.

Hollis shook off the reminder of her abduction and stood in front of the bullet-proof, double-locked case. She frowned. Something was wrong.

"Stevie, come over here. Look at this."

Her friend walked up to her side and looked into the case. "What the… We didn't put them that close together."

"No we didn't. We had at least nine or ten inches between them and they were not in line with each other."

Sveyn growled—he was now looking over her shoulder with a very disturbed expression. "This is bad, Hollis."

"That looks more like six or seven inches," Stevie estimated. "How did that happen?"

Hollis felt for her key. "Who has access to this case besides me and Miranda?"

Stevie regarded her with wide eyes. "I don't know."

Hollis moved around to the back of the case and punched in the code. After the light turned green she inserted the key and opened the lock.

"I'm putting them back where they belong," she said as she opened the case.

"You don't have gloves on!" Sveyn barked.

"Screw the gloves," Hollis grumbled.

"Hollis!"

"Hush!"

"I didn't say anything, Hollis." Stevie looked over her shoulder. "Who are you talking to?"

Crapola. "No one."

Sveyn threw his hands up and stomped to the other side of the room.

Stevie glanced in his direction and shuddered. "He's here, isn't he? Your guardian angel?"

Hollis said nothing. She simply moved the halves of the icon back to their original places. Jaw clenched, she lowered the lid on the case and double-locked it again.

Stevie laid a hand on Hollis's arm. "I won't think you're crazy. I promise."

Hollis gazed across the acrylic case at her friend. "Stevie, I don't know what to tell you."

"Tell me this, at least: is there a spirit of some sort following you?"

Hollis hesitated. The desire to be honest with her co-worker overwhelmed her. Besides that, she and Sveyn agreed last night that he could be marginally proved without putting Hollis in danger.

Here goes.

She drew a deep breath. "Yes."

As confident as Stevie was a moment ago, now the blood drained from her face. "Did he just walk past me?"

Hollis nodded.

"Is he evil?"

"No!" Hollis almost laughed. "He is the opposite of evil."

"Thank you for that, at least," Sveyn said from across the room.

"How, I mean, when—" Words failed the normally talkative blonde.

"He just appeared one day." Hollis swallowed the lump that suddenly lodged in her throat. "And one day he'll disappear, I expect."

"What's his purpose?" Stevie pressed. "Does he have a mission?"

Hollis decided to punt this answer. "I think he came to save me from Everett."

Sveyn crossed his arms and wagged his head. He leaned against the opposite wall. "And yet I was as surprised as you at what occurred."

Stevie risked a tentative look over her shoulder. "But he's still here."

"Tell her I guard the icon."

Hollis flicked a glance at Sveyn. It was a good suggestion. "Maybe I'm wrong to call him a guardian angel. He's probably attached to the icon, not to me."

"Oh." Stevie looked at Hollis with obvious relief. "Well that would make sense."

"It would, wouldn't it," Hollis mused. "That's the logical explanation." *Thank you, Sveyn*.

Stevie heaved a sigh. "I guess we should get to work."

"Yep." Hollis walked past the half-filled display cases. "But first, I'm going to talk to Miranda and see who's messing with the Blessing."

Chapter Eight

"The icon pieces were moved?" Miranda opened her desk and reached for the other key to the case. She lifted it up, still attached to a four-inch rubber Saguaro cactus by a thin steel cable. "My key's here, right where I left it."

She dropped the key back in the drawer. "Are you sure the pieces were moved?"

Sveyn leaned down to Miranda. "Yes," he said in her ear.

Miranda brushed her hair away from that ear.

Hollis hesitated, wondering if that was more than a coincidence. "Um, yes. Both Stevie and I agreed they were not where we left them."

Miranda's brow furrowed. "Maybe the case was moved and the pieces slipped. I know the AC crew was working until late last night."

That was certainly possible. "Who was with them?"

"The security guys worked late." Miranda flashed a wry grin. "With Christmas coming, they were happy about the overtime."

"I guess that's what must have happened." Hollis was vaguely unsatisfied, but there was no basis for claiming that anything else had occurred. "But can you *please* tell them to be more careful? It's not like we can order replacements if something gets damaged."

"You're right about that." Miranda scribbled a note. "And I certainly will."

"Thank you."

Miranda looked up from her desk. "What are you bringing on Thursday?"

Thanksgiving.

Hollis named the first thing that came to her mind. "Stuffing."

Sveyn looked puzzled. "What are you stuffing?"

Stop talking, Viking. "I don't know what size of turkey you're getting, but in my experience there usually isn't enough room inside for the amount of bread stuffing people want."

Sveyn chuckled. "You put bread inside the turkey?"

"You're right." Miranda made a note on a different pad of paper, then pointed the eraser end of her pencil at Hollis. "Remember—not out of a box."

"Of course not," Hollis lied.

"Because that's the whole point," Miranda pressed. "A home cooked dinner with friends."

"I make it with sausage," Hollis dug her hole deeper. *What are you doing?* "Is that all right?"

"Absolutely! As long as there aren't any oysters, I'm fine with that." Miranda grinned. "I'm so glad you're coming."

Hollis grinned back at her boss and lied once more. "Me, too."

Wednesday
November 25

"They moved again." Stevie stared into the brightly lit case holding the Blessing.

Hollis frowned. Stevie was right. "Someone is playing a trick. They have to be."

"It's not a trick, Hollis." Sveyn deigned to stand beside the case, though he looked nervous. "The damned things want to be joined to each other."

"They're nothing but wood and steel," Hollis objected. "They can't be doing this on their own."

"Are you sure?" Stevie turned wide eyes to Hollis. "Did you ask their guardian?"

Startled by the question, Hollis snapped, "Do you think *he's* doing it?"

Stevie's hands started to shake visibly and she rolled them into fists. "Could he?"

"No." Hollis waved a hand in Sveyn's direction without thinking about it. "He doesn't have a physical body. He can't push things around."

Stevie looked back into the case. "Should you move them back?"

Sveyn's gaze cut to Hollis's. "Yes. And put something between them."

She sighed. "I suppose."

Retrieving her key, she punched in the code, waited for the beep, and unlocked the case.

"What are you doing, Ms. McKenna?" Mr. Benton strode toward her and Stevie. "Is everything all right?"

Crapity crapsalot.

This was not going to go well.

"The halves of the icon keep moving," Stevie blurted.

Hollis's shoulder dropped.

Oh, Stevie.

"What?" The museum's General Manager stopped in front of Hollis. "By themselves?"

Hollis squared her shoulders and spoke with confidence. "Of course not, sir. We believe some workmen have been careless and bumped or moved the case."

"Hmph." Benton looked disappointed with her explanation.

Hollis opened the top of the case and moved the halves until they were about a foot apart. Then she placed the engraved placard, which told their story, in between them.

"How's that?" she asked Sveyn without looking at him.

"Better," he answered.

"That looks a little awkward, if you want my opinion," Benton stated.

Hollis pressed her lips together and waited. She wouldn't move the placard unless Benton ordered her to.

"We can rearrange it on Sunday before the tea," Stevie offered. "And in the meantime, we'll see if they move again."

Hollis closed the case before Benton could say anything else. "If they *are* moved again, I'll want you to look at the security tapes, sir."

Benton shook his head. "The cameras aren't working in here yet."

Hollis looked at the GM, surprised. "Why not?"

"Some wiring issue." He appeared unconcerned. "But we still have time before the opening gala next Tuesday. And the wing's not open to the public until Wednesday."

Hollis bit her lips between her teeth and stuffed the key into the front pocket of her jeans. She looked around the space, trying to think of something to say.

She came up with, "We'll be ready. The interns have been very helpful."

"Good."

Stevie's expression brightened. "Are you coming to the Jane Austin Tea on Sunday, sir?"

Benton considered the petite blonde. Hollis could practically see the wheels turning in his head. "I hadn't planned on it. But I might come after all."

"We'll all be in costume," Stevie effused. "Even Hollis."

"Will she?" Benton turned his attention back to Hollis, his eyes narrowed in thought. "In that case, I'll be sure to attend. What time does it begin?"

"Three o'clock." Stevie looked as pleased as a cat who outsmarted a dog. "It's going to be amazing."

"Yes. Absolutely." A clearly distracted Benton turned on his heel and left the wing without another word.

Hollis sighed and looked around the space. "I'm going to run to the grocery store before all the food's gone. I have to make stuffing for Miranda's dinner tomorrow."

"Not from a box," Stevie chastised.

"Why does everybody keep saying that?" Hollis groused. "It's better than homemade."

"Miranda will know." Stevie shrugged. "I don't know how she does, but she does."

*****

Hollis wore her Bluetooth earpiece in the grocery store so she could talk to Sveyn. She had explained the concept of stuffing to him in the car on the way over, so now that he understood what she was making, he didn't have any comments about the items she tossed in her basket except to ask, "Isn't that a box?"

Hollis grabbed a second one. "I'm using these as a starting point."

"Stevie says Miranda will know," he warned. "Do you wish to risk the wrath of your superior?"

Hollis flipped the box over. "The ingredients are bread crumbs, spices, and dehydrated onions and celery. It's more efficient to buy those things this way."

She tossed the box into her cart. "But I'm adding fresh celery, fresh onion, extra croutons, and sausage. So that counts."

"What is dehydrated?"

"Another word for dried out."

"And croutons?"

"Seasoned cubes of bread that have been toasted—until they are dry."

Sveyn nodded. "So the stuffing is dry?"

"It's supposed to absorb the fat that melts inside the turkey as it bakes." Hollis headed toward the meat counter. "But because my stuffing won't ever see the inside of the bird, I'll have to add fats and liquids."

Sveyn shook his head. "I never understood this when I was with the soldier. I only saw the bowls of unrecognizable food on the tables."

Hollis looked up at the Viking. "You never asked about it?"

"He was a soldier. He never cooked anything." He grinned at her. "And men do not speak about these things."

"True, and what would be the point?" *You can't taste anything anyway.*

Hollis selected a two-pound package of fresh pork sausage, set it in her cart, and pushed it toward the wine aisle. "It's polite in this case to bring the hostess a bottle of wine for the meal."

Sveyn nodded. "I saw that you only have two bottles left in your condo."

Hollis's cheeks warmed. "Wine is good for you. Especially red wine."

"But you drink quite a lot of white wine." The statement was actually a question, judging by Sveyn's expression,

"It's hot in Phoenix. Iced whites are very refreshing." Hollis turned down the aisle lined from bottom to top with a seemingly endless array of choices. "But now it's winter, so…"

Sveyn wandered down the aisle, his hands clasped behind him. "How will you decide which ones to purchase?"

"In this case, by the label," she admitted. "No one could know how all of these taste, so since it's a gift, I'll pick a cute label."

Hollis put several bottles of chardonnay and red zinfandel in her cart as she searched the shelves for a label that stood out.

"What's this?" Hollis bent down and lifted a bottle with a California red blend. "*I Love You* wine?" She smiled at Sveyn. "Now that's adorable!"

"Do you love Miranda?" he asked.

"Yes, but probably not like they mean it." She set the bottle in her cart. "I wonder if it comes in white."

Hollis scanned the bottles for a matching label. "Here—a moscato that's called *Thank You*."

"That seems appropriate, does it not?" the Viking asked.

"Yes. I'll get two so I can keep one." Hollis set the bottles in her cart.

"Here's another." Sveyn squatted and pointed at the shelf.

"It's a chardonnay called *Congrats*. What does that mean?"

"It's short for congratulations." Hollis turned the bottle over and read the label. "Golden Glass Wines. Such fun!"

She put the bottle in her cart. "Are there any more?"

"I don't see any."

"All right. Then let's get going." She turned the cart around and hurried toward the long lines at checkout. Everyone was cooking or baking for the holiday and most seemed to be shopping today. "I have to finish up at the museum before I go home and make my not-from-a-box stuffing."

Sveyn snorted a chuckle.

*****

Hollis's eyes watered as she chopped the onion and it stung her sinuses. The celery was already sizzling in the pan in a bath of butter and olive oil. The sausage was browning in a separate pan.

Sveyn stood in the middle of her small kitchen, his six-and-a-half foot frame completely in her way, whether it had substance or not.

"Excuse me?" she said as she stepped around him to dump half of the onion into the pan with the celery. "Could you stand somewhere else?"

"No."

Hollis looked up at the apparition. "No?"

He shook his head. "I cannot smell this from over there."

She almost dropped her little cutting board. "What do you smell?"

He leaned toward the steaming pan. "Onion. I smell onion. I remember this."

"I don't understand, Sveyn." Hollis set the cutting board on the counter. "How can you smell anything if you don't breathe?"

He straightened and looked down at her. "You act as if I know everything about my condition. When I was impaled by the broadsword and this happened to me, I understood nothing. I did not know what had happened to me, or how this all transpired."

"I know that, but—"

"But *nothing*, Hollis. All along, I have discovered as I go. As I manifest from, from…" He paused, his brow twitching. "Time to time, and from man to man."

Hollis knew all of this, but it felt inconsistent as he began to regain some of his—self. "Only now you manifested to a woman, and everything is altered."

"Yes." He shook his head. "I do not believe you understand how much."

"Stevie can sense you. The cameras caught your essence. And you can smell some aromas if they're exceptionally strong." Hollis leaned back against the counter. "What does this all mean?"

Sveyn looked as flummoxed as she felt. "Damned if I know, Hollis. Damned if I know."

• • • • • • • • • •• • •

Friday
November 27

Hollis walked into her office, dressed for a day of manual labor. She wanted to personally oversee the set-up for the tea in the Glass Pavilion, an area of the modern museum building that was the closest to anything remotely Regency. She didn't want to come to work tomorrow if that could be helped, and setting up today left that possibility open.

Yesterday was more fun than she expected it to be. When she rang Miranda's doorbell, she reminded Sveyn that, "I'm wearing the earpiece, but please be careful about what you say to me."

"Yes, madam, Sveyn teased. "I shall be on my best behavior." And thankfully, he was.

Miranda made a big deal over the wine, declaring it was way too cute to drink. But when Hollis assured her there was plenty more available, she uncorked the bottle and they enjoyed the unexpectedly crisp and delicious moscato together.

The partially box-originated stuffing apparently flew under

Miranda's radar—and if it didn't, her boss said nothing.

Sveyn was fascinated by the football games the men in attendance were watching. As he caught the gist of the play, he chose whichever side Hollis said she favored and cheered along with them.

Hollis smiled at the sight of the tall, leather-linen-and-fur clad figure getting excited over the contests. At one point, he brushed his hair back. And it actually moved.

Something was going on with the not-dead, not-alive Viking, but whatever that might be was way beyond the scope of her experiences.

Maybe the ghost hunters will know.

For the first time, she found a reason not to dread their appearances.

"We're setting up for a hundred guests," Hollis told the interns. "So ten tables with ten chairs each."

"And how many at the head table?" Tom, her favorite intern, asked.

Hollis ticked them off on her fingers. "Benton, Miranda, Stevie, and me, I guess."

"Will Stevie not sit with George?" Sveyn asked.

Good question.

"Stevie might want to sit with George," Hollis told Tom. "But it's better to have a chair we don't need, than scramble for one if we do."

"Gotcha." He ambled off.

Miranda appeared at one end of the space. "Do you need help?"

"No, I think we have it covered." Hollis flashed a quick smile. "My only concern is that everything matches Stevie's instructions and turns out the way she expects."

"I wonder how she's getting along with George's family." Miranda's expression was wistful as she approached. "Those two are so smitten."

Hollis stifled a sigh. Stevie connected with George after her own connection with the lawyer didn't spark and the rest was rapidly becoming history.

"They are really cute together," she admitted. "I'm happy for both of them."

"You're a good person, Hollis." Miranda patted Hollis's shoulder. "One day your knight in shining armor will appear."

Hollis's gaze shifted to Sveyn, and she burst into completely unexpected tears. Those tears quickly descended in the dreaded ugly cry, complete with loud, gulping sobs.

My knight did appear.

But that was all he was: an apparition.

"Oh, sweetie!" Miranda pushed Hollis down onto one of the chairs. A tissue was pressed into her hand. "Please don't cry."

"I—I don't know wh—why I am," Hollis stammered as she tried to staunch her flooding eyes. "I guess my emotions are— are raw right n—now."

Miranda rubbed Hollis back. "I know why. It's that Everett Sage business isn't it?"

Hollis sniffed and wiped her nose, but didn't reply.

Sveyn kneeled beside her, his face drawn. His deep voice rumbled impossibly in her chest. "I am so sorry, Hollis."

"Shut up," she growled.

"I won't shut up, Hollis," Miranda said softly. "You can't blame yourself. We all thought he was charming."

Ah, crap.

Do not answer the Viking.

"He terrified me," Hollis managed then blew her nose. Wiping her tears was a still futile effort. "I've never been so scared."

"I can understand that. Believe me." Miranda continued her soothing touch. "But he isn't the norm, by any means."

"No." Hollis sniffed wetly. "Apparently the norm is a man who wastes ten years of my life, dumps me, and marries someone else four months later."

Miranda nodded sympathetically. "Matt was clearly an ass."

Though her boss was trying to be helpful, Miranda's evaluation of Hollis's live-in boyfriend ricocheted back and shot Hollis in the chest.

"And that makes me the bigger fool for hanging on so long,

Whoa! :)

waiting and hoping for something that was never going to happen!"

Another wave of tears swamped her. Hollis was on a steep downhill roll. "And then, when my knight *does* show up, he ends up being nothing more than a damned smudge on a video tape!"

"Hollis—"

She jumped to her feet. "I need minute."

Managing not to collide with any tables or chairs in spite of her tear-blurred vision, Hollis hurried out of the Pavilion and toward her office with its solid, lockable door.

Sunday
November 29

Hollis straightened her shoulders and walked into the Glass Pavilion. Dressed in the yellow gown, she did her hair up in a loose bun the way Sveyn imagined it in her dream. To complete the stark Regency look, she applied a light coat of mascara and pale lip gloss—though normally she just added a touch of eyeshadow to that duo only when she wanted to look dressy.

"You are stunning, my love," Sveyn purred. "You look perfect in every way."

Hollis tucked the scarf deeper into her cleavage. "I hope I pass muster with the JASNA people."

"If you do not, then they are the mistaken ones," he assured her.

"Hollis!" Stevie's excited voice crossed the glass-enclosed space. "Look at you!"

A beaming Stevie wove between the tables and chairs with George in tow. "That dress is gorgeous!"

Hollis laughed. "Me? Look at George!"

The lawyer did a slow turn followed by a courtly bow once the couple reached her. "I assure you, Miss McKenna, that this is no mere costume."

"No it's not, I can see that." Hollis smiled. "Are you Mister Darcy, or Mister Knightly?"

George leaned forward and gave her a conspiratorial grin. "I am whomever the lady requires me to be."

"Isn't he fantastic, Hollis?" Stevie gushed. "He's so good at every part of this."

Sveyn spoke in her ear. "He is. She's right. That ensemble is perfectly tailored."

Hollis's gaze swept the enclosure, evaluating the progress of the set-up. The caterers seemed to have everything well in hand, and she relaxed a little. "Are you happy with everything?"

"Yes, thank you." Stevie looked over her shoulder. "Everything turned out just like I hoped it would."

Hollis was pleased too, if she was honest. "I'm glad. So how was your Thanksgiving?"

"Stevie was an even bigger hit than my grandmother's pecan pie recipe." George smiled at Stevie. "Though I shouldn't have expected less."

The blonde's cheeks flushed. "Oh, stop."

Miranda entered the pavilion wearing a burgundy dress which was perfect for her dark hair and eyes. "Hollis, you look absolutely fantastic."

Hollis raised her brow. "If you didn't sound so surprised, I'd take that as a compliment."

Mr. Benton strode into the room and gave her a very obvious once-over. Then he nodded, looking pleased. "Ms. McKenna, will you come with me?"

"Yes, sir." She glanced at Miranda and Stevie, both who looked as puzzled as she felt.

With Sveyn at her side, she followed the General Manager out of the pavilion and toward the new wing. A hum of voices behind the plastic made her wary. What was Benton up to?

Crap. Crap. CRAP.

Hollis pasted on a smile as she entered and faced a trio of cameras and reporters.

Really?

"Here she is once again, gentlemen," Benton effused. "Our Lead Collector for the Kensington Collection."

Hollis clasped her hands in front of her and waited for the

barrage of questions.

"How did it feel to discover a signed Jane Austin novel?"

"How did you authenticate it?"

"Has the Jane Austin Society concurred that it is real?"

"Did you find any other Austin memorabilia?"

Luckily, Hollis was prepared to talk about all of those things in her keynote. The answers ticked off as if she had known this press opportunity was going to happen.

She'd make a Benton doll later and stick fat pins in it. Lots of them.

"What about the icon with the curse?" one of the reporters asked suddenly. He had a national logo on his microphone, not one touting a local station.

"I'm sorry, but I do have an event about to start," Hollis deflected.

Benton stepped forward. "Over this way." As he led the crews toward the case he said, "We have the two halves of the *Blessing of the Gods* in a bullet-proof acrylic case with a double lock. It requires both a combination and a key to open it."

When she looked into the case, Hollis's pulse surged. She felt the blood drain from her face.

"Oh my God," Sveyn murmured. "The damned things moved again."

"That's impossible," Hollis replied.

One of the reporters whirled around and stuck his microphone in her face. "What's impossible?"

Think. Fast. "I thought I heard someone ask if it was possible to break the case."

"And of course, it's not," Benton boomed.

"Why take such extreme precautions?"

Hollis stepped in front of the case, blocking the reporters' view. "Because there are crazy people in this world who believe the myth, and they will go to extreme lengths to get their hands on these pieces."

"Weren't you kidnapped last month by one of those crazies?"

Hollis felt her composure precariously near to breaking. "If that's all, I'll be returning to our tea. The Jane Austin Society is why I am here today."

Hollis didn't wait for permission from Benton, but lifted her skirt and walked as quickly as she could from the wing. She slowed her pace once she neared the Glass Pavilion, needing to calm herself before facing the crowd that was streaming into the building.

"Only three or four inches separated them, Hollis."

Hollis nodded, but didn't look at the Viking. "I know. I saw."

"You cannot allow them to join."

She shot him an angry look. "There is nothing I can do about it right now!"

"Before you leave this evening." Sveyn's expression shifted to fear. "Will you move them again? For your own sake?"

Hollis's brow wrinkled. "My sake?"

"You are the owner. This is what the pieces believe."

Hollis scoffed. "You're the crazy one."

Before he could respond, she darted into the Glass Pavilion and joined the Regency gathering.

*****

Her speech was very well received—and easily delivered thanks to her impromptu rehearsal. Benton had his own speech, of course. Miranda did little more than introduce Hollis to the attendees.

The tea was drawing to a close when George approached the head table where Stevie had decided to sit after all. "My I say something to everyone?"

Hollis looked at the other museum employees. "He *is* a member of JASNA."

Benton was obviously in a good mood, having had his day with the cameras. "I have no objection."

"Thank you." George took the wireless microphone from its stand. Hollis noticed his hand was shaking.

He straightened his jacket and cleared his throat before he

Cut scene

began. "Hello everyone. First of all, I would like to thank the Arizona History and Cultural Center for providing us with this generous opportunity. I don't know that any of us would be able to hold one of Jane's signed books if they had not invited us to do so."

had they not

A round of gloved applause swelled in the glass enclosure.

"Secondly, Jane Austin wrote about romance. Chance meetings or planned assignations, it made no difference. She made certain that love bloomed before the last page."

Heads bobbed around the room. The attendees smiled.

"And thirdly, no JASNA gathering would be complete without a little romance of its own." George turned around and held out his hand. A red splotch formed on each cheek of his otherwise pale face. "Miss Phillips, will you join me?"

Looking stunned, Stevie rose to her feet and walked around the end of the head table. "What are you doing, George?"

"I know what he's doing," Sveyn whispered.

Hollis nodded.

Me, too.

When Stevie reached him, George took her hand and bent down on one knee. A delighted gasp shivered through the audience. Stevie's eyes rounded and she covered her mouth with her free silk-gloved hand.

Hollis could no longer see George's face, but she heard the tremor in his voice. She thought that being a trial lawyer he would have more confidence.

I guess love can *fell the mightiest men.*

"Miss Stevie Phillips, would you do me the honor of becoming my wife?"

Stevie's eyes sparkled with happy tears. "Yes. Oh, yes!"

George set the microphone down before he unbuttoned the glove on her left hand and pulled it off. He reached into the small pocket on the front of his jacket and pulled out a glittering ring. He slipped the impressive bit of jewelry onto her finger as people stood at their tables to get a better look.

When he regained his feet, he kissed her.

This time, the applause wasn't hampered by gloves.

Chapter Ten

Monday
November 30

"The opening's tomorrow," she reminded Sveyn needlessly. "I have a lot to do today."

"Check the icon again." He didn't look away from the windshield as they wove through the rush-hour-crowded parkway and toward the museum.

"When I have time." She stayed behind yesterday and moved the pieces apart after the tea. Truthfully, the thing was creeping her out and the less time she spent in its presence, the better. Denial was a wonderful thing.

"Do not wait too long, Hollis. They must not touch."

"I know."

"Promise me."

"Yes," she hissed. "Now be quiet and let me think."

Stevie was already in the office hallway, flashing her diamond engagement ring and telling the story of George's public proposal.

"Want to see a picture?" She pulled up the photos on her

phone and showed them to the employees who worked in the public areas of the museum, while they all made the appropriate coos and comments.

Hollis smiled as she scooted past the crowd and into her office. There was too much to finish for her to waste time this morning—not that congratulating Stevie on her abundant happiness was wasting time exactly, but Hollis had toasted and hugged her friend yesterday. And tomorrow evening the proof of her worth as a Lead Collector would be displayed to the world.

That meant that she had to be focused today. Details were key.

"What the hell is this?" Tony Samoa stormed into Hollis's office holding up his phone.

"Good morning, Tony." Hollis stepped behind her desk and dropped her purse into the drawer. "What are you all worked up about now?"

"This." Tony thrust the phone in front of her. "Don't play dumb, Hollis. It doesn't suit you."

Hollis stared at the headline on the Arizona Central website: *Cursed or Blessed? Icons have a will of their own.*

"What the—" Hollis fell onto her chair and pulled the site up on her computer. As she read the copy, a shudder of foreboding tripped up her spine.

A six-thousand-year-old icon, which will be on public display beginning on Wednesday at the Arizona History and Cultural Center, seems to be trying to fulfill its own legend.

"Oh my god." Hollis framed her forehead with her hands as she read the short article, which claimed that the pieces mysteriously inched closer together on their own in their special case.

"Every morning when we return to the display, the halves are closer together than the evening before," states the museum's General Manager Isaac Benton. *"It's undoubtedly eerie."*

Hollis rose to her feet, so angry she could hardly see straight. "Don't say anything!" she growled at Sveyn who was giving her an angrily smug look.

"Like what?" Tony demanded. "Like this is a cheap trick—which it is!"

Hollis leaned her hands on her desk and glared at Tony, who recoiled a little. "This is all Benton's doing, and I'm going to call him on it." She straightened. "You want to come?"

Without waiting for an answer, Hollis strode from her office toward Benton's, assuming the museum's permanent Collector and the Viking apparition were both close behind.

*****

"Ms. McKenna, I don't like your tone." Benton sat behind his desk, the offending article displayed on his screen.

"I'm sorry, Mr. Benton." Hollis struggled to pull back her irritation. "But I don't like my work ridiculed."

"No one is ridiculing your work," Benton objected. "On the contrary—you've done an excellent job."

Hollis threw a thumb over her shoulder in Tony's direction. "He's ridiculing it. My *peer* thinks this is a joke. And he's right."

Benton's eyes narrowed. "What exactly is the joke here?"

Hollis turned around and faced Tony. "Tell him. You called it a cheap trick."

The Hispanic man flinched. "What I meant was—"

"Trick?" Benton stood and pinned Tony with a hard gaze. "Are you suggesting that I am moving the pieces myself?" His gaze shifted to Hollis. "Is that what you're saying?"

Hollis was gob smacked. There was only one way to respond to the question. "Are you saying that the pieces actually moved on their own?"

Benton raised his hands. "Well I've never touched them!"

Hollis felt all the fire drain from her, and another shiver of fear took its place.

"I told you, Hollis," Sveyn murmured in her ear. "That thing has power."

She wagged her head. "This isn't possible..."

"Go check them now," the Viking urged.

Hollis spun on her heel and left Benton's office, practically running through the halls to the Kensington wing. She heard footsteps behind her; apparently Tony and Benton were both following her.

She stopped in front of the case, staring in disbelief. "After the tea, I moved them apart."

Tony appeared on her left. "How far?"

"A foot."

The icons were so close that barely an inch separated them. Hollis whirled to face a panting Benton. "How did you know about this?"

"About what? That the pieces move?" He scowled at her. "I know everything that happens in this museum."

"Who has the combination and keys besides me and Miranda?"

"I do."

"Who else?" she pressed.

He folded his arms over his chest. "No one."

The realization punched Hollis in the chest. "And you told the reporters about this yesterday afternoon while I was at the tea."

"I believe it's newsworthy. Don't you?"

"I believe it's ticket worthy." Hollis dragged her fingers through her curls. "What's really going on here?"

Benton lifted one eyebrow. "What's going on here is that this wing opens tomorrow night. And this icon is the most unique object in the man's collection. And thanks to your research, Ms. McKenna, we know that there is a legend attached to the pieces."

Hollis shifted her gaze to Sveyn. His expression was somber and otherwise unreadable.

"I assure you, I have never touched these pieces," Benton continued. "I can't tell you anything more than that."

Tony's face was pale. "I, uh, apologize, Hollis. I thought it was your doing."

"Apology accepted," she mumbled. Shooting a glance at Benton, she fished the case's key from her pocket. "I'll move them apart again and then get back to work."

*****

Hollis was exhausted, probably more from the unease prompted by the day's revelations that the actual tasks she completed for tomorrow's gala opening.

It's not possible. The pieces can't move themselves.

"Could it be magnetic?" she asked Miranda. "Maybe the steel is magnetized."

"That's an easy test," her boss pointed out. "Did you try it?"

Hollis did.

Nothing.

She sat slumped in her office chair with her feet on her desk. "There has to be an explanation, Sveyn. Someone is moving those pieces."

The Viking sat on the corner of her desk. "Though I disagree, there is a way to discover if that is true."

Hollis shook her head. "Benton would never release the security video. It's to his advantage to keep the possibility alive."

"I am not speaking about the security video."

Hollis tilted her head up toward Sveyn's. "What then?"

"Me."

Of course. "How?"

"My tether has grown long enough that I can easily remain inside the museum while you are outside." He tipped his head in the direction of the back door. "You leave and scan your card. Park your car as far from me as you can, and stay there. If I see someone move the pieces, I will tell you."

Her brow puckered. "Could be a long night."

"Or an early morning."

"Yes... Someone could be arriving very early to move them." Hollis pressed her lips together and nodded. "That's obviously what we need to do."

"When shall we do this?"

Good question.

"The sooner the better, I think." Hollis stretched. "Tonight."

Sveyn looked at her like she was nuts. "You are too tired."

"I'll sleep in my car." Hollis swung her feet down from her

desktop. "I won't be able to sleep at home anyway, just thinking about it."

She reached for her purse. "I'll go home now and get a pillow and blankets. And I'll tell everybody that I'm coming back after I get something to eat, and staying late to finish some paperwork."

Hollis followed through with that plan, returning to the office just after six o'clock. Stevie had tried to talk her out of working late, and Miranda insisted that any paperwork could wait until after the gala. But Hollis stood firm.

"I'll be out of here by eight. Nine at the latest." She held up three fingers. "Scout's honor."

She sat at her desk, looking busy as she typed a chatty email to her parents, and waited until everyone had left the property except her. Tom the intern was the last to leave.

"I just wanted to say, before tomorrow night and everything, that I have really been honored to work with you." Tom's cheeks reddened. "I have learned so much about handling pieces, and how objects are researched, and how displays are chosen…"

Hollis smiled at the twenty-something young man. "Your help has been amazing, Tom. Thank you."

"I wish…" He paused as if deciding to choose different words. "Well, I wish everything goes perfect tomorrow."

Hollis couldn't help herself. "Perfect*ly*."

Tom grinned. "Yeah."

Now that the intern was gone, Hollis sent the email and finally relaxed. "I'll wait about half an hour before I go out to my car. Just in case anyone checks the log."

Sveyn nodded. "That is a good plan."

"Meanwhile—" Hollis stood. "—I'll wash my face, brush my teeth, comb my hair, and get ready for bed."

Sveyn followed her to the ladies room and inside. "What do you expect to discover?"

"That someone, maybe even Benton, is moving the pieces." She looked at Sveyn in the mirror while she brushed her hair. "What about you?"

The Viking appeared honestly confused. "I do not know

what to expect. I do believe the legend, and I know that thing is evil, but…" He shrugged. "Can it connect itself? Or must the owner of the halves do so? This I do not know."

Hollis tied her hair into a ponytail and washed her face. Sveyn's unshakeable stance on the Blessing seemed foolish to her, yet she had grown to know the Viking well over the last three months. He was intelligent and logical, even while his belief was not.

Not in the modern world, anyway.

And yet, in this modern world, I'm talking to a man caught between.

This was going to be a very interesting experiment, of that she was certain.

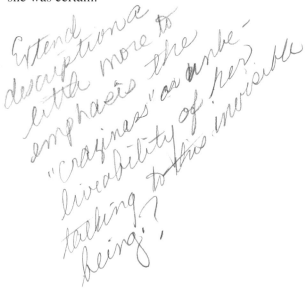

Chapter Eleven

Tuesday
December 1

"Hollis! Wake up!"

Startled, Hollis opened her eyes. The top half of Sveyn's body was sticking through her car door. "What?"

"Get up! Tom just went into the museum. You have to hurry!"

Right. I'm in my car. At the museum.

Tom?

Hollis threw her blanket aside and opened the back door of her car. A blast of forty-degree air rudely woke her the rest of the way up. She slid out the door, reclaimed the blanket because it was freaking freezing outside, and slammed the car door shut.

"Let's go." She ran around the corner of the construction trailer—which she hid her car behind, just in case—and toward the employee entrance, trying not to trip on the blanket. "What time is it?"

"It is just after six o'clock."

And dark this time of year.

Hollis swiped her employee key card and opened the back door. "Where is he?"

"He was heading toward the new wing." Sveyn ran ahead of her. "Let me see if I can find him."

Hollis re-wrapped the blanket around her as she walked down the office hallway. The only lights in this part of the museum were the security lights in the corners of the ceilings, and they were only on because she swiped her card and opened the door. She was on video, and she knew it.

Hopefully that would not come back and bite her.

"In here, Hollis!" Sveyn's muffled shout came from the Kensington wing.

The translucent plastic veil still covering the wing's entrance was abruptly thrown back and Tom stepped into the dimly-lit lobby. He jumped back with a little grunt, startled to see Hollis where he certainly expected to see no one at all.

"Hollis? What are you doing here?" he demanded.

She walked up to him. "I might ask the same, Tom."

He frowned. "Why are you wrapped in a blanket? Are those pajamas?"

"Yoga pants."

"What—"

"Just turn around and head back where you came from." She gave him a little shove. "We need to talk."

Tom hesitated as if debating his options.

"I know you've been moving the pieces, Tom," Hollis offered. "Let's go talk about why."

He didn't move. "Were you spying on me?"

Hollis tightened the blanket. "Yep."

"How? You weren't in your office..." Poor Tom was clearly confused, and rightly so, but Hollis certainly wasn't going to enlighten him.

"That's for me to know." She pushed him again. "Let's go talk, Tom. I'm sure you don't want the police involved with this."

That seemed to sink in. "No. I'm sorry. Okay."

Hollis followed Tom around the curve of the wing to the

Blessing's case in the back. Sveyn was pacing nervously in front of the display.

"Calm down," Hollis said to both men. "Give me the key, Tom."

A sheepish Tom placed the key to the case in her palm.

"Did Benton give you this?" she asked.

"I guess so, but I don't know for sure. It was in my employee mailbox with instructions to move the pieces closer together." Tom's expression sank; he looked worse by the minute. "And every day that I did, there would be an envelope with a fifty-dollar-bill in my box."

"No one else has a reason to do this," Sveyn muttered.

"No one else has the finances to do this," Hollis countered.

Tom nodded. "That's what I thought."

Hollis laid the blanket over another display case and went around to the back of the bullet proof display. She punched in her code, and then unlocked the top.

As she lifted it, she looked at the intern. "Why did you do it, Tom? Was it just the money?"

"No…" He shrugged, guilt plastered all over his face. "If it *was* Benton, I wanted to stay on his good side, you know?"

"Move them and close the top, Hollis," Sveyn said. "Then we can be rid of this business."

Hollis looked down at the two halves of the Blessing, and something inside her snapped. This icon was being given way too much attention. Enough was enough.

She grabbed one half in each hand and lifted them from the case.

"Put those back!" Sveyn barked.

"These are just wood and metal!" Hollis walked around the case to face Tom, though her words were meant for both of the men. "They aren't magic. They have no power. They're not alive—they're dead."

Sveyn stepped closer. "Put them down. Now."

"The myth is just that. A myth. Made up by a superstitious culture that existed hundreds—"

"Thousands!" Sveyn interrupted.

"—of years ago. Long before science and technology explained the things that they were terrified of. Like the Northern Lights, for example." Hollis looked at the carved and pierced pieces in her hands. "How could any modern person with a functioning brain cell believe otherwise?"

Put us together. The words were whispered into her right ear.

You know that you want to. Those words were in her left ear.

Hollis's hands began to shake. She lifted her gaze. "Which one of you said that?"

Tom frowned. "Which one of who? It's only you and me here."

"Hollis," Sveyn pleaded. "Put them down."

You see how we fit. That whisper was in stereo.

Her right ear: *Go on.*

Her left ear: *You are so close.*

Hollis felt the pieces begin to vibrate in her hands. They grew warm. The urge to connect them overwhelmed her. "How do they go together, do you think?"

Tom gave her an odd look. "I don't know."

"Stop!" Sveyn shouted.

"Like this?" Hollis touched the pieces together.

Images flooded her mind, swirling with increasing speed and separated by blinding flashes of light. Past. Present. *Future.*

A roar of thunder rumbled her frame.

Her breath came in sudden staccato gasps.

"Hollis, let go! *Hollis, let go! HOLLIS! LET GO!*" Sveyn bellowed. He stood close in front of her, futilely batting at the icon, his hands passing through the object with no effect.

Tom launched himself at her, knocking her against the acrylic case. It slammed shut as the force of his weight bent her backwards over it. The ancient pieces of the Blessing clattered angrily to the floor. She swore she heard them scream.

"Hollis? Are you all right?" Tom's worried face hovered over hers.

Her mind cleared slowly. "What?"

"Can you breathe? Are you hurt?"

Her core was still trembling. "Let me up," she croaked.

Tom retreated and offered his hand. "I'm sorry. I didn't mean to tackle you."

Hollis unsteadily regained her feet. "Why did you?"

Tom's expression looked like he didn't believe his own words. "Something was attacking you."

She squinted at him in the dim light. "Attacking me? Was it the Blessing?"

He shook his head. "No. It looked like a man. Seven feet tall. All in brown." Tom swallowed and glanced to the side where Sveyn stood glaring at her. "But he wasn't *really* there, was he."

Hollis wouldn't say one way or the other on that. "Did it look like the smudge on the security video?"

"No. That image looked like the whatever-it-was had wings. But this thing didn't have wings. And it was clawing at you." Tom shuddered. "Couldn't you see it?"

In truth, she couldn't see much past the explosion of visuals in her head. "No. I just felt a surge of energy when the pieces touched. It dazed me, like an electric shock."

"I told you, woman," Sveyn scolded, scowling at her. "But you were too damned stubborn to pay heed."

Hollis couldn't face him; the Viking was right about one thing—those two halves created some sort of energy force when they touched.

Tom took another step back and looked at the pieces on the floor. "What now?"

Hollis rubbed her face with both hands as she formed a plan. "First, we put them back in the case and at least a foot apart," she said from behind her palms. "You can go ahead and do that now."

Hollis moved out of the way while Tom picked up one piece at a time and laid them in place. Then she came around to the back of the case and locked it.

"Next, I'm going home to wash up and change clothes." She collected her blanket from atop the other case. "You are going to start making a rustic looking barricade to lay between those pieces in the case."

"Rustic looking?" Tom asked. "Like what?"

"Like out of old wood and tin, or whatever you can find." She waved toward the outside wall. "Maybe there's construction trash out there you can use."

"Okay." Tom's brow furrowed. "But why, exactly?"

Hollis faced the intern. "We are going to support Benton's contention that the pieces move by preventing them from ever touching."

"Oh-kaaay..." It was another question.

"Then third, we are going to speak with Mr. Benton, and tell him that we know all about his little scheme." Hollis was mad enough about the whole situation that she didn't care if he fired her.

He wouldn't. But Tom didn't know that. "No, Ms. McKenna, please don't. I really need this referral."

She shook her head. "Don't worry. We have the upper hand. First, we'll tell him about the barrier you will have made by then which proves *his* story."

Tom nodded. "I get it now."

"Then we tell him that if the security video from this morning is not deleted while we watch, then you and I will go public to expose that scheme, and claim that both security videos are frauds."

He still looked unsure. "But they aren't frauds. Right?"

"Doesn't matter. It's our word against his."

Sveyn leaned toward her. "He wants to know for certain that he did not imagine me."

"I know."

"Well, if you know..." Tom rested his hands on his hips and his head dropped. "I'm really sorry, ma'am."

Hollis didn't want to let the intern off too easily, lest he be tempted to falsify museum happenings again sometime. "This was a very unwise choice, Tom. It would be a career-killer under different circumstances. Do you realize that?"

He looked like he was going to cry. "Yes, ma'am."

"We can't mess around with the truth," she pressed. "We have a responsibility. People trust us."

Tom nodded and wiped an eye. "I'm going to get started on that barrier."

"I'll see you in a while." Hollis threw her blanket over her shoulder. "Be ready."

*****

Once back inside her car, Hollis finally let her tears loose. "What the hell was that?"

Sveyn was clearly still angry with her. "Do you believe me at last that the thing is evil?"

"I do. I think. I don't know what to believe, to be honest with you." Hollis wiped her eyes with a shaking hand and started her car.

"What did you experience?" Sveyn demanded. "Tell me everything."

Speaking past the irritating constriction of her voice caused by her uncontrolled crying, Hollis described her experience as best she could while she drove to her condo. First she told Sveyn about the directional whispers, the pieces' vibrations, and the way the icon literally warmed up in her hands.

At a stoplight she pulled a paper napkin from the stack in her glovebox and blew her nose. Then she described her sudden difficulty breathing, the flashes of light, and the feeling of thunder causing her chest and gut to tremble.

Last were the images—past, present, and what had to be the future—cycling rapidly through her mind.

"I can't say that the blessing makes a person immortal. That seems too far-fetched," she stated, still wiping her nose. "But there is something eternal embedded in it, I think."

Sveyn nodded. "The sons of god who made it were eternal."

"Were?" Hollis glanced at her passenger. "How does that stop? Isn't that an oxymoron?"

"What is an oxymoron?"

"That something that was *temporarily* eternal," she repeated. "That doesn't make any sense."

Sveyn waved one hand. "No, what does the word oxymoron

mean?"

Hollis coughed a laugh, the first lift of her spirits on this fraught morning. "Sorry. It means two words which describe one thing, only that one thing can't embody both words used to describe it."

He still looked confused. "Give me an example."

"Plastic glass. Paid volunteer. Bitter sweet." Hollis smiled. "Alive ghost."

Sveyn smiled a little at that. "I understand. So temporarily eternal seems to be an oxymoron."

Hollis turned into her condo complex's parking lot. "Seems to be? How is it not?"

"I tell you again, Hollis, read your Bible. The sons of god are mentioned in Genesis, and their demise is foretold in the Psalms."

She sighed. "Fine. I'll give you that one."

When she parked her car and turned off the engine, Sveyn held out a hand to stop her from getting out. "Hollis, it is important to me that you admit you were wrong about the Blessing. It is not a blessing in any way. Instead, it holds a curse."

For the first time in her three-month relationship with the Viking apparition, Hollis realized she was not the dominant one. Sure, she had the physical body, and that gave her an upper hand at times. But Sveyn possessed both greater general knowledge and a stronger personal will than she did.

Well, he is nearly a thousand years old.

When she bent her will to Matt's, she always felt he respected her less for it.

She felt nothing like that now. She knew without a doubt that Sveyn would respect her more.

"You were right, Viking. I was wrong. This blessing-curse thing is so far outside of my modern existence that I dismissed it as impossible." She heaved a shuddering sigh. "I should not have done that. I'm sorry."

A slow smile spread across his handsome scruff-bearded face and his eyes glowed purple in the pink light from the rising sun. "I love and respect you, Hollis. I fervently wish that I could kiss you right now."

Me, too.

"Let me get through today and tonight," she said, opening her car door. "And then, when I go to bed at last, you can have you way with me."

Chapter Twelve

Mr. Benton was watching the early morning security video when Hollis and Tom walked into his office unannounced. The look on his face when he saw them hovered somewhere between excitement and apprehension.

"Good morning. What can I do for you two?" he asked, flashing a grin that was not at all convincing.

Hollis squared her shoulders and pointed at the computer screen. "We need to talk about that, sir."

He leaned back in his custom chair. "What about it?"

Hollis stood in front of the general manager's desk, forgoing a chair of her own. She needed to take the dominant stance in this exchange if she and Tom were to achieve what they hoped.

"First of all, I am asking that the security video from this morning be permanently deleted."

The grin faded. "First of all?"

"Yes, sir."

"What comes second?"

"That depends on how you respond to the first."

Benton leaned forward and planted his elbows on the desk. "What exactly did happen, Ms. McKenna, when you touched the two pieces of the icon together?"

Sveyn stepped around the desk and stood next to Benton. "Hold steady, Hollis."

"What did you see, sir?" she countered.

The man's eyes narrowed. "I saw what looked like a ghost of some sort attacking you. And then Tom here scared it away."

She gave a little shrug. "Then you saw more than I did."

Benton scowled. "What sort of game are you playing?"

Hollis drew a deep breath and measured out her words. "I have agreed to cooperate with the ghost hunters and the other kooks who asked to come do whatever sort of research it is that they do—"

"For a nice extra income, don't forget," Benton interrupted

Hollis ignored the comment. "But I never agreed to be made a spectacle of, nor be party to deception. If this video is not permanently deleted, then we will hold a press conference of our own and expose your scheme for moving the pieces of the icon."

He shook his head, chuckling. "I never touched—"

Now Hollis interrupted. "No. But you paid someone else to."

Benton's gaze shifted to the silent intern at her side and back to hers. "There is no proof of that."

"Maybe not." Hollis shrugged. "But our story will be believed because a real scandal always trumps fake ghosts."

Benton glared at her. "And if I do agree, what comes second?"

Hollis smiled a little. "Then we'll show you the new antique-looking barrier that Tom is making, which will be placed inside the display case between the halves of the icon, and will prevent them from moving close enough to touch."

"You will perpetuate the story?" He looked skeptical, as he should have.

"The myth is historical. And it's written on the plaque." Hollis lifted one shoulder. "The barrier only helps illustrate that."

"We don't ever say the pieces actually moved," Tom added. Clearly the intern was beginning to feel like his position at the museum might survive this interview. "So we aren't messing with the truth."

Benton tapped his steepled fingers against his lips. "What about showing this video to those ghost hunters and kooks?"

Hollis shook her head. "I would really rather not, because you know as well as I do that if it's not deleted, it will eventually end up on YouTube."

Hollis crossed her arms and waited. She wasn't going to speak again until Benton did. She and Tom had the upper hand, and yet they offered the general manager a way to insinuate that the legend might hold some truth.

But there's no way in hell I'll ever tell him how much.

Hollis forcefully stifled a shudder.

Mr. Benton shifted in his chair. He turned his monitor so Hollis and Tom could see it. He selected the video section in question and hit delete. When asked if he was sure he wanted to delete that portion of the video, he hit enter.

The video disappeared.

*****

Hollis went to her office, relieved to some extent. There was certainly a way to retrieve the video clip from wherever it was that deleted files went, but Benton seemed to believe her when she said she'd expose the trick.

"You handled that very well, Hollis," Sveyn complimented.

"Thank you." She looked at the navy blue cocktail dress hanging on the back of her office door. Ten hours remained until the gala, and then most of the insanity would be over.

She lifted her still-to-do list and mentally triaged the tasks.

"There you are, Hollis!" Stevie bounced into the office. "Where were you?"

"Last minute meeting with Benton." Hollis looked up from her list. "And now I'm deciding what we need to do and in what order."

"In case it helps, the museum is closing at three today so the caterers can set up in the lobby." Stevie waved the hand weighted down by her glittering engagement ring. "Benton made the call yesterday and Miranda had it posted on the website last night."

Hollis wrinkled her nose. "I'm assuming the TV stations will be here. Again."

"Only outside. Miranda made a point of that." Stevie grinned. "Too many socialites and local celebrities are attending. She told Benton he wouldn't want his thunder stolen by letting them hog the press."

Hollis laughed. "Well for once his hubris is working in our favor."

"Is that your dress?" Stevie closed the office door so she could get a full view. "It's beautiful."

"Thanks." Hollis tamped down the memory of the last time she wore it: Matt's office promotion party. A month before he broke up with her, and five months before he married someone else.

"I told George he didn't have to rent a tux." Stevie smiled wistfully. "I'm just so happy to have him by my side."

While Hollis didn't begrudge Stevie a moment of joy, her friend's happiness shined a glaring spotlight on both Hollis's current lack of a functional relationship, and that there were no visible options on her horizon.

Sveyn was watching her carefully, as if he could read her thoughts. Hollis turned away from his pitying gaze.

"We better get to work if we're going to get finished in time for me to get gorgeous," she quipped.

*****

Hollis examined herself in the restroom mirror and fussed with her hair. She decided to put half of it up in the loose bun again, and leave the rest of her curls spilling over her shoulder.

Sveyn smiled at her in the mirror. "That dark color looks good on you."

Hollis smiled back. "Redheads don't generally look good in black, so navy is my go-to."

"It complements your eyes and your hair very nicely." Sveyn

heaved a breathless sigh and frowned.

Hollis froze. "What's wrong?"

"I think I smell lavender." He waved his hand. "But there are no flowers here."

Hollis turned around to face him. "Is it this?" She lifted her wrist to his nose.

He leaned down and sniffed. "Yes. I believe so."

She smiled at him. "It's the lotion I put on. It's scented with lavender."

"So once again I am not imagining this." Sveyn stared at her. "And yet I have not discovered what this means."

Hollis turned back to the mirror. She certainly had no explanations for the Viking, and no time right now to think about it. "How does my hair look in back?"

"There is one place that requires one of those metal pins."

Hollis grabbed a bobby pin. "Where?"

"Lower. To the left. There."

Hollis felt the errant lock and pinned it in place. "How's that?"

"Perfection, my lady." Sveyn's smile in the mirror warmed her throughout. "You looking stunning."

Hollis tucked her makeup and hair paraphernalia into her tote bag and retrieved the gold pumps and chunky necklace that completed her outfit. Donning both, she zipped the bag closed.

"Let's get this party started," she muttered. "The sooner it starts, the sooner it ends."

The looks she received from her co-workers as she carried the tote bag and her work clothes to her office surprised her.

"You look amazing, Ms. McKenna," Tom said.

"Thank you." She felt herself blush a little.

Even Tony Samoa appeared impressed. "I have to admit, you clean up nicely, Hollis."

Not quite a compliment, but more than expected. "Thanks."

After stowing her bag and straightening her already straight dress, Hollis walked out of the administrative office area and into the museum. With half an hour remaining before the doors were opening, the loud hum of conversation was surprising.

"Ah—here you are." Mr. Benton grabbed Hollis's elbow. "Let's step into the pavilion and talk to the press."

A brisk winter breeze threatened rain, so the reporters had been allowed into the glass-walled entry way. Hollis stood next to Miranda, who stood next to Benton, who spoke in glowing terms about the collection and the opening and how proud he was that the Arizona History and Cultural Center had been selected by the late Ezra Kensington the Fifth to house his treasured collection.

"Ladies and gentlemen, I have a catalogue for each of you to take with you so that you can highlight any pieces that catch your eye."

While Miranda handed out the glossy booklets one reporter asked, "Is that Blessing thing in there?"

Hollis decided to answer that one herself. "The *Velsignelse av Gudene*—Blessing of the Gods—is most certainly included."

"Has there been any more unexplained activity?" another asked.

"No. And it's very likely there never was," Hollis stated before Benton could say anything incriminating. "But just in case, we have placed a barrier between the two halves."

"We do wish to honor the legend," Benton added, stepping in front of her. "Our ancestors certainly did."

Miranda looked at her watch. "Do any of you have more questions? If not, our guests will be arriving soon."

Glances bounced and heads shook. Cameramen turned off their lights, microphone cases were opened, and Hollis reentered the museum proper with Miranda right behind her.

"Glad that's done," Hollis said. "Now there it's just two hours of schmoozing to get through."

"You look amazing, Hollis," Miranda gushed. "That dress fits you like a sexy glove."

Hollis looked at her boss and chuckled. "Good. Because this dress needs a new memory. It's way too expensive to get rid of."

The museum doors were propped open at seven on the dot. The hundred-plus invited guests—all of whom made a minimum donation for the right to attend the wing's opening—began to enter.

They were greeted in the lobby with trays of champagne flutes and canapés, and directed by uniformed museum employees toward the now-uncovered entrance to the Kensington wing.

Hollis grabbed a flute of champagne. "Here's to us, Miranda. We deserve to make the best of the evening."

Miranda accepted a flute of champagne as well, and touched the rim to Hollis's. "We certainly do."

When her stomach rumbled, Hollis waved a waiter over and selected a couple of the hors d'oeuvres. "I just realized I forgot to eat dinner."

"Well, there's plenty." Miranda mimicked her actions again. "Good thing, because I did too."

Hollis grinned. "There's always pizza on the way home."

"And garlic knots," Sveyn added with a wink. "I am going exploring."

Hollis watched the towering Viking move through the crowd and around the corner into the new wing. Damn but he was handsome.

Miranda popped the canapé into her mouth. "Shall we go inside?"

Hollis drained her champagne flute and traded it for a full one. "Let's go. I'm ready."

The first hour went fairly quickly as Hollis was barraged with questions about the entire collection. It seemed that those in attendance held themselves above the controversy, and asked instead about the more traditional objects: the signed Mansfield Park, the English criminal's tricorn, the Viking sunstone, and the stone dildo.

"We can't be certain what the exact purpose was for this object, other than to know by the carving that it was linked with fertility," Hollis explained to a trio of smiling older women.

"That's the official line, isn't it dearie." The woman patted Hollis's arm. "But we all know what this was used for don't we?"

Hollis smiled as well. "We are all certainly free to come up with our own possibilities."

"Well, I think you should sell them in the gift shop," another stated. "You'll make a fortune."

Hollis laughed at the mental image of the phallic-shaped carving on display in the museum store. "I will pass your suggestion on, ladies."

Hollis turned toward the lobby with the intent of replacing her long-emptied champagne glass.

She smiled at the waitress who accommodated her and lifted the flute in a toast. "One hour done. One hour to go."

The girl smiled politely. "Yes, ma'am."

"Hollis?"

"Yes?" She turned toward the voice, and her jaw dropped. "What the *hell* are you doing here?"

Chapter thirteen

Sveyn was at her side in a blink. But even his looming presence couldn't calm her heart—which had decided to buck and pitch like a bronco gone berserk.

"Who is this?" Sveyn demanded.

"Matt. Matt Wallace." Hollis's grip on the champagne flute tightened.

He flashed a nervous grin. "In the flesh."

Don't lose it.

No matter what.

Hollis shifted her stance. "I'm serious, Matt. What are you doing here?"

"I came to see you, of course."

"How did you find me?" *Okay,* that *was a dumb question.*

Matt chuckled. "I Googled you. You're a little famous, you know."

Damn the media whore.

Hollis waved her free hand. "How did you get in tonight? This is a private event for donors."

Matt gave her one of those condescending looks she always hated. "Yes, Hollis. It is."

Crapola crapsalot. "Well, then. Thank you for your support."

Matt dipped his chin. "You are very welcome."

She sipped her champagne to keep from saying anything she probably shouldn't. Instead she managed, "How is Suzan?"

"Um, great. She—"

"It was a polite question, Matt. I really don't give a rat's ass." Hollis gulped her champagne and handed the empty glass to a surprised Matt who accepted it. "If you'll excuse me?"

Whirling on the heel of one of her golden pumps, Hollis strode across the lobby with her shoulders square, head high, and a little extra swing in her hips. She knew he would be watching.

Once in the ladies room, however, her tenuous composure made a hasty exit.

She locked the restroom door and stood in front of the mirror, blotting tears as soon as they appeared and trying to protect her makeup.

Sveyn sat on the counter, facing her. "Why is he here, Hollis?"

"To torture me?" she snapped.

"And why would he want to do that?"

"Who the hell knows?" She cut her glance to his. "Whose side are you on?"

"Do not be foolish," Sveyn chided. "I am asking you serious questions."

Hollis continued to blot her eyes, but Sveyn's inquiry was already pulling her out of the abyss.

"Okay, I don't really think he came here to torture me." She pressed the tissue into the corners of her eyes. "Why would he? He's ecstatically married to a beautiful woman and has an amazing job at some hoity-toity ad firm."

Sveyn's brow twitched. "What's an ad firm?"

Hollis dropped her hands from her eyes. "You know hoity-toity, but can't puzzle out ad firm?"

The Viking looked offended. "Hoity-toity is an old expression. I have heard it many times."

"Sorry." Hollis turned back to the mirror and dabbed fresh

tears. "I didn't mean to make fun of you."

Sveyn dipped his chin. "You are forgiven. Now, could 'ad' be short for advertisement?"

Hollis nodded. "Yes."

"So Matt works for a revered advertisement firm, and yet you are the one who, as he said, is a little famous."

Hollis snorted and regarded the apparition again. "Are you suggesting he's jealous of me?"

Sveyn gave her a one-shoulder shrug. "Is that truly so impossible?"

Hollis's tears slowed as she considered the unexpected suggestion. "I don't know."

Sveyn twisted a little, pulling one bent leg onto the counter. "Matt had a reason to come all the way here and give the museum enough money to be able to attend tonight. That reason is you."

"But why go to all that trouble?" Hollis shook her head. "If he wanted to talk to me, he could just email me or pick up the phone."

"Would you have talked to him?"

He has me there. "Maybe."

Sveyn leaned an elbow on his knee and stroked his scruff of a beard. "It is much harder to dismiss someone when they are standing in front of you."

Hollis stared at Sveyn as the impact of his words wormed past the shock of Matt's sudden appearance. "He wants something from me."

"I believe he does. At the least, his actions strongly suggest it."

"What could he want?" Hollis mused. "He has everything. All I have is a temporary job, and I live alone in a city where I barely know anyone."

One corner of Sveyn's mouth lifted. "Not entirely alone."

"My relationship with you only makes me more of a loser," Hollis huffed. "I've apparently replaced all living men with an undead one."

The Viking's expression grew somber. "I cannot argue with

you on that count."

Hollis felt a pang of regret. "I'm sorry, Sveyn."

He met her gaze with a regretful one of his own. "I wish I could be more than I am for you, Hollis."

"I know." She ached to take hold of his hand, knowing that to try would hurt more than ignoring the urge.

Sveyn slid off the counter. "It is time to find out what he wants."

Hollis drew a deep breath and examined her face in the mirror. "Do I look like I have been crying?"

Sveyn stepped behind her and smiled at her reflection. "You look beautiful. As you always do."

Hollis rolled her eyes. "Give me a serious answer."

"No, you do not. But if he asks you, tell him that something else made your eyes water," the Viking hedged.

Hollis threw the tissue in the trash and straightened her dress. "Like what? Onions?"

Sveyn chuckled. "You will think of something."

A rattle of the doorknob made her jump. "Hollis, are you in there?"

She flipped the lock and pulled the door open. "Yes, sorry."

Stevie looked past her, her concern obvious. "Are you alone?"

"Of course. I just needed a minute." Hollis stepped past the normally perky blonde.

Stevie, however, didn't budge. "I thought I heard a man's voice."

Hollis turned back slowly. "You did?"

Stevie faced her squarely. "What's going on?"

Sveyn looked at her over the top of Stevie's head. "Tell her about Matt."

Duh.

"We have a guest this evening who I never in a million years expected to see." Hollis wrinkled her nose like something smelled bad. "It caught me off guard and I needed to compose myself."

Stevie's brow plunged. "Who?"

"Matt."

"Matt, who?" Realization exploded her expression. "*Your* Matt?"

"Yep. That's the one."

Stevie was obviously still confused. She pointed a thumb over her shoulder. "Were you talking to him in there?"

"No. I was planning what I was going to *say* to him in there." Hollis looked purposefully sheepish. "I was saying what I expected him to say, and then coming up with my responses."

"So that deep voice was you?" Stevie's skepticism dripped from her words.

"It's really stupid. I know," Hollis diverted; she would think about the fact that Stevie could hear Sveyn's voice at another time. "But you know how it is when you think of a great comeback way too late? I just wanted to have some snark pre-loaded in my arsenal."

Stevie gave a reluctant grin of acceptance. "You'll have to introduce me."

"Absolutely. And Miranda." Hollis started walking back to the gathering. "You both need to see what I was up against."

Matt was still in the lobby. Clearly he didn't want to miss seeing her return.

"Is that him?" Stevie whispered. "Be still my heart..."

Hollis had to admit that Matt Wallace was a handsome man. Just shy of six feet, he had neat dark hair and rusty brown eyes highlighted with gold streaks.

In that custom tailored tux, he was to die for.

"Ah, you're back." Matt handed Hollis one of the two flutes he held. "I took the liberty."

Hollis accepted the glass. "This is Stevie Phillips. She's the Registrar I have been working with on this project. Stevie, this is Matt Wallace."

Matt grinned charmingly at Stevie, offering the second flute. "And so this is for you."

Stevie smiled. "Thank you."

Matt gave them a hint of a bow. "Please excuse me while I get another. Would you ladies like any canapés?"

Hollis shook her head. "No. Thank you."

"Stevie?"

"No, I'm fine."

As he walked away, Stevie whirled to face Hollis. "Okay, now I understand why you stuck it out for ten years. He's charming and drop-dead gorgeous."

"It's true," Hollis admitted. "And out of my league, as it turned out."

"*Pfft*. Not even!" Stevie sipped the champagne and glanced back at Matt. "But I do have another question."

"And that is?" Hollis prompted.

Stevie faced her again, her expression comically bemused. "Were you really willing to become Mrs. Hollis Wallace?"

*****

Even Sveyn laughed. "If you were a criminal, you would be the lawless Hollis Wallace!" he quipped.

Hollis bit her lower lip. "I, uh, wasn't going to change my name."

"And your beauty is unsurpassed!" Sveyn howled. "Flawless and lawless Hollis Wallace!"

Hollis coughed to hide her laugh.

Stevie frowned. "Are you all right?"

"Fierce as a lioness, but in actuality harmless..." Sveyn dropped to his knees, holding his belly. "Flawless and lawless, Hollis Wallace is clawless!"

"Shut up—or you'll be jawless," Hollis said through clenched teeth.

Stevie glared at her. "Why are you threatening me?"

Sveyn flopped on the floor, kicking his feet. "Stop! I can't breathe!"

"No kidding!" Hollis scrubbed her palm over her mouth. Her hilarity surged behind her hand and she was losing the battle to contain it.

Stevie stomped a foot. "Hollis, you're not making sense."

Matt returned with his drink. "What's going on?"

Sveyn sat up. "I'll end up jawless for saying it, but the flawless and lawless, Hollis Wallace, is clawless!"

Hollis succumbed, laughing at apparently nothing. "Well you look like a walrus!"

Sveyn bellowed his glee. "And you are found out!"

Heads began to turn in her direction as Hollis realized her blunder. "A—a silly sentence popped into my head. Rhyming."

"What was it?" Matt asked.

Hollis snorted, then covered her mouth. "If I married you and became a criminal, I'd be the lawless Hollis Wallace."

People around them smiled faintly, looked at her like she was a few bulbs short of a chandelier, and then went back to their conversations as they edged away from her.

Sveyn climbed to his feet. "Oh my God—when did I laugh so hard?"

"Oh my god!" Stevie jumped back. "Did you see that?"

"What?" Matt asked. His gaze swept the area.

"Your angel!" Stevie pointed at Sveyn. "He was right there!"

Matt frowned at her. "Are you saying that's real?"

"No!" Hollis stepped in front of the still-heaving Viking. "I mean, there is some sort of—something—that showed up. But no one here has actually *seen* him. I mean *it*."

Matt faced Stevie. "What did it look like?"

"A tall, brown, smudge of smoke." Stevie tipped her head toward Hollis. "She says it's here to guard the Nordic icon."

"The Blessing of the Gods?" Matt turned to Hollis. "Is that true?"

Intense emotion made Sveyn momentarily visible.

And apparently the emotion didn't have to be negative. That was an interesting new twist.

If that was true, Hollis needed to cap this precarious well of speculation and pretty darn quickly. "First of all, I have no idea what is true. I've never had any experience with anything otherworldly before, so I'm no expert."

"Have you seen it?" Matt pressed.

"I've seen the video," was all she would admit to.

"What's second of all?" Matt was always good at pushing

for details. The man never let anything slide past him.

Hollis took a gulp of her champagne to buy herself a steadying moment.

"Starting next Monday, we'll have weekly visitors doing paranormal research." She forced a smile. "If they actually find anything, we'll let people know."

"Who's coming?"

Let it go, Matt. "I'm not sure about next week. But the week after is *Ghost Myths, Inc.*"

Matt let out a low whistle. "That's impressive. Those guys don't go just anywhere."

Hollis looked at her watch. "Well I need to get back to the paying customers."

Matt leaned toward her. "I paid."

Hollis leveled her gaze at him. "I mean those whose opinion of the wing *matters*."

Chapter fourteen

Even the insult wasn't enough to dissuade Matt, apparently. Though Hollis stood at the door at nine o'clock, and personally thanked everyone who attended, Matt waited for her until the last guest—other than himself—had left.

"You need to leave now," Hollis held the door open. "And please hurry. It's been a long day and I'm exhausted."

Matt paused in the doorway. "Can I take you to dinner tomorrow?"

"No."

"No?" He actually looked hurt. "Why not?"

Hollis rolled her eyes. "What's the point, Matt?"

"I came all this way to see you," he cajoled. "How about lunch, then? I'll come here and pick you up."

"I'm not working tomorrow."

"Ms. McKenna!" Benton's voice echoed through the lobby as he wound his way through the scurrying caterers who were packing up. "There you are. What a triumph!"

Hollis smiled tiredly. "Thank you sir."

"When you get in tomorrow come see me first off. I have news."

Crappity crap-pants. "Of course."

Benton exited through the door Hollis still held open for Matt.

Matt flashed a smug smile. "See you tomorrow at noon."

Hollis pulled the door closed behind him and locked it.

Wednesday
December 2

The line waiting for the museum to open was astounding.

"We never have a line—unless it's a school group, of course." Hollis drove around to the employee parking lot. "I guess the new wing was more anticipated than I expected."

"Hmph." Sveyn hadn't said much last night, spending his time scowling silently at the television. Between Matt's appearance, and Stevie being able to hear him, and then see him when he was laughing so hard, the Viking seemed a bit off-kilter.

"My existence no longer makes sense to me," he said as they drove home. "I can smell things. And I can be seen at times by people to whom I did not manifest."

"That happens when your emotions are high." Hollis stifled a huge yawn. "But I'm too tired tonight to think about it any more."

When she let herself into the museum's back door, Stevie virtually pounced on her. "I need to talk to you."

"I'm supposed to go see Benton." Hollis walked down the hall to her office. "Can it wait?"

Stevie followed so closely that her leg bumped Hollis's. "No. I'll lose my mind if I have to wait any longer. Hurry up and get inside before Miranda sees you."

Hollis closed her office door and crossed to her desk. Though she dreaded the answer, there was no skirting the issue any longer. "What's going on, Stevie?"

Her friend stood in front of the desk, staring hard at her. "No, the question is what is going on with *you*."

Hollis opened her mouth to speak, but Stevie didn't give her the chance. "Be honest with, Hollis. I really need some answers."

"I do believe she means it," Sveyn opined.

"I know I heard a man talking to you in the ladies room last night," Stevie continued. "And I saw—something—in the lobby. Something more clear than the shadows I thought I saw before."

Hollis sank into her chair, pushed down by the weight of the truth. Stevie now had enough of her own experiences with the apparition that she was not going to accept an *I don't know* sort of answer anymore.

"Oh, Stevie," Hollis moaned. "You're going to think I'm crazy. And then you'll start avoiding me. That'll lead to more questions, and rumors. And then I'll end up having to leave the museum."

Stevie's face paled. "I don't want that to happen."

Hollis felt the prickle of tears. "Neither do I."

Stevie pulled the other chair around Hollis's desk, so nothing separated the two women. She grabbed Hollis's hand. "I feel like *I'm* going crazy. And if you don't tell me the truth, I'm going to completely lose it, I swear I am."

Hollis looked up at Sveyn. "What should I do?"

His expression was resolute. "Tell her the truth."

Stevie looked in the direction Hollis was. "Are you talking to him?"

"Yep." Hollis returned her attention to her petite friend and drew a deep breath. "All right. I'll tell you everything. All I ask is that you remember how sane I was for the first six months that you knew me."

Stevie quirked a smile. "Of course."

Hollis began her tale with, "It started when I went to that romance book weekend that Miranda paid for…"

Over the next quarter hour, she told Stevie everything: how Sveyn was tethered to her, that she was the first woman he ever manifested to, that he bounced forward in time, never backwards, and that he had no control over his manifestations.

Stevie looked stricken. "You mean he could disappear at any moment?"

Hollis nodded.

"How did he end up like this?"

"He was run through the gut by a broadsword in ten-seventy." Hollis glanced at the unchangeable bloodied slice in Sveyn's leather vest. "As he lay on the ground dying, the priest was at his head giving him last rites. But the devil was pulling at his feet."

"Oh dear…" Stevie's eyes widened.

"He says there was a boom of thunder and a flash of lightning, and when it cleared he was like he is now."

"A ghost?"

"No. He didn't die. He's caught in between."

Stevie leaned back and let go of Hollis's hand. "What will happen to him?"

Hollis couldn't look at the Viking or she would not be able to speak. "Someday he'll leave me and manifest to someone in the future."

Stevie's eye welled with tears. "That's so sad."

Hollis nodded, but said nothing.

"Has anyone else seen him?" Stevie reached for a tissue.

Hollis decided to lie, lest Stevie decided to run to Tom the intern and compare notes. The fewer people who knew about this situation the better. "No."

"I guess I'm special, then." Stevie blotted her eyes. "My grandma had the *gift*, as she called it. Said she could talk to spirits."

Hollis chose not to encourage that possibility. "The thing is, he says this is the first time this has happened."

She stopped dabbing. "What?"

"The first time others can see evidence of him."

"Or hear him?" Stevie's hands fell to her lap. "I did hear him, didn't I? In the ladies room with you?"

"Yes. But how?" Hollis tried to remember exactly what Sveyn said.

"Intense emotion."

Hollis looked up at Sveyn. "What emotion?"

Stevie turned her head in the same direction.

"When I said I wished I could be more than I am for you." Sveyn smiled softly. "And then I said you looked beautiful. My God, but I ached for you."

Stevie sucked a slow gasp. "How tall is he?"

Hollis turned to her friend. "Six feet and five or six inches."

Stevie's gaze shot back to hers. "Why is he brown?"

Hollis felt a wash of relief so strong she was glad to be sitting; her knees would have buckled from it. "You can see him now?"

"I did. Just for an instant."

Hollis sighed, glad to finally be able to talk about the Viking. "He looks as he did at that moment. Nothing can change. So he is dressed in leather pants, a leather vest, a linen shirt, and furry boots."

"What color is his hair?"

"Dark blond."

"And his eyes?"

"Blue."

"What's his name?"

"Sveyn." Hollis smiled softly. "Sveyn Hansen."

Stevie gave her a sheepish look. "Is he handsome?"

Hollis felt a knife slice through her heart. "He is the most beautiful man I've ever met. Inside and out."

Sveyn snorted, clearly embarrassed by the praise.

"Really? Better looking than Matt?" Stevie looked skeptical now. "Are you being honest, or are you just mad at Matt?"

Hollis chuckled. "Both."

Someone knocked on Hollis's door. "Come in."

Miranda opened the door. "So you are in here." Her gaze bounced between Stevie and Hollis. "Am I interrupting something?"

"Just a super-secret planning session," Hollis said the first thing she thought of and punctuated it with a laugh. "Some possible tweaks for the display."

"You'd better talk to Benton before you touch a thing," Miranda warned. "He's as giddy as a girl over last night. He sent me to find you and send you to see him ASAP."

Hollis stood. "Tell him I'm on my way."

Miranda gave them another odd look, then left the door open when she walked away.

Hollis regarded Stevie with the sternest expression she could manage. "Not one. Single. Word. Do you understand?" she whispered.

"Cross my heart." Stevie moved her index finger over her chest.

"I *mean* it, Stevie." Hollis pulled a steadying breath. "My professional life will be finished for good if anyone hears about this."

*****

Hollis sat in front of Mr. Benton's desk and listened to his seemingly unending recap of the previous evening's gala, complete down to who said what about the collection in a long list of people she wasn't acquainted with and probably never would be.

"And did you know that there was a line of people outside the museum this morning waiting to get in?" he effused. "A line! We haven't had a line since the museum opened!"

"Yes, sir."

The grinning General Manager wagged a finger at Hollis. "It's because of you and that Blessing."

"I beg to disagree," she demurred.

"No—it is. You have such a presence, and it comes across beautifully on the small screen." He chuckled. "Either on television or a computer monitor, you are captivating."

"Thank you, sir."

"And when *Ghost Myths, Inc.* starts taping here, you'll be representing the Arizona History and Cultural Center on an even larger scale!"

Oh joy of joys.

"If I might offer another opinion about the interest in the Kensington collection?" Hollis ventured.

Benton gave her a dispensational wave. "Of course! Is it

anything I can use to promote the museum?"

"Maybe." Hollis shifted in her chair. "As you know, I've been in Phoenix for less than a year, and as a museum professional I was disappointed in the options here, especially for such a large city."

Benton frowned. "What do you mean?"

"Well…" Hollis swallowed. "It's my opinion that the popularity of the new collection might be rooted in the fact that nothing in it originated in Arizona."

One brow lifted. "Local market's flooded?"

"Yes." Hollis winced, afraid to offend but pressing onward nonetheless. "Ezra Kensington collected from all over Europe and America, so now Arizona residents can see things like the signed Jane Austin, or the Viking sunstone, or any number of other objects without having to fly back east, or even Europe, to do so."

Benton's brow smoothed and he drummed his fingers on his desk. "Experience Europe without leaving the Valley…"

Hollis nodded. "Something like that."

"Brilliant."

Hollis relaxed. "Really?"

Mr. Benton nodded. "Almost every museum in Arizona focuses on this region exclusively—our campuses included. To market this particular location as the one museum that stands apart is nothing less than genius."

"Thank you, sir." Hollis rose to her feet. "Is there anything else you needed from me?"

Benton stood as well. "No. Just keep up the good work." He dismissed her with a distracted smile.

Hollis stifled a chuckle as she exited the GM's office.

The media whore is at it again.

Chapter Fifteen

Hollis stared at the menu. She had no appetite at all with Matt once again sitting across the table from her, but after a decade spent with the man she knew him well enough to know that he would continue to hound her until he got the chance to talk with her. At least Sveyn consented to stay out of her line of sight.

She finally ended up scanning prices and picking the most expensive thing among those offerings which she felt she could stomach today.

"I'll have the salmon Caesar salad, and a glass of this Chardonnay." She pointed to the priciest glass. "Make it the eight-ounce, not the five-ounce, please."

Matt lifted one disapproving brow but made no comment. Then he sighed and closed his menu. "I'll have the same."

He waited until the wafer bread and spicy butter was served before starting the conversation. "You seem happy here, Hollis."

"I am." She smiled at the waitress as she served their glasses of wine. "Thank you."

"No thoughts of returning to Chicago? Or Milwaukee?"

Hollis made a face and shuddered. "Do you know how *cold*

it is there? No, I expect to be offered a permanent position here when my contract expires."

Matt winced. "Would you accept?"

"If the offer's a good one." She shrugged. "And maybe even if it's not." She sipped her wine and steeled herself to jump in. "And how are things with you?"

"My marriage is a disaster."

And there it is.

Hollis sipped her wine again to keep from laughing. Then she pinned Matt with an accusing gaze.

"Do you mean to tell me that the enormous and expensive wedding that you had, only one-hundred-and-twenty-seven days after moving out of our apartment, didn't lead to the eternal bliss that you expected it would?"

He recoiled. "You counted?"

Hollis ignored him. "You said you wanted some space to find yourself. How'd that work out?"

"You sound angry."

Hollis glared at him. "Why are you surprised, Matt? After a decade of false promises, followed by you bailing out, did you honestly think I'd be all unicorns and rainbows for you?"

Matt leaned forward, his beautiful gold-streaked eyes glittering with unshed tears. "Hollis, I was an ass. A selfish, foolish, short-sighted, frightened, pompous ass."

Yes. You were.

"Go on."

His brow furrowed. "Go on?"

"You forgot insecure, domineering, and a really, really bad listener." She lifted her wine glass. "And cheap. You never would have sprung for eighteen dollars a glass before."

Matt looked at his own glass, horrified. "Is that what this costs?"

"Yes." Hollis smiled. "And I plan to have two."

Matt scrubbed his clean-shaven face with his palms. The voice that emanated from behind his hands sounded hollowed out. "God, Hollis. Can you ever forgive me?"

"Sure. Why not."

Actually, she realized with a start, she could. It would be much easier to let go of her anger and pain, now that she saw him suffering the consequences of his own actions. He ran off with the pretty new rope and hung himself. And he knew it; she didn't even have to say *I told you so.*

Matt's eyes peeked over his hands. "You forgive me? Really?"

"Whatever you think of me, I'm not a cruel or vindictive person." *I never actually sent that crate of feral cats to your door, after all.*

Matt's hands fell to the tabletop. "I never thought that you were, Hollis. I just know how much I hurt you."

Something inside her recoiled. She rested her elbows on the table and stared at him. "I didn't curl up and die, you know."

"I didn't mean that."

"What did you mean?"

"I meant that, well, I made a mistake. A big one."

Oh, God. Hollis narrowed her eyes. "What mistake?"

Matt reached for her hand, but she pulled it back and laid both hands in her lap.

"What mistake, Matt?"

"Caesar salad with salmon?" the waitress trilled as she set the big, shallow bowls in front of them. "Would you care for fresh ground pepper or parmesan cheese?"

Matt spoke first. "No, thank you."

"I would like the parmesan, please," Hollis said quickly before the girl walked away. "No pepper, though."

Hollis let the waitress grind more cheese onto her salad than she initially wanted, just because the girl was willing to take Matt's dismissal as a table-wide decision.

"Thank you," she said eventually.

The waitress gave Hollis a stiff smile and walked away.

Hollis lifted her fork. The server's interruption had allowed her to recollect the bits of her composure which were as shredded as the cheese.

"What were you going to say?"

Matt picked up his fork as well and began to poke at the

grilled salmon steak. "I said I made a mistake. When I broke up with you, it was the stupidest thing I've ever done."

Hollis's inner justification meter soared. She shrugged and spoke more casually than she felt. "Hindsight. Twenty-twenty, and all that."

She ate a bite of her salad. *Delicious.*

"It's more than that, Hollis." Matt lifted his eyes to hers again. "I want to know if there's any hope."

She paused, her fork hovering in midair. "Hope for what?"

"Us."

The fork sank back into the salad. "There's no *us*, Matt."

"There was, once." He tried to smile. "I'm hoping there could be again."

Hollis lifted her wine glass and took a long drink. There was a time she would have jumped at this chance to reunite with him, but not anymore. Too much had happened since she moved to Phoenix for her to want to go back.

Hollis set the glass down. "You're married."

"I'll get a divorce."

That was an odd way to say it. "What do you mean you *will* get a divorce?"

"I mean, if you say yes, I'll file for divorce," he said.

"And if I say no, you'll stay married?" she accused. "Is that your plan?"

Matt blanched. "No. Of course not."

Something here didn't make sense. "So why didn't you file for divorce before you came to Phoenix?"

"It's the holiday season." He waved his as yet unused fork. "I didn't want to ruin it for Suzan."

"Well that's completely messed up, Matt." Hollis shook her head. "You still *are* an ass."

"Why?" He looked genuinely confused. "I thought it was nice of me."

Hollis drained her wine glass, lifted it, and caught the waitress's attention. The girl nodded.

Hollis returned her consideration to Matt. "So you think it's acceptable for her to spend a cozy December with you, her husband, celebrating with family and friends at a dozen parties, all of you sharing toasts to the past year and best wishes for the coming year, then kissing under the mistletoe and on New Year's Eve at midnight, before you tell her it's all a sham and you want out?"

Matt paled. He grabbed his wine glass, still more than half full, and drank it all.

"Would you care for another Chardonnay as well?" the waitress asked as she set down Hollis's second glass and collected the empty one.

"No!" he coughed, handing her his glass. "I'm good."

Hollis took a bite of her salad. The conversational ball was in Matt's court—if he had enough balls to pick it up.

"When you put it that way," he managed. "I do sound like an ass."

"Yep." Hollis refilled her fork. "You need to file for divorce when you go back, no matter what my answer is. Suzan deserves that much consideration."

"You're right." His brow twitched. "But if I had already filed before I came to see you, would you have said yes?"

Hollis's heartbeat stuttered. "I don't know. I don't think so."

"Why not?" Matt demanded. A wave of understanding shifted his expression. "Is there someone else?"

Hollis was a little offended at his tone. "Would that surprise you?"

"Oh, uh, no. No!" Matt shook his head. "You're very date-able."

He was just digging another hole, in her opinion. "Date-able, but not marry-able?"

"I didn't say that," he groused. "Stop twisting my words."

Hollis unclenched her jaw, deciding. "Yes. There is. Someone else."

Matt blinked. "Was he at the opening last night?"

Tell as much truth as you can.

Less chance of screwing up that way.

"Yes."

"Did I meet him?"

Hollis looked at Matt like he was nuts. "How should I know?"

"What's his name?"

Hollis chuckled softly. "Oh, no you don't."

Matt frowned. "What's wrong?"

"I'm not going to have you go Google-stalking him." *Good save.*

Matt's mouth twisted. "How did you meet?"

That was an easy answer. "We were at a conference together over Labor Day weekend."

Matt started playing with his fork. Though Hollis's salad was half gone, Matt hadn't eaten a bite. "Is he in the museum business as well, then?"

"No. Not really."

Matt's brows lifted in question. "Not really?"

"He's a history buff. We have that in common." Another good save.

Matt was like a pit bull with a rat. "So what does he do?"

Yikes. *How do I make this true?* "He's in trade."

"Trade?"

"International trade. Shipping. He's a captain." From the corner of her eye, Hollis saw Sveyn enter the dining room and walk slowly toward her table. He was looking at her like she had just admitted he actually *was* a thousand-year-old Viking.

Matt leaned back in his seat. "Captain of a ship. Living in Phoenix. In a desert."

"Right. I see where you're going with that." Hollis took a gulp of the expensive white wine.

Matt screwed up his expression and wagged his head. "Hollis, I'm worried. How much do you really know about this this guy?"

Time for another tactic. She heaved a sigh of resignation. "Okay, fine. He was a captain in the navy. Special Ops. He can't tell me more than that."

Sveyn stood next to Matt. Both men were staring at her with wide eyes under concerned brows.

"Was?" Matt pressed. "Is he retired?"

Hollis pointed her index finger in the air. "Yes! A retired special ops navy captain with a fascination for history. Who sails a trade ship."

"And you're sure about this?"

Now Hollis looked at Matt like he was the crazy one. "Of course. Why wouldn't I be?" She forked another bite of salmon into her mouth.

"What does he look like?"

Damn pit bull. "Why?"

Matt shrugged. "I want to see if I remember seeing him there."

"Well he's very handsome. Over six feet tall. He has dark blond hair. Blue eyes." Hollis shrugged. "Do you remember him?"

Matt shook his head. "I don't think so."

"Hmm. Too bad. This salad is delicious." Hollis pointed her fork at Matt's untouched lunch. "Aren't you going to eat yours?"

He ignored the question, looking at her with a troubled expression. "Hollis, I have something to ask you, and I want you to be very honest with me."

"Okay."

"Does this navy captain really exist?"

Hollis set her fork down. There were two ways she could go with this; scorched earth was her choice.

"Let me get this straight: you think I made this guy up because I'm so pathetic that only a loser shooting for his second choice would want me?"

"No!" Matt barked.

"Do you know anyone in special ops, Matt?" she pushed.

"No, but—"

"Have you seen a movie? A TV show? Read a book?" Hollis was on a roll. "Special ops guys are forbidden to talk about anything they do. So *obviously* I don't know everything about his past. It's called national security. Look it up."

Matt looked like the cornered weasel that he was. "I'm sorry, Hollis. It's just that—"

"It's just that what? You think that I've been pining away for these last two years because you left me, when the truth is that *you* are the one that has been pining away for *me!*" Hollis gasped at her own words, her eyes rounding. "That's true, isn't it?"

Matt's mouth opened and closed like one of those singing trout novelty plaques.

Sveyn's stance relaxed. "I was worried about where this conversation was going, Hollis, but I do believe you now have him dead to rights."

Damn right I do.

"Are you going to say anything, Matt?"

Matt signaled for the check. Then he folded his napkin and set it by his untouched salad before his eyes met hers once again.

"Yes, Hollis. It's true. I have pined for you ever since my honeymoon."

Her jaw dropped. "What?"

"I should've never married Suzan. But her life was so glamorous and so exciting. Traveling first class. Eating at the best restaurants." Matt heaved a heavy sigh and rubbed his eyes like his head was beginning to pound. "You were always sincere, honest, trustworthy. Down to earth. No pretense."

"You make me sound like a faithful dog," Hollis grumbled.

If Matt heard her, he ignored the comment. His hands fell away from his rub-reddened eyes. "I should have known better. I mean, really. Who spells Susan with a Z?"

The waitress brought the check and pointed at Matt's salad. "Would you like me to box that up for you?"

"Yes," Hollis said before Matt declined. "Thank you."

Matt pulled out his wallet and put a wad of cash inside the padded black folder. He looked so miserable that Hollis felt like taking care of him. *Just like old times.*

"Why didn't you eat?" she asked gently.

Matt stood. "I hate salmon."

Then he reached for Hollis's glass of wine and drained it.

Chapter Sixteen

Thursday
December 3

Hollis looked at the caller ID on her screen then answered the phone. "Hi, Mom."

"Hi, sweetie. How has your day been?"

Hollis smiled. "Well, it's only noon, but so far so good."

Her mom's frustrated laugh made Hollis chuckle as well. "Oh, dear. I'll never get this straight."

"Just remember that in winter I'm only one hour behind you. The rest of the year it's two."

"Why doesn't Arizona do daylight savings time like the rest of the civilized world?" her mom grumbled good-naturedly.

"If you were here in the summer, you'd know why, Mom. In fact, I think they'd invent daylight 'spending' time if they could!" *There's an idea.* "So how are things with you?"

"Well... that's why I called."

Hollis sat up straighter. "Is Dad okay?"

"Oh, yes! Better than okay, actually."

Hollis was literally on the edge of her chair. "What does that mean?"

"It means... Well... it means he was awarded the seven day Caribbean cruise at last night's company dinner."

"Mom! That's great!" Hollis paused. "So why don't you sound happier?"

"Because it sails at the end of this month... From the twenty-third to the thirtieth."

Ah. "Over Christmas."

"I'm sorry, Hollis. I'd say skip it, but your dad has worked so hard this year, that—" Hollis shook her head as she listened.

"Mom. Stop. Of course you are going. And you are going to have a fabulous time."

"Are you sure?" Both concern and hesitant joy were evident in her tone.

"Yes!" Hollis relaxed in her chair. "But I feel bad now that I couldn't come home for Thanksgiving."

"No, please don't. We missed you, of course, but we understood."

"Mom, I want you and Dad to go on that cruise and have enough fun that missing our Christmas together will be worth it. Do you understand?"

"If you're really sure."

"I am, Mom. I have friends here to spend Christmas with. Don't worry about me." Hollis flipped a page in her mostly unused day planner. "In fact, I'm looking at my calendar now. I can probably take a week off at the end of January and come visit."

"That would be wonderful!" Happy tones were back.

"We can wait and exchange presents then, if you want." Hollis grinned. "That gives me a chance to shop the after-holiday sales, and you to buy me something fabulous in the Caribbean."

Her mom laughed. "Sometimes I wonder where you get this practical streak. You are so unsentimental."

"It's true. Logic over tradition." Hollis shrugged. "Must be a throwback to some ancestor. Like my red hair."

"I suppose." Her mom sighed. "Now that everything's settled I'll let you get back to work, sweetie. I love you."

"Love you, too, Mom. Give my love to Dad. And my hearty congratulations."

Hollis hung up and leaned back in her chair. She bought her Christmas ticket from an airline with no change fee, so that was good. It was just a matter of changing the dates when she knew what the new dates would be.

"So I will not meet your family at Christmas, after all." Sveyn leaned down so his head was at her level. "Are you saddened by this news?"

"Yes. And no." Hollis set her phone on her desk. "My parents deserve this treat."

"Perhaps I can show you a Norse Christmas." Sveyn smiled. "Will you cook if I teach you?"

Hollis laughed. "Really?"

"Why not?"

That actually sounded fun. "Sure. I'd like that."

Her office phone buzzed.

"Yes?"

"I have a gentleman at the front desk who wants to speak with you, if you have a moment."

"What's his name?"

"Matt Wallace."

Hollis sighed. "Sure. I'll be there in a minute."

"I wonder what he wants of you now." Sveyn did not look pleased.

"Heaven only knows." Hollis stood. "I guess I'll go find out."

*****

Matt stood in the lobby, acting casual, looking at postcards. But when his eyes met hers, she saw the stark circles under them.

"Thanks for letting me interrupt your day, Hollis," he said. "I'm on my way to the airport and I wanted to say goodbye."

"Okay." Hollis shrugged. "Goodbye."

Matt glanced around the busy lobby. "Will you walk me to my car?"

"Um, sure." Hollis had left her jacket in her office, but standing in the sun would make the sixty-degree December day tolerable.

Matt held the door for her, and she walked in silence beside him to the public parking lot. When he stopped at a generic silver sedan, he turned to face her.

"I made a decision last night, Hollis. You were right. I'm going to file for divorce before Christmas."

Hollis nodded. "I'm glad. As hard as that is, sooner really is better."

"I'll let you know how it goes."

Hollis wasn't sure why that was necessary, but she said, "Okay."

Matt fiddled with a button on his jacket. "Once that's done, I'm wondering if you'll give me a chance to win you back from the captain?"

Hollis honestly didn't know how to answer that. "Back? What do you mean back?"

Matt looked contrite. "I know I hurt you, Hollis. I'm sorry about that."

"He didn't win me *away* from you, Matt," Hollis stated. "You were already long gone."

"I know—"

"So what you *mean* to ask," Hollis interrupted, too startled by his suggestion to be polite. "Is would I consider giving you a second chance at being the kind of man I deserve?"

Matt blanched. "Um, yes. I guess that's what I'm saying."

To say yes made the most logical sense. Considering her long and familiar history with Matt, reconnecting with him should only be a matter of updating each other on their experiences while they were apart. With the lack of any viable future with Sveyn, she might be foolish to let this opportunity pass.

Still, her heart objected.

"Why don't you call me once the papers are actually filed?" Hollis suggested, buying herself time. "Until then, all of this is moot anyway."

Matt looked defeated. "I understand."

"Besides, you don't know how Suzan will respond. Maybe you can still work things out."

Matt shook his head. "I doubt it."

"She's your wife, Matt. You have to try." *And if you don't, how can I believe you'll try with me?*

Hollis stood on her toes and kissed Matt on the cheek. He hadn't shaved today and his beard stubble stabbed her lips. "Thanks for coming to see me, Matt. No matter how this all plays out, it was good to see you again."

*****

Stevie was driving her insane. Between her co-worker's giddiness over her engagement to George and the resultant wedding planning, and her fascination with Sveyn and all which that situation entailed, the woman never stopped bouncing.

She slipped into Hollis's office after she returned from her conversation with Matt, and closed the door. "Is he here?"

"Stevie, you can't do this. People will get suspicious." Hollis reopened the office door. "And then we'll end up having to create some big surprise to justify all the secrecy."

"But is he?" Stevie followed Hollis to her desk.

Sveyn chuckled and Hollis sighed. "Yes."

"Where?" Stevie turned in a circle.

"You won't be able to see him because he's calm."

"Just tell me."

Sveyn stepped up right behind the petite Stevie and grinned at Hollis over the blonde's head. "How is this?"

Hollis rolled her eyes. "He is standing right behind you."

Stevie whirled around. "Here?" She stuck her arms out then yanked them back. "Oh my god—I felt something."

Sveyn rubbed his belly. "And I felt her. I think."

"I don't know what's going on with any of this," Hollis snapped. "But I do know that we have a job to do, and enough of this day has been wasted." She glared at Stevie. "Are you coming?"

With a glance around the office, Stevie hurried after Hollis. "That was so strange, Hollis. Can anyone feel him?"

"If they walk through him, I think."

Stevie grabbed her arm. "Walk through him? Like, literally?"

Hollis pulled another sigh. "They can't see him, and if he doesn't move out of the way of course they'll walk through him."

"That is so weird..." Stevie murmured.

Welcome to my world.

Hollis walked into the Kensington wing, which was packed with sixth graders on a school field trip. Several of the group were clustered around the Blessing—of course—talking about Vikings.

"They were a bunch of brave warriors," one boy stated.

"They had women warriors, too," a girl added.

"Yeah but they robbed and killed everyone wherever they went," another girl snipped. "They were barbarians."

"I like the helmets with the horns."

"I wonder why they don't have one here?"

"You know they discovered America, not Christopher Columbus."

"Nuh uh."

"Yeah huh."

Stevie nudged Hollis. "Can he hear all of this?"

Hollis glanced at Sveyn who was standing behind the case with a bemused look on his face. "Yep."

She then stepped into the fray. "So you all are interested in Vikings?"

Heads turned toward her and the commentary halted.

"Did you see the Viking sunstone?" Hollis continued, pointing their attention toward the next case. "This rectangular piece of calcite allowed the Vikings to navigate by the sun even on cloudy days."

As the small herd of students flowed toward the next case Hollis added, "And that was how they discovered North America five hundred years before Christopher Columbus found the islands south of Florida.

One boy elbowed another. "Told ya."

"Shut up."

Stevie grabbed Hollis's arm. "I have an idea!"

Hollis glanced at her and tossed off one last bit of info before allowing Stevie to pull her away. "And we don't have a horned helmet because the Vikings never wore them."

Hollis followed the registrar out of the wing and into the much quieter lobby. "What?"

Stevie spun around to face her. "Let's write a kid's book. For the museum to sell. About Vikings."

Hollis thought she was following Stevie's train of thought, but still asked, "Why?"

"So we have a reason to be talking about you-know-who." Stevie's eagerness was palpable.

"You do realize that we would have to produce an *actual* book at some point," Hollis warned.

"I concur with Stevie." Sveyn stepped around Hollis and faced her. "The amount of misinformation these children have about my life and my people is appalling."

"We can do it. Or at least claim to try." Stevie spread her palms and stated the obvious. "We do have a legitimate source, after all."

It wasn't a bad suggestion, Hollis realized. Not only would it be a cover for her to talk about the apparition with Stevie, but they might actually end up writing a decent little book.

"Who would do the illustrations?"

Stevie clapped her hands and started bouncing. Again. "We could hold a contest! Ask students to submit drawings for each chapter."

Hollis was getting behind the idea now, and not only as an excuse. "If we covered—I don't know—say twelve common ideas about Vikings, we could even make a calendar."

"I love it!" Stevie twirled in a circle.

"Okay, then. I'll dictate his answers, but it's your baby to organize. You handle the actual contests and production." Hollis started walking toward their offices. "I have to deal with the ghost people starting on Monday, so I'll be losing a day of work every week until they stop coming. And the hoard isn't adequately sorted or catalogued yet."

As they entered the back hallway, Stevie asked, "So how did things end with Matt?"

Chapter Seventeen

Hollis felt the need to get out of buildings for a while, so when she left the office she drove to a nearby park. Even though the sun had set and the air had grown chilly, she wanted to go someplace outside of her normal routine and think.

Sveyn had been quiet most of the day and Hollis assumed it was because he was either thinking about ideas for the Viking book, or he was contemplating her conversation with Matt.

Either way, she switched on the Bluetooth earpiece and got out of her car. "I just want half an hour of fresh air to clear my head."

Sveyn moved through the passenger door and walked around the car to her side. "I understand. I do miss feeling the wind and the cold. They do refresh the soul."

Hollis stuffed her hands into the pockets of her jacket in part to keep warm, and in part to keep from reaching for Sveyn. Taking his arm or holding his hand felt obvious at the moment, and the reality of that impossibility irritated her.

"What weighs on your mind, Hollis?"

She walked in silence for a while before answering him. So many thoughts were charging around in her mind that she was having trouble organizing them into any sort of coherent statement.

She finally settled on, "Matt."

Sveyn nodded, his sober expression barely visible in the low lamps along the gravel walkway. "As I suspected."

"Did you hear the whole conversation?"

"I came out and stood behind you when I heard you say that I didn't win you away from him." He turned his head to look at her. "At the least, I assumed you meant me."

"I did." Hollis sighed. "Before that, he said he's not going to wait and he's going to file for divorce now. Then he said he wants another chance with me."

Sveyn stared at his booted footfalls and clasped his hands behind his back.

"I would be a fool to go back to him…" Hollis left the sentence hanging.

Sveyn's voice was stern. "From what you have told me, I believe that to be very true."

"But we have so much history together. So much time invested in each other's lives."

"And yet, he left you to marry someone else."

"The grass looked greener," Hollis countered. "And now he knows it wasn't."

Sveyn's brow twitched as if he was working out the idiom. "And what happens when another field of grass looks greener?"

"He'll remember this disaster, of course." *I hope.*

Sveyn stopped walking. A pair of joggers trotted by them, nodding a greeting. "And what if your grass is not as green as he remembered?"

Hollis glared up at him. "My grass is actually way greener now." *Crap—that sounds like a personal issue.* "I mean I'm a better person than I was when he left me. I've grown."

Sveyn's expression twisted. "And what if he is not happy with how you have changed?"

The Viking's questions were infuriatingly obvious. "So what are you saying? That I should let this opportunity go?"

He folded his arms. "What do you think?"

Hollis stomped further down the trail. "I think you don't trust me to make a good decision."

Sveyn followed her. "I am only pointing out the situations which are possible. Or probable."

"Of course you are," she snapped. "But everything you said was a question. How do you expect me to find the answers if I don't explore the possibility?"

Apparently, he didn't have an answer for that.

Hollis halted and looked up at him. "What if I miss the best thing that ever happened to me because I was too scared to risk being hurt again?"

Sveyn stared down into her eyes, his darkened by the night. "Was he truly the best thing that has ever happened to you?"

Hollis felt the Viking's words like a spear through her chest. "Sveyn… That's not fair."

He shook his head. "No. It is not fair. Not for either one of us."

Hollis rubbed her eyes before tears could form. "What do you expect me to do?"

"Expect? That I cannot say." He paused and drew an impossible breath. "But what I desire for you to do is not fair either."

Hollis stepped into the breach. "Tell me what you desire, Sveyn."

His gaze fell away. "I believe you know."

"Tell me anyway. I need to hear it." She wiped her eyes again. "I can't make a decision without it."

The apparition walked into the glow of the next footlight and turned to face her. "I will be fully honest, Hollis. No matter how hard this might be for you to hear."

"Please do." She wrapped her arms around her waist. "I'm ready."

He nodded. "I want you entirely to myself. I do not want your attentions pulled away from me by any other man who walks this earth."

Hollis's pulse sped up.

"In all of my experiences—and I have had many centuries of

them—I have never come to know a woman like you. You are so intelligent. And kind. And brave." He wagged his head. "And I am wholly immersed in my admiration and love for you."

Now her palms were sweating. "Oh, Sveyn…"

He put up one hand to silence her. "Because we can come together in your dreams, those nights are what keep me from going completely insane. I ache for you, Hollis. I want to father your children. I want to grow old with you."

The soft breeze chilled Hollis's wet cheeks. "I want that, too, Sveyn. You have no idea."

His gaze flicked aside briefly. "If you feel but half of what I do, then I am sorry to have brought this upon you."

"No. Don't apologize." She sniffed and wiped her cheeks. "I can't imagine my life without you now."

Something in her words caused a sudden shift in Sveyn's demeanor. His cheeks hollowed and his eyes widened,

"What is it?" she asked.

He dragged his hands though his long hair. "I am being far too selfish."

"No, you're being honest," she objected. "And I want the same things you do."

"But they can never be!" Sveyn turned in a tight angry circle. "Do you not see that?"

Hollis scrambled unsuccessfully for a response.

He stilled and pointed at her. "I will never change. I will never age. You know this!" he shouted. "But if I somehow remain with you for the rest of your life, you will. And in the end, you will hate me for it."

"I could never—"

"If you never marry, and never have children, you will end up alone, Hollis." Sveyn shook his head fiercely. "If I truly love you, I cannot condemn you to that."

Hollis desperately wanted to argue the point but she couldn't. The future he just outlined was realistic. And what if he stayed with her for less than her whole life—say thirty years and then disappeared? She would be a single, sixty-one-year-old woman, deeply grieving a lost love that no one could understand.

She sank to her knees on the path, the crumbled granite pressing sharply through her jeans. "What do you expect me to do?" she asked again.

Sveyn squatted in front of her. "As much as it angers me, I must expect you to continue your search for a husband."

"In spite of how we feel about each other?"

Sveyn wiped his eyes, though the apparition couldn't actually produce tears. "Because of how we feel about each other. This love we share must not ruin your life."

Her brow plunged. "What if I fall in love with another man?"

Sveyn touched the bloodied gash on the side of his vest, as if it pained him anew. "If he makes you love him more than you love me, then it was meant to be so."

Hollis reached for Sveyn's cheek, and felt the faint tingle when she touched it. "I don't want to hurt you."

He laid his hand over hers. "I came to you unbidden, Hollis. You did not ask for, nor desire, my presence in your life."

"But that's not your fault."

"Neither of us is at fault. My singular situation was created by God, and will only be resolved when He allows me to die." Sveyn's expression begged her understanding. "Until then I am at His mercy."

Hollis dropped her hand back into her lap. "So... Matt."

"What do *you* want to do about him?"

There it was. *The million dollar question.*

She heaved a resigned sigh. "If he actually files for divorce, and Suzan-with-a-Z doesn't contest it, then I guess I'll let him try and woo me."

Sveyn stared at his hands, his laced fingers twisting together until his knuckles were non-apparition shade of white. "You must understand that I deeply and violently despise that idea."

"Because it's Matt, specifically."

"Yes."

"He does have an uphill battle, you know." She smiled softly when Sveyn looked at her. "I'm afraid I've met the man of my dreams—literally."

Sveyn's lips quirked at that, but his eyes narrowed. "Because this is important to you, I promise to play fairly as much as I am able. But I cannot pretend to like it."

"Thank you." Hollis's eyes welled again, blurring her vision. "I don't think anyone has loved me so selflessly in my entire life."

Sveyn's expression turned pensive. At that moment the wisdom of his years was apparent. "While I do find it unlikely, you might be surprised some day."

And there's another selfless comment.

"I love you, Viking."

"And I love you, Hollis."

She climbed stiffly to her knees and brushed tiny bits of granite from the knees of her jeans. "I'm hungry. I'm going to stop at the pizza place on the way home."

Sveyn grinned. "Garlic knots."

"Yeah." Hollis laughed. "What can I say? I'm addicted."

As they walked back down the path toward her car, Sveyn leaned down and spoke in her ear. "Where shall I love you tonight?"

Imagined breath in her ear sent a shiver of pleasure over her skin. She gave him a seductive smile. "Surprise me."

Chapter Eighteen

Monday
December 7

The middle-aged woman in flowing robes swept into the museum's lobby on a cloud of patchouli. She stuck out her hand as soon as she spotted Hollis, who blinked rapidly to keep her eyes from watering as she approached. "You must be Hollis McKenna!"

Sveyn wrinkled his nose. "Is that her that I smell?"

The white-haired woman's hippy-ish perfume was really strong if the apparition could detect it.

"Yes," Hollis answered both the seen and unseen entities with a single word. She held out her hand as well. "Welcome to the Arizona History and Cultural Center."

The woman gave Hollis's hand a firm, dry shake. "I know I'm a little early, but I wanted to make sure that the séance was correctly arranged."

Hollis smiled politely. "And what was your name?"

"Oh, I'm sorry!" The woman smoothed her shoulder-length pageboy haircut and flashed a toothy smile. "My name is Ether."

"Ether?" Hollis repeated. "Really?"

The woman chuckled. "Well, originally it was Esther. But in my profession, I believe Ether is much more appropriate, don't you?"

"Oh, yes. I have to agree." Hollis tried not to look at Sveyn, who was leaning over Ether and sniffing her with puzzled look on his face, lest she break into inappropriate laughter. "Will you be running today's session?"

"Yes, I am the medium of the day." Ether looked around the space as if trying to discern who—or what—might be present.

"And you have four ladies joining you?"

"Three now, I'm afraid." Ether returned her regard to Hollis. "One went into labor."

"Oh!" With a start Hollis realized she expected only older women to attend. "Um, let me show you the collections storeroom where we have you set up."

"Wonderful." As Ether fell into step beside Hollis, she said, "With all of these fabulous old objects here, I'm sure we'll have many spirits eager to establish contact."

Sveyn walked on Ether's other side. "Ask her if they are here now."

"I've never been to a séance before. Where are the spirits before you contact them?"

"Oh, they're all around us, dear." Ether waved her arm and Sveyn dodged it. "They wait for us to invite them into a conversation."

"Can you feel them?" Hollis probed. "I mean, do they hover nearby when they know something is happening?"

"Yes. Sometimes."

Hollis opened the door to the administration offices. "Can you feel any of them now?"

Sveyn walked backwards in front of the medium, waving his hands and grinning like a fool. "Hello, Ether. It's nice to meet you."

The medium stopped walking. "I do sense something."

"You do?" Hollis and Sveyn said in tandem.

"A woman."

Sveyn's jaw dropped.

Hollis bit back her laugh. "A woman. Are you sure?"

"Yes. You have her dress here."

We have a lot of dresses here. "Whose dress is it?"

Ether waved a hand and resumed walking. "She's gone."

"She left without being here in the first place," Sveyn said. "Now that *is* amazing."

Hollis shot him a warning glance. "Well I hope you encounter more cooperative spirits when you get started."

She swiped her employee card and opened the door to the collections storeroom. Inside the doorway to the crowed space were a rectangle table and six chairs.

Hollis folded one up and set it by the door. "Is this going to work for you?"

Ether turned in a slow circle. "Yes. This should be very fertile ground."

"I meant the table."

"Oh!" Esther winced a little at the generic plastic table. "It's serviceable, I suppose."

Hollis almost rolled her eyes. Like the spirits would care—if any showed up. Besides Sveyn, of course. "Do you want the lights on or off?" she asked.

"Off. The spirits get shy in the light."

Guess that quality would put the Viking in a different category. "Remember—no candles are allowed."

Ether reached into her oversized hemp bag and pulled out a plastic bag of LED candles. "Got it covered."

Hollis nodded. "Let's go back to the lobby and wait for the others."

*****

Hollis sat at the table with Ether and three perfectly normal looking women. The storeroom lights were off and half-a-dozen LED candles flickered dully in front of them. Sveyn hunkered down beside her.

"Don't say anything to get me in trouble," she warned him

earlier when she excused herself and went to the ladies room.

"Do you believe she will be able to hear me?" he asked.

"Don't you mean, do I think she's a wacko?" Hollis snorted. "No. she won't hear you."

Sveyn grinned. "I assume that you will want me to tell you if I hear or see anything."

"Yes, please."

Ether asked everyone to hold hands and instructed the women to close their eyes and, "Concentrate."

"Concentrate on what?" Sveyn asked.

Hollis shrugged and cracked one eye open to see if Ether reacted to his voice.

Nothing.

"Friendly spirits—are you here with us today?" Ether asked.

Silence.

"Don't be afraid, dear hearts. We mean you no harm."

"How does one harm a spirit, exactly?" Sveyn grumbled. "*Give* them a body?"

Hollis coughed to cover up her laugh.

"Sorry," she whispered with her eyes closed.

"We come here with respect, and hope you will engage with us…"

"That stinking woman cannot hear me, can she?"

Hollis shook her head slowly.

Ether jerked and the table shook. "Hello?"

Hollis opened her eyes to see if Sveyn might have done something, but he was still squatting beside her.

"Yes!" Ether said. "Thank you for coming!"

"Do you see anything?" she asked the Viking. He shook his head.

"No, but we usually don't expect our visitors to manifest." Ether's voice had that tone of strained politeness which screamed *shut up*. "It's far too exhausting for them. Isn't it, dear?" she addressed the air.

"Can we open our eyes?" the woman to Hollis's left asked.

Ether ignored her. "Are you the spirit who was seen on the camera?"

Hollis looked to her left and met the woman's open-eyed gaze. Hollis mouthed: This is my first time.

Mine, too, she mouthed back.

Ether tilted her head as if she was listening. "Yes? You are? You are the spirit we saw on the camera?"

"This should prove interesting." Sveyn stood and walked around the table to stand behind the colorful medium.

"Do you have anything you want to say to Hollis?"

Hollis stiffened. While she insisted that she be present at anything which took place in this fragile space, she expected to be a silent witness, only there to protect the museum's collection. She certainly didn't expect any of the attention to focus on her.

Ether looked at Hollis. "It's a man. He says he knows you."

That's creepy.

Hollis faced the four pairs of expectant eyes. "And, uh, what else does he say?"

Ether seemed to be listening. Then she nodded. "Of course."

"What?" the woman on her left asked. "What did he say?"

"He says he was very powerful and important."

Sveyn frowned. "Of course he does. Ask him to show himself."

"Can he show himself?" Hollis flashed a hopeful expression. "I want to see if he looks the same as he did when I saw him."

Ether shook her head and gave her an apologetic expression. "He says that is not allowed unless you are in danger."

Hollis frowned. "How does he know me?"

"He is an ancestor, several generations back."

So she wouldn't know his name anyway.

Neat trick.

Hollis decided to push the woman in regards to Sveyn. She looked at the apparition, hoping he would catch on to what she was doing, and squinted. "I think I can see him."

"Where?" the woman on her left asked.

Hollis pointed. "Right there, behind Ether."

"Really?" The medium twisted around in her seat. "Are you there?"

Sveyn started to chuckle. "Keep on it."

"He's getting clearer." Hollis looked at the other three women. "Can any of you see him?"

One was staring hard. "Maybe…"

"He's tall. Dressed in brown. I can't make out his face." Hollis jumped up. "I'm going to turn the lights on."

"We don't normally—"

Hollis flipped the switch before Ether could finish her objection. "But his clothes are so dark, he's hard to see."

"What is your name?" Ether asked, despite her obvious irritation.

"Make it a good one," Sveyn prompted, grinning.

The group waited.

Hollis gasped. "Did you hear that?"

Ether looked stricken. "No. What did he say?"

"He said Wallace." Hollis pressed her lips together to keep from smiling.

Sveyn whooped. "Excellent."

"Wallace?" Ether pleaded, closing her eyes. "Will you speak again?"

Sveyn leaned down and spoke directly in her ear. "My name is Sveyn Hansen and I'm a Viking caught between life and death."

"Please?" she asked again.

Sveyn was laughing hard now. He spoke into Ether's other ear. "You are a fraud, madam. There is no one here but I."

Hollis started to giggle. "Can any of you see him?"

Ether glared at her. "Are you making light of this process?"

"No!" Hollis put up her hands. "There is definitely some sort of spirit here."

"We paid a lot of money to hold this séance and contact the spirit on the security tape, you know." Esther narrowed her eyes. "I certainly hope this wasn't some cheap trick the museum has played."

Hollis shook her head. "It was no trick. I can definitely see and hear something here in the room with us."

"Does he have long hair?" asked the intently staring woman.

Hollis gave her an incredulous look. "Yes. He does."

She nodded. "I see him. Sort of. Maybe."

Sveyn did a quick spin. "Here I am!"

"Where do you see him?" Ether demanded.

The woman didn't shift her gaze. "Right behind you."

Ether swung her arm in an arc around her chair. Sveyn didn't move this time and allowed her hand to pass through him.

"That tickles!" he laughed.

"Oh my goddess…" Ether did it again. "There *is* something there."

The look on the medium's face was so disbelieving, so shocked, and so funny that Hollis could barely contain herself.

"Are you surprised?" she managed with only a few coughed chuckles escaping. "Wasn't that the point?"

Two of the women exchanged bemused glances, while the third continued to stare silently in Sveyn's direction.

"She *is* surprised!" Sveyn guffawed. "This is *such* fun!"

Hollis stood, hoping that what she said next would throw Sveyn into such a state of hilarity that he would become momentarily visible. She started laughing at the thought, and almost couldn't say the words.

"Flawless and lawless—" she began before doubling over and leaning on the table, hooting with glee.

"Yes!" Sveyn looked like he was about to wet himself. "The flawless and lawless Hollis Wallace!"

"Is clawless!" Hollis squeaked, gasping for breath. "Oh my lord!"

Sveyn fell on top of the table, curling in a hilarity-defined ball of leather and fur.

"There he is! One the table!" the staring woman shouted.

Ether jumped to her feet and let out a scream that would shame a banshee. Then she bolted for the door.

*****

"I only saw him for a second."

"I didn't see anything."

"Neither did I."

"Well Miss Ether sure did, and it scared the crap out of her."

A smiling Hollis collected the LED candles and put them in Ether's big hemp bag. "Would one of you ladies carry this to the front door?"

"I will," said the woman who saw Sveyn. "And I'm asking for my money back."

Hollis gave her a puzzled look. "But you said you saw him."

The woman shouldered the hemp bag. "No thanks to her. That was all you."

Hollis laid a hand on the woman's arm, suddenly afraid she had gone too far. "What will you tell people? About today, I mean?"

The woman looked into Hollis's eyes as if she understood her concern. "What do you want me to say?"

The truth is always the best plan. "Would you be willing to say only that the medium wasn't able to make contact with the spirit?"

She nodded. "Yep. That's the truth."

"And, in spite of everything, neither of us saw anything," said the obviously disappointed woman who sat on Hollis's left.

The third woman shuddered. "I'm glad I didn't if it scared Miss Ether so much. I won't do anything like this again."

Sveyn stepped up beside Hollis as she watched the trio head toward the lobby. "As fun as that was, I do not believe I will laugh so hard the next time."

"That's okay. I think I was playing with fire." Hollis sighed. "No matter what sort of frauds and kooks walk in here from now on, I won't interfere."

Chapter Nineteen

Monday
December 14

A week had gone by since the séance with the fake medium, and ten days since Matt went back to Milwaukee.

Not the slightest peep had been heard about either.

Yay.

And crap.

Hollis drove to the office earlier than usual so that she could get some work done before the *Ghost Myths, Inc.* crew arrived. Benton had struck a deal with the cable TV show, allowing them twenty-four continuous hours of access starting at nine this morning, and ending an hour before the museum opened on Tuesday. Of course, that meant Hollis was working for more than twenty-four continuous hours as well.

At a hundred dollars an hour for sixteen hours of overtime.

If Sveyn had not been so tender and caring as he loved her in her dreams last night, she probably wouldn't be in such a good mood now in spite of the extra money. The man had skills—or at least, a very good imagination. And because of the uniquely nonphysical nature of their lovemaking, repetition didn't wear either of them out.

An adult sleep and dream cycle was about ninety minutes on average. Five cycles in a normal eight-hour night.

Hollis smiled.

"You are pleased this morning?" Sveyn asked.

"How could I not be?" Hollis glanced at her handsome passenger. "How do you think of all that?"

He grinned. "Many, many, *many* years of contemplation."

Hollis pulled into the employee parking lot and parked closest to the back door. She reached into the back seat for her overnight bag. She wasn't going to sleep while the show was being taped, but she brought some personal care stuff plus comfy non-work clothes to change into later.

Never underestimate the value of a toothbrush.

A white van pulled into the parking lot before she even got out of her car.

"Crap. They're early." Hollis got out of her car and locked it, wondering if she should speak to the guys in the van now, or go inside and come back out at the scheduled time.

The decision was made for her when a guy opened the van door and climbed out. "I know I'm early," he called out. "I'll wait out here."

"Well now it feels rude to leave him here," she muttered.

Sveyn looked down at her. "You have no obligation to extend his hours, Hollis. Go on inside."

Hollis nodded, gave the guy the *thanks* wave, and headed into the building.

*****

Stevie came bouncing over while Hollis was showing the *Ghost Myths* camera crew where Benton wanted the interview shots to take place. "Guess what? I have the best news!"

Hundred to one it's about the wedding. "You're eloping?"

Stevie giggled. "Where's the fun in that? No—we have our location. And a date!"

"Oh, good." While Hollis really *was* happy for her friend, the topic of conversation wore on her. At least now, with two major decisions apparently made, some of the stress should ease.

She opened the calendar on her phone. "When and where?"

"Sunday, February seventh. At four o'clock."

Hollis punched in the time on that date. "Got it. Where?"

"At the Chocolate Affaire in Glendale."

Hollis looked up from her phone. "What?"

Stevie was practically glowing. "George booked the last hour on the main stage. We're going to demonstrate a Regency wedding ceremony, in full costume, and actually get married in the process."

Hollis blinked, searching for a response. "Well... from what I've heard that event *is* dedicated to romance."

"Right? It'll be amazing!" Stevie clapped her hands. "And the best part is that we can invite everyone we want. All of JASNA. Unlimited space!"

That was actually true. "What about the reception?"

"Don't know for sure yet, but there is an adorable little event place called Virginia's House nearby. George and I are meeting with them this week to talk about having the wedding dinner there." Stevie winked. "Separate invitation, of course."

"Of course." Hollis saved the calendar entry. "Well I think it sounds like a '*ton*' of fun."

Stevie laughed, delighted by the pun. "And now that we have that decided..." She clasped her hands in front of her waist, her eyes twinkling. "I have a question to ask you."

Hollis held her breath, anticipating the question. She wasn't sure whether she wanted to be right—or wrong.

"Would you be one of my bridesmaids?"

Yep. *That's the question.*

Stevie was so excited, Hollis found herself being pulled into the vortex. "I would be honored."

"Thank you!" Stevie attacked her with an enthusiastic hug. "None of this would be happening if it wasn't for you."

Hollis hugged her back, then disentangled from her petite friend. "We'll talk more later. I need to get back to these guys."

Stevie turned to look at the crew as if seeing them for the first time. "Oops. Sorry!"

"Congrats." The man driving the first white van—whose name was Cody—gave her a tight-lipped smile and turned to Hollis. "We're ready for the next set-up."

*****

Justin Howard, founder of *Ghost Myths, Inc.*, strode into the collections storeroom like he owned it. "How're we doing, fellas?"

"We're just about finished." Cody, whose official title was Director, climbed down his ladder. "Give us thirty minutes to wire the last couple cameras and clean up, and we're good to go."

Justin turned to Hollis. "And you're the lady that started all this, aren't you?" He stuck out his hand. "Justin Howard. Pleased to meet you, Ms. McKenna."

Hollis shook his hand, wondering if she should tell him to call her Hollis, or just enjoy his gentlemanly Southern charm. "Welcome to the Arizona History and Cultural Center, Mr. Howard."

His deep brown eyes crinkled at the edges when he smiled, the single indication that this man was approaching forty. "Please call me Justin, ma'am."

Sigh. "And you can call me Hollis."

Justin rested his hands on his hips and scanned the space. "Your husband worried about you spending the night with a bunch of strange men?"

"I'm not married."

Justin looked at her again, his smile softening. "Lucky for me."

Sveyn snorted. "I do not trust this man."

Hush.

He's pretty.

"Can you come to my office and review the guidelines for being in the storeroom?" Hollis asked. "I know we sent them to you, but in case there are any questions."

"Happy to." Justin stretched out one arm. "After you."

Hollis led Justin to her office and pulled a copy of the list of *Collection Storeroom Dos and Don'ts* from her Paranormal Guests folder. Justin sat in front of her desk and she leaned forward as they read through the list together.

"The room is strictly climate-controlled, as you know," Hollis said. "Which is why your regular lights and cameras are not allowed inside."

"Right. And the room has sensors for humidity and temperature, and that data will be fed to us." Justin pointed at the list. "The museum also has thermal vision cameras in place. They'll be turned on for us, I assume?"

"They are never off." Hollis looked up from the paper. "Mice are a museum's worst enemy."

"Understood." Justin met her gaze. "I understand that the lights will be off, so the room is actually pitch black?"

Hollis nodded. "Yes."

"Perfect. We have a few quarter-watt night lights to plug in so the night vision cameras will work."

"Not a problem." Hollis reached for a pen and tapped the bottom of the document with it. "Will you sign here?"

"This is going to be fun, I think." Justin signed the page with a strongly slanted signature. Then he looked at her again. "I hope your protector shows himself."

Hollis gave a wan smile. "I have a good feeling."

*****

Miranda was in the storeroom when Hollis and Justin returned. "Welcome to the Arizona History and Cultural Center."

Justin flashed his killer smile and Hollis saw Miranda's jaw sag. "Thank you. And you are?"

"Yours."

Justin's smile faded. "What?"

Miranda startled. "Your curator. Your expert. Hollis's boss."

"Oh. Nice." Justin pointed at the mid-thirty-ish man

descending a ladder. "Cody there is my director. He'll want both of you to do some on-camera interviews."

Ugh. Hollis made a face. "What about?"

"Your experiences in the museum. Your experiences with the apparition. Things like that." Justin shrugged. "You'll just sit and talk. Answer questions. We'll edit it later."

Cody came to stand beside Justin. "We're set here."

"Good. Ready to do the interviews?"

"Almost."

Miranda gave Justin an inquisitive smile. "What sort of equipment are you using?"

Justin lit up like he just won the lottery. "Come here and I'll show you."

As Justin explained how the infrared depth camera and the all-spectrum camera worked, Hollis began to get nervous. It seemed obvious to her that Sveyn would not be able to hide from all the technology—four kinds of cameras in all—and he would be fully exposed.

As she was talking herself down off the wall, however, Justin showed them the Ovilus—a device which supposedly registered what he happily called, "EVPs. Electronic voice phenomena."

Hollis felt a full-blown panic attack looming.

"I, um, forgot something. Be right back." She hurried toward her office, and closed the door before she faced Sveyn.

The apparition looked pale. "I did not expect such a variety of equipment."

"Neither did I. I guess we should've watched the show a few times and prepared for this."

Sveyn dragged his fingers through his hair. "It seems that would have been helpful."

Hollis lifted her brow in hope. "Maybe because you aren't actually a ghost, they won't work on you."

"No." His blues eyes met hers. "I fear they will be even more accurate."

I was afraid of that.

Hollis considered the array of elaborate cameras, monitors,

and microphones which were all in place in the storeroom. "I don't think you should speak."

"I agree."

"We have to figure out which of these are likely to register your presence, and which ones we can keep you off of."

Sveyn waved one hand. "I can always simply leave the building, remember. My tether is long enough."

For a moment, Hollis wondered if that wasn't the best plan. "No. We talked about this. A little proof is best."

She drew a deep breath. "But until we see how all of these things work, you will have to stay out of sight and quiet."

Chapter twenty

If she wasn't so nervous about how this night was going to turn out, Hollis would have laughed. Miranda sat in the hot seat, answering the questions Cody asked about the security videos that showed evidence of something being in the storeroom with Hollis, while Miranda tried to sound both professional yet awestruck.

But that wasn't the funny part.

The lights in the back hallway were turned off. Miranda's face was lit from below, reminding Hollis of the spooky flashlight trick. As Hollis stood behind the cameras, she saw them using the shaky-frame sort of shot that became popular with the old paranormal movie, *The Blair Witch Project*.

Though early and heavy-handed copycats made audiences nauseous at first, the trick was now widely and much more subtly used to ramp up the viewers' anxiety levels to match the intended mood of whatever they were watching.

Obviously the *Ghost Myths, Inc.* guys wanted their audience to feel uneasy. As if their subject matter wasn't creepy enough already.

"Thank you, Miranda." Cody gave her his hand to guide her

through the lights and wires that created a messy obstacle course on the hall floor. "That was very well done."

Miranda looked pleased. "Really?"

"Oh, yes. You were very helpful." The director turned to Hollis. "Are you ready?"

Hollis nodded and accepted the same assistance from Cody to navigate the impromptu set. She settled in the chair and squinted toward the cameras. "I can't see you."

"You don't need to. Just talk toward my voice."

"Oh." Hollis turned a little to the left, where Cody's voice was coming from. "How's this?"

"Great. Now I'm going to ask you questions, and I want you to answer like we were friends discussing this over coffee."

Hollis huffed a little laugh. "So rambling is acceptable?"

"Rambling is preferred," Cody said with enthusiasm. "The more you say, the more we have to work with."

Sveyn squatted in front of her. "Be careful, Hollis. Think before you speak."

"Can you say a few sentences so we can get a voice level?" Cody asked. "Anything is fine."

Hollis cleared her throat. "Like this? I will think before I speak."

"Uh, sure."

"Okay. Then I'll tell you what I can—and won't tell you what I can't." She shifted in her seat. "Are we good?"

"Let's do it."

Hollis heard paper rustling a few feet from her, then Cody asked, "Tell us what happened that night right before the manifestation."

Hollis wasn't expecting that question. "What?"

"Tell us where you were when the phenomenon occurred."

Her pulse surged and roared in her ears. "Don't you know?"

"Easy, Hollis." Sveyn's calm voice was close to her ear. "You are safe."

A swarm of gnats danced in front of her eyes. She felt weak.

More papers rustled. "My notes say you were locked inside the storeroom."

"It was a hell of a lot more than that!" she cried. Her voice sounded strangled. "I almost died!"

Sveyn's face moved in front of hers. "Tell them you don't want to talk about that."

She focused on his eyes. "Huh?"

"Tell them you don't want to talk about that," he said again.

Hollis nodded. The Viking's big, close, and calm presence was pulling her back from the brink of hysteria. "I—I don't want to—to talk about that."

From very far away, she heard Cody say, "Are you getting this?"

"Yep."

"What do you want to talk about, Hollis?"

Sveyn was still between her and the cameras. "Tell them what happened when the motion detectors went off."

She nodded again and kept her attention on Sveyn. "I was scared. Terrified. And I couldn't move."

"Then what?" Cody prompted.

"Tell them I was angry. But do not say my name."

"The—the apparition—was there, and he was angry." Her gaze shifted to where Cody was standing. "He was frustrated because he couldn't help me. Do you understand?"

Cody grabbed the opportunity. "How did you know that?"

"Because he was shouting."

"At you?"

Hollis scowled. "No. About his lack of a body."

"Okay. That makes sense." Cody stepped closer and she could see him now when she looked past Sveyn. "Then what?"

"I will stay here, but do not look at me," Sveyn said.

Hollis nodded a third time and gripped the arms of the chair. "Then somehow he set off the motion detectors."

"How, do you think?"

"I think it was his anger."

Cody took another step closer. "He is here, isn't he?"

Hollis recoiled. "What do you mean?"

"It seems he is talking to you. Calming you down."

"Can you hear him?" She leaned to the side and looked at

the cameras. Sveyn moved out of her way, but stayed by her side. "Can *you* hear him?"

"I can't," one of the crew blurted.

Hollis was regaining her composure, and along with it the realization of what the crew might have just seen. "Then why do you think he's talking to me?"

"You have been looking at something close to you," Cody said softly. "And you nodded three times when no one asked you anything."

Oh crap.

Crappity crappity crapsalot.

Hollis rallied her inner strength and pinned as stern a gaze as she could conjure on Cody. "Have you ever been close to losing your life? I'm mean, like really, honestly, close?"

"No, I can't say that I have," he admitted.

"Well when something like that happens to a person, they panic when they remember it. And they have to talk *themselves* out of completely losing it."

Sveyn nodded. "Good. Well said."

Hollis tilted her head. "Does *that* make sense, Cody?"

"It does."

"Good." Hollis pulled a deep breath and stilled, closing her eyes.

"Hollis, are you okay?" Cody asked gently. Someone pressed a bottle of cold water against her hand.

She opened her eyes and accepted the water, taking a long drink before answering. "I'm sorry. I wasn't prepared for the direction of your questions and it caught me off guard."

He nodded. "I understand."

"I'm feeling better now. Thanks for the water."

"You're welcome."

"All right then." Hollis recapped the water and set the bottle on the floor next to the chair. She pulled a long, slow breath, combed her fingers through her curls. and smoothed her blouse. "Let's start over. Ask me the same questions, if you want. I'm ready now."

Cody looked skeptical. "Are you sure?"

Sveyn asked her the same thing.

"Yes, I'm sure. Just promise me you'll erase the first try." She flashed an embarrassed expression which was completely sincere. "Please? I really don't want anyone watching me in full blown panic mode. Especially on television."

"Of course." Cody nodded at the two cameramen. "Do it."

When the second interview was finished, Cody let Hollis watch the entire thing. She made an effort to be more forthcoming about Sveyn in the second round, adding a few extra details in hopes that the director would keep his word about her first debacle.

"That looks great," she said.

Cody smiled. "Yeah, it does."

Hollis faced him and gave him her most charming smile. "Thank you again, Cody. That first go was really embarrassing."

"Can I ask you something? Honestly?"

In spite of a stab of trepidation, Hollis said, "Sure."

"Do you think he'll appear while we're here?"

That's a loaded question. "I'm afraid I can't answer that."

"But you have seen him since that night?"

Hollis shrugged her acknowledgement. "Several people have caught glimpses."

"Under what circumstances?" he prodded. "Anything we can recreate for the cameras?"

"He's not a trained monkey, Cody. I can't haul him out to perform on command."

"But you will call for him?"

Hollis was afraid of where this conversation was going. "I will fully cooperate with you guys. I promise."

Cody looked defeated. "I guess that's all we can ask of you."

Hollis waved a hand toward the storeroom. "You have more equipment in there than I could ever imagine. If he decides to show himself, I'm sure you'll be able to capture it."

"Yeah." Cody scratched his head. "If he showed up on regular security equipment, theoretically he should light up like a Las Vegas sign on ours."

Oh. Great.

"What about that Ovilus thing?" she asked. "How does that actually work?"

"It takes readings from the environment and puts them into words," Cody explained.

Hollis laughed. "Really?"

"It measures the electromagnetic field, the extremely low frequency field, and the temperature, then through an analog digital converter, assigns those readings a number. Each number is assigned a word."

Aside from the astronomically high reading on her bullshit monitor, Hollis noticed something else. "So it doesn't pick up words spoken normally."

"No. It doesn't need to, does it?" Cody shifted his stance. "I mean, if the human ear can hear what's being said, then that's enough."

Another question surfaced. "Have you ever actually heard something that wasn't picked up by your devices?"

Cody shook his head. "If any one of us heard something, so did at least one piece of our equipment."

"Interesting." Hollis clapped her hands together. "If we're done here, I'll go see how things are coming in the storeroom."

"Great. And I'll clean up here."

As Hollis walked away, she whispered to Sveyn. "I don't think they'll hear you."

He spoke in her ear. "We shall see."

*****

Command central was set up in the administration hallway. Miranda was adjusting the amount of light in the hall, trying to make it dim, but not dark. The guys had to see their control boards, after all. She opened her office door and Hollis's, then switched off the overhead fluorescents. Indirect light seeped through the open doors.

"Perfect!" one tech guy said. "Can we leave it like this?"

"Yes, of course." Miranda smiled at Hollis. "You don't mind do you?"

Hollis shook her head and looked at the monitors. Each was labeled with the camera's type—all spectrum or infrared, for example—and a number. Right now, the central and most open area of the collections storeroom could be seen from six distinct angles.

"Holy Mother of God," Sveyn swore softly. "I shall have to enter the room through the back wall, until we know for certain if I can be seen."

Stevie came in the back door with two trays from Starbucks.

"Salvation!" the same tech said, grinning at the blonde registrar. "These all-nighters are brutal without the right kind of sustenance."

"I'm happy to stay and be your caffeine and food runner," Stevie offered as she passed out the drinks.

Justin walked out the storeroom door in time to hear the proposal. "Great! You're hired!"

Stevie grinned and handed him his iced coffee, no cream.

Hollis knew how badly her friend wanted to be there, but there was one issue in the way. "It's fine with me if you want to stay and volunteer your time."

"I think it'll be fascinating," Stevie replied. "I don't expect to be paid."

"What about work tomorrow?" Hollis had the day off.

"I won't stay all night. Unless exciting something happens, of course." Stevie winked at Miranda. "Then I'll call in sick."

Cody walked into the hallway, loops of cables over his shoulders. "I smell coffee."

Stevie handed the director a cup with his name on it. "The guys told me your usual order."

"Thank you—"

She blushed and smiled, dimples showing. "Stevie. Phillips."

"Thank you, Stevie." Cody sipped the soy latte, as his drink was labeled. "Are you one of the people here who has seen the ghost?"

Hollis startled. She hadn't thought to tell Stevie that, for the purposes of this production, Sveyn must be called a ghost.

"Ghost?" Stevie looked puzzled. She tilted her head. "Are

you sure about that?"

That caught Justin's attention. "What would you call it?"

"There isn't really another name for him," Hollis prompted. "*Is* there."

Stevie gave a little shrug and tossed Justin a flirty smile. "Well, he could be called a guardian angel. Couldn't he."

Excellent creation of tension throughout these last scenes! Fun!

Chapter Twenty One

Two hours later, Hollis stood in the darkened storeroom wondering what to do next. Justin stood near her, an earpiece linking him to the control center in the hallway beyond the closed steel door. This was the first time she had been in here at night since…

"Why do you guys always do this stuff in the dark?" she snapped much more harshly than she intended.

"Because most of the phenomena can't be photographed in bright light," he answered as he adjusted his earpiece. Then he chuckled. "And, of course, it's scarier that way. But don't worry, I'll keep you safe."

"And scarier means better ratings, I suppose." Hollis grumbled. She looked around the space. Sveyn was nowhere to be seen.

"If I'm honest, you don't seem scared, Hollis." Justin stepped closer, his earpiece secured at last.

She lifted her chin and silently told Everett Sage to go burn in hell for a very, very long time. "There's nothing in here to be scared of, Justin."

He grinned at her. "So you're not afraid of ghosts?"

Oh, please. *Ghosts aren't real.* "The only 'ghost' I've ever encountered saved my life, so I'm with Stevie on this one."

"Guardian angel?"

Hollis shrugged. "Makes more sense."

"Well, you have me on that. Most of the phenomena we encounter are very angry and hurtful. But then, they all died in very unpleasant ways, as a rule."

"And angels don't die, so…"

"Another point for your theory." Justin turned around and addressed the cameraman with a huge night vision camera on his shoulder. "Are we set?"

"Yep."

Justin pressed his earpiece. "Sound check. Are we good?" He turned back to Hollis. "Could you say something so they can check the level of your mike?"

"Sure. What exactly will you want me to do?"

"Got it?" Justin gave her thumbs up, and then faced her fully. "Just do what I ask. Mostly I'll be prompting you on what to say."

Hollis nodded, still not clear on how this evening was going to play out.

"Three, two, one." Justin faced the camera. "I'm here at the Arizona History and Cultural Center with Hollis McKenna, the museum's Lead Collector. We are hoping that the apparition, which saved her life by setting off motion detectors, will cooperate and let us see him tonight."

"I'm *one* of the lead collectors," Hollis corrected, trying to avert another Tony Samoa rant. The Kensington collection and her role with it had the man enough on edge as it was.

Justin acted like she hadn't spoken. "Hollis, have you seen the apparition since that night?"

Umm. "There have been a couple sightings."

"Have you made actual contact?"

"There was a situation with one of the museum pieces," she admitted.

Justin brightened. "The Blessing? The one with the legend attached? What happened?"

"Do you need me to explain the legend?"

"No, we'll do that in an interview later." Justin repeated his question, "What happened?"

Hollis felt a chill skate up her spine. She mimicked the action with her empty hands. "I was holding the two halves of the icon, and when they touched, one of the interns tackled me and knocked them out of my grasp."

"Why would he do that?" Justin prompted.

"He said I was being attacked by some sort of figure."

"Could you see it?"

Don't tell him the truth. *Or I'll be deeper into this than I already am.* "I did see something."

"Why was this figure attacking you?"

"He wasn't attacking *me*; he was trying to knock the pieces away."

Justin was practically giddy. "To save you from the legend?"

Hollis nodded. "I assume so."

"It appears you do have a guardian angel, Hollis." Justin addressed the camera. "We haven't encountered an angel before. If we can coax him to appear, this will be an epic episode."

Hollis rolled her eyes.

The good stuff just keeps coming.

"All right, Hollis. Do you see him now?"

Hollis did a slow turn, looking down the long rows of crowded shelves on both sides. "No."

"Will you call him?"

Hollis drew a breath. *Don't use his name.* "Hello? Are you here?" She turned around again. "Will you let me see you?"

Sveyn appeared at the end of one row and started walking toward her.

Hollis made eye contact with him, and then pretended she didn't see him.

"Ask if he'll speak," Justin prodded. He held up the Ovilus. "We usually get verbal contact more easily that visual."

She nodded. "Will you speak to me?"

Sveyn stopped in the aisle still out of the cameras' view. He lifted his hands in question.

Hollis turned her back on the cameraman and gave a slight nod of encouragement. "If you're here, please say something."

Sveyn spoke from the shadows. "What shall I say?"

Hollis waited.

The Ovilus was silent. She didn't expect that.

Interesting.

"Please speak to us," Hollis urged. "I want to thank you for watching over me."

"That little box didn't respond." Sveyn took a step closer. "Can they hear me?"

Hollis looked over her shoulder. "Do you hear anything?"

Justin shook his head. "Neither does the Ovilus or it would be speaking."

"Huh." Hollis looked up at the ceiling. "We can't hear you. Are you even here?"

"What do you want me to do, Hollis?"

That was the million dollar question. There was only one action that made sense. "Can you show yourself?"

"Are you absolutely certain, Hollis?" Sveyn asked. "If any of their cameras see me somehow, there will be no denying my existence any longer."

True. Hollis gave another small nod. "If you are here, please come out of hiding."

Sveyn hesitated.

"Whatever happens, you'll be safe," she urged.

"Safe from what? Death?" Sveyn snorted. "That water has long passed beneath all possible bridges."

Hollis bit back a smile, then turned to face Justin. "How long do we wait?"

"We have all night." He gave her arm a reassuring squeeze. "This is very common. It seems to require quite a lot of effort for the apparitions to cross over."

Justin jerked away from her, eyes wide. "Where?"

Hollis's heart thumped. "What?"

"He's on the infrared depth camera." Justin touched his earpiece. "He's right behind you."

Hollis whirled around and made a sudden decision. She

looked up at Sveyn and winked. "How close?"

"Can't you see him?"

"No."

"Is he showing up anywhere else?"

"I can't see anything," the night vision cameraman behind her said.

"What about the all-spectrum camera?" Justin asked excitedly. "No? Nothing? Anything from the thermal vision?"

Hollis pressed her lips together. *He won't create heat when he's calm.*

"So only the infrared, then?" Justin's excitement dropped a notch.

Sveyn smiled. "And no microphones."

"So it seems." Hollis felt a surge of relief and shifted into full paranormal support mode. "What does he look like?"

Justin stepped to her side and removed his earpiece, holding it so that she could hear the response. He was less than a yard from Sveyn.

"He's huge, Justin. Half a head taller than you…"

Hollis looked at Justin, ignoring the Viking. "How tall are you?"

"Six feet." He shook his head, irritated by her distraction. "What else?"

"Hair to his shoulders? Maybe a beard? Details are hard to see…"

"He's close enough for you to touch him, Justin," another voice added. "Stretch your right arm toward the back wall."

Justin's eyes narrowed. He lifted his hand. "Here?"

Sveyn held his ground.

Justin's hand reached right into the Viking's gut, then jerked backwards. "Oh my god."

Hollis looked at him. "Did you feel something?"

Justin nodded and did it again.

The earpiece barked, "What do you feel?"

"Thick air. An electric tingle." The *Ghost Myths* star took a step back. "There really *is* something here."

Watching his reaction, it occurred to Hollis that Justin was in the middle of the realest paranormal encounter that he had ever experienced.

"What's he wearing?" she prompted.

"Uh, we aren't sure. There's no color on this camera."

"What does it look like?" she pressed.

A disbelieving snicker crackled through the earpiece. "To be honest? He looks like a Viking."

Hollis flashed a crooked smile. "Well I guess it's official. Norsemen really were the original heroes."

Justin seemed to be recovering from his shock. "What's he doing?"

A pause. "He's just… standing there."

Justin turned to Hollis. "Ask him why he's here."

"But we can't hear him," she pointed out.

"Right." Justin looked at the useless Ovilus and handed Hollis the earpiece to hold. He shoved the device in his back pocket. "Yes and no questions, then."

She frowned a little. "Like what?"

Justin folded his arms over his chest and looked unconvincingly nonchalant. "Like—are you an angel? Right hand for yes, left hand for no."

An incredulous producer spoke through the earpiece. "He's raising his left hand, Justin."

"He is? Are you recording this?"

"Every bit."

"Okay. Right on." Justin's fingers tightened visibly on his arms. "Are you a ghost? Did you die?"

Hollis watched an amused Sveyn wave his left hand again. "This will surely confuse them," he said.

"Left hand, Justin."

Hollis tried not to laugh as Justin shook out his hands and jammed them on his hips. "What are you—I mean, are you attached to Hollis in some way?"

"Right hand this time."

Justin looked at Hollis. "Why is he attached to you?"

She shrugged. She wasn't going to give him anything he couldn't puzzle out on his own.

Justin blew a sigh. "Have you always been attached to her?"

"Left."

"Will you be attached to her for the rest of her life?"

A long pause. "Ask him ag—never mind. Left."

Hollis's amusement dimmed with that reminder. *Don't think about it.*

Justin's expression shifted. "Will you be sad to leave her?"

The voice in the earpiece held an unexpectedly tender tone. "Right hand."

Hollis lifted her eyes to Sveyn's. *Me, too.*

When she said nothing, Justin asked, "How will you feel Hollis?"

"I don't know how I'll know when he's gone." She turned to face Justin. "I guess when I'm in danger and he isn't there."

"I'm walking away now," Sveyn said behind her. "I believe they have enough evidence."

Hollis nodded, still facing Justin. "He just showed up with no warning and I imagine he'll leave the same way."

The voice in the earpiece interrupted them. "Speaking of leaving…"

Justin reached his arm out, swinging it in an arc. "What? Is he gone?"

"He turned around and is walking toward the back wall—oh my god! He just walked *through* it!"

*****

Justin and Hollis—and Sveyn—joined the production crew in the hallway and watched the playback from all of the synced cameras. Stevie and Miranda were still there, and Stevie was gripping Hollis's hand so tightly that Hollis could feel Stevie's engagement ring against her knuckle.

"This is so exciting!" Stevie stage-whispered loud enough to be shushed by a producer.

Miranda's face was pale and drawn. "I never believed in ghosts before…"

"He's not a ghost, Miranda," Hollis reminded her boss. "He

said so."

"Well if he's not an angel, and not a ghost, then what the hell is he?" Justin snapped, his eyes on the monitors. "And why can't the Ovilus hear him? Why can't the other cameras see him?"

Hollis motioned for Stevie and Miranda to follow her and led them into the ladies room—which seemed to be her best meeting place of late.

"I don't think he's going to show himself any more tonight," she said. "I'm going to change into my comfy clothes and try to get a little rest."

"You're suggesting we go home." Stevie sounded even more disappointed than she looked.

Hollis shook her head. "You can stay as long as you want. But I have to stay, and you both have to work tomorrow."

"Well I'm going home." Miranda glanced in the mirror and straightened her bangs. "This has been more than enough spookiness for one night." She turned on a heel and grabbed the door handle. "Good night, ladies."

Once their boss was gone, Stevie stared hard at Hollis. "Everything you told me is true."

Hollis smiled sadly. *If you only knew.*

chapter twenty two

Wednesday
December 16

After doing the interview where she explained the Blessing of the Gods legend to a producer, Hollis changed her clothes and spent the rest of that night watching a lot of nothing. Stevie stayed through the interview, then went home after Hollis assured her that Sveyn was not going to be seen again.

Sveyn focused on the production process, so fascinated by the technology that he kept asking Hollis to ask questions on his behalf. As he did, her hopes for a chance to nap evaporated, and she resigned herself to a night with no sleep.

She made up for it yesterday, spending the day luxuriating on the sofa with popcorn, hot chocolate, and a string of Christmas movies with Sveyn by her side.

"You will miss your parents, will you not?" he asked as she reached for her sixth tissue while watching *Love Actually*.

"I'll be fine," she lied. "They really do deserve this trip, and I'll see them in less than eight weeks. Right after Stevie's wedding."

Today she walked into the office refreshed and ready to take on whatever life or her job decided to throw at her.

Stevie walked up and handed her an overnight envelope. "It's from Matt Wallace."

Except that.

"Oh, Lord." Hollis accepted the envelope and carried it into her office, Stevie behind her, Sveyn in front of her. She dropped her briefcase and jacket on her chair and, with a silent prayer for strength, tore it open.

"What is it?" Stevie asked.

Hollis pulled out a small stack of papers. Her heart rate surged when she realized what the contents were. "Copies of his petition for divorce."

Stevie gasped. "He was serious."

"Apparently." Hollis looked inside the cardboard folder and pulled out a handwritten note. Her hands trembled a little as she read it out loud.

Dear Hollis,

As you can see, I took your advice. Suzan was served yesterday and I moved out of the house. I was surprised at how well she took it, which does make me wonder if she was contemplating the same action. Maybe I should have waited. It would have cost me less in the long run if she had filed.

"Men," Stevie scoffed.

Hollis nodded. "Always about the end game, not how you actually get there."

"Anything else?"

Hollis refocused on the letter and continued.

Because you are not going to be here for Christmas, I am coming to you. I know you haven't agreed to give me another chance, but I can't think of a better way to prove my sincerity.

"Where does he expect to sleep?" Sveyn growled.

Hollis looked at Stevie. "I hope he doesn't expect to move in with me!"

"Just tell him that when you talk to him," Stevie said. "Would he be so presumptuous?"

"I hope not." Hollis returned to the letter.

And while I would love nothing more than to pick up where we left off, I have leased an apartment through January while we take time to reconnect.

"There's a relief." Hollis fanned herself with the letter and glanced at Sveyn. His expression eased.

Stevie frowned. "Can he leave his job for that long?"

"Who knows." Hollis shrugged. "Who cares? That's his problem, not mine."

"Is there anything else?"

Please call me when you have a chance.
Love, Matt

"Love, huh?" Stevie gave Hollis the stink-eye. "You know, men never leave a marriage, or even a long-term relationship like you guys had, unless they have someplace else to go."

Hollis folded the papers and stuffed them back inside the overnight envelope along with the letter. "So you think he had Suzan in his pocket before he left me?"

"Don't you?"

"I always wondered. Their wedding happened so fast." Hollis dropped the envelope in the trash. "And now he thinks he has me to run back to."

"Or so he hopes." Stevie walked over and retrieved the envelope from the plastic bin. She held it out to Hollis. "Keep this. You never know what you'll need to know."

*****

Miranda loved the idea of the children's book. "Will it be a coloring book as well?"

Hollis shook her head and looked at Stevie. "No, we didn't plan anything like that."

Stevie shrugged. "We could think about it."

"No, we couldn't," Hollis stated. "One extra project at a time. Let's see if we can get this done before we take on anything else."

"When will it be finished?" Miranda asked.

"As soon as we finish the contest and choose the illustrations." Stevie grinned at Hollis. "But we'll have the copy written before that."

"Good. The sooner the better." Miranda turned to Hollis. "By the way, I spoke with Mr. Benton yesterday. I don't think I have to tell you how thrilled he was when he heard that the *Ghost Myth* guys got footage of the apparition."

"I can only imagine."

Sveyn chuckled.

Shut up.

"I'm sorry you couldn't see him." Miranda gave her a sympathetic look. "You must have been disappointed, knowing he was there but…"

"I'm fine, Miranda. Really. I am."

"Anyway, Benton wants to do a big-screen viewing here when the episode airs in January."

Hollis huffed. "I'm not in the least bit surprised."

Stevie's expression turned puckish. "Matt will be here then."

Miranda's jaw dropped. "Which Matt?" She looked at Hollis. "*Your* Matt?"

"Tell her," Stevie urged.

Hollis folded her arms and gave her boss the abbreviated version. "Yep. He filed for divorce, and is coming for Christmas. Staying through January. Not with me."

Miranda blinked. "Got it. When did this happen?"

"This morning. In fact," Hollis looked at her watch, "I have to call him and tell him I got his letter."

"Before you go—" Miranda opened a drawer and pulled out

two business-sized envelopes. "Some guy from the Renaissance Festival brought these by yesterday."

"What are they?" Hollis asked as she accepted one of the envelopes. Stevie took the other one.

Miranda grinned. "Two free tickets for each of you to the Festival on opening day, plus passes for a behind the scenes tour."

"Wow. Why?"

"Because we're a museum. And we have the new collection. And you two pulled it together."

"We can double date!" Stevie gushed. "Me and George, you and Matt!"

"Ugh," Sveyn grunted.

Hollis opened the envelope and looked at the date—January 9th. "We could, I guess. If I haven't sent him packing before then."

Sveyn snorted. "One can always hope."

Hush.

Stevie smacked Hollis's arm with her envelope. "Stop it. You need to think positively."

Hollis flashed a wry smile. "I am positive that I will have more fun with you and George than I would with Matt alone."

"It's a start," Stevie conceded. "Now go call him before he slips out of your life forever."

*****

"Hello, Hollis."

"Hi, Matt." *Deep breath.* "I got your packet."

"Yeah." Pause. "So what are you thinking?"

"I'm sorry she wasn't more upset."

"Really?" He sounded confused.

"Yes. For your sake," Hollis clarified.

"Oh."

"I mean, aren't you a little hurt that she didn't fight for you?" *I did. Remember?*

"To be honest, Hollis? I'm actually relieved."

Hollis could understand that; clean breaks were ultimately less unpleasant. "So… you rented an apartment? In Phoenix?"

"Tempe, actually. I figured staying with you might piss off the captain."

Who? She glanced at Sveyn.

Oh, right.

"And you weren't *invited* to stay with me," Hollis pointed out. "There's that."

"Well, I thought maybe—nope. Never mind." Matt cleared his throat. "So I'm leaving this Saturday. Driving down. Should get there by Monday afternoon."

Driving made sense, in spite of the distance. He'd need a car when he got here, not to mention packing along all his clothes and stuff. "Is the apartment furnished?"

"Yeah."

"That's good."

Another pause. "What are my chances, Hollis?"

"With me?" she asked, stalling for time.

"Yes."

Hollis dropped her head onto her hand. "I honestly don't know how to answer that, Matt."

"Let's start with a ranking. On a scale of one to ten, how much do you forgive me?"

How much, indeed. "You *really* hurt me, Matt."

His voice got very small. "I know."

"I felt like all those years we were together were a lie. You didn't follow through on anything you promised me. Not *any* of it." *Dang.* It really felt good to say that. "I wasted an entire decade waiting for you to man up. You know?"

"I was scared, Hollis."

"That's not an excuse." She had no intention of letting him off easy. Why should she? He didn't deserve it.

"No. It's not." Matt sighed heavily, blowing on the receiver. "But I'm manning up now. I promise."

Stevie's supposition echoed through her thoughts. Might as well throw everything on the table; there was no point in dancing around any of it now.

"Were you with Suzan before you left me?"

"Hollis—"

"I need to know, Matt. And I need the truth." Hollis pounded her fist on her desktop. "And if I find out you lied to me again, I *will* cause you physical harm."

"Hollis…"

"I'm not kidding, Matt."

He sighed again. "I wasn't dating her before I moved out."

Aww crap. "But you were talking?"

"Yes."

Hollis's hand sagged. She sat back in her chair and stared at her phone. The temptation to hang up on him nearly pushed her to do so.

"Hollis?" his thin voice called through the tiny speaker. "Are you still there?"

"Yes," she answered from a distance.

"You sound far away."

"I *am* far away, Matt. It's where you *put* me."

Silence.

Hollis waited, watching the seconds tick by on her screen; proof that Matt had not hung up.

"I'm sorry, Hollis. I was wrong," he finally said after more than a minute had gone by. "I was so completely wrong. It was all me. I was one hundred percent at fault."

Hollis returned the phone to her ear. "I needed to hear that, Matt." She heaved a sigh. "And I needed to know about Suzan."

Another long pause passed in a wordless void was punctuated by Matt's sniffling. "What now?"

That's the million dollar question. She would not look at Sveyn, though the Viking was next to her listening to every word of the conversation.

"What do you mean?" she stalled again.

More sniffing, followed by another throat clearing.

"Should I stay in Milwaukee?" he asked at last.

Hollis wiped her own eyes. She knew what she should say. And she knew what she wanted to say. The problem is, they were not compatible answers.

"Hollis?"

Hollis muted her phone and looked at Sveyn. "I have to do this."

He straightened and walked to the other side of her office, clearly distressed. He nodded slowly and stared at her with pain-filled eyes.

She un-muted her phone. "No."

"No?" Matt hesitated. "No, what. Exactly. Just to be clear."

"No. Don't stay in Milwaukee, Matt." Hollis drew a slow, steadying breath. "Come to Phoenix. Let me know when you get here."

Chapter
twenty three

Sveyn stared across the office at her, his eyes dark as his mood. "Are you truly convinced about what you re doing?"

"Sveyn—"

"Hollis." He strode toward her. "From the start of my manifestation here, you have not said one good thing about that man."

"I know, but—"

"There is no 'but' which applies, Hollis." Sveyn jabbed a stiff finger at her. "Are you absolutely confident that there is good reason for you to encourage this man's attentions?"

Hollis felt her anger surging to dangerous levels. "There *is* a reason! And it's ten years!"

"Ten years wasted, you said," he threw her own words back at her. "And let us be clear, by inviting him to come you are considering wasting even more."

"Ten years *invested*," she snapped. "When you were living, you never spent that much time with one person. You can't possibly understand what a big deal that is!"

Sveyn flinched.

Hollis felt a stab of regret at the accusation, but she couldn't stop now. "Besides, if he's telling the truth and he's really sorry for what an ass he's been, then the pain of his leaving will be worth it!"

The Viking's gaze narrowed. "How?"

Hollis rolled her eyes; though a good man overall, Sveyn was stubbornly contrary sometimes. "He's had his fling. The grass wasn't greener—it was dead. He knows that now."

"What you do not see, Hollis, is that it will not be different. It cannot be." Sveyn dragged his hands through his hair—which moved and tumbled across his shoulders this time. "The sad truth is that men do not change."

"What are you talking about? Of course they do." She scowled at him and tossed an intentionally belittling spear. "At least modern, civilized men do."

Sveyn snorted. "I have been watching men—dozens of them—for a thousand years. I do believe I can speak with more authority on that subject than you can."

Hollis recoiled, unwilling to listen. "You're saying that because he strayed once, he'll stray again? You don't even know him!"

"I know his actions, however, do I not?" Sveyn narrowed the gap between them. "He said he loved you, but he never married you. Why? He thought he might meet someone better than you."

The Viking ran Hollis through the heart with that sword. "How *dare* you!"

"You were not good enough for him then." Sveyn threw his arms wide. "So why is he back?"

Tears stung her eyes. "Why are you being so mean? Can't you just give him—and me—some credit?"

Sveyn folded his arms. "And if you take up with him again what will you expect? Marriage?"

"Of course." That was the only logical reason to consider reuniting with Matt.

"How soon?" Sveyn pushed.

She swiped at her eyes. "Well, I'm not going to wait another ten years. I'm not stupid."

"How soon?" he asked again.

"I can't answer that yet!" she cried. "Can you please just back off?"

He didn't. "And what if he leaves you again?"

Hollis would have slapped him if she could. "Stop it!"

"You are *inviting* this man to hurt you again."

"Don't you get it? I want a future!"

"Then you should look elsewhere." Sveyn stared hard into her eyes. "This man will not give you one."

"Oh! And you will?"

Hollis clenched her fists and quickly moved away from him. She couldn't look into his eyes, so filled with pain that it spilled over her and burned in her chest. Everything Sveyn was saying could very well be true. But Hollis couldn't see another path to follow at this point.

Then without warning a horrible, terrible, devastating thought occurred. *Of course.* She turned slowly to face the angry apparition.

"You don't want me to go back to Matt because *you* don't want to be stuck with him," she accused. "That's what this is all about!"

A shadow passed over Sveyn's brow. "Of course I do not wish to be stuck, as you say. But that is not why I am giving you this advice!"

Hollis shook her head "I don't believe you."

Sveyn closed the gap between them, fury turning his face impossibly red. "I have never lied to you, Hollis! And I never will! You know that!"

"You're jealous!" she shouted. "Admit it!"

Her office door opened and Stevie stuck her head in. "Are you all—" Her eyes rounded and she stared straight at Sveyn. "*Oh my god!*"

Stevie slipped through the partially opened door and leaned on it to close it. "Is that him?"

Sveyn fell back, his eyes fixed on Stevie's. He looked as shocked as she did.

Stunned, Hollis's anger turned to disbelief. "Do you see him?"

Without waiting for Stevie's answer, Sveyn whirled around and disappeared through the office wall.

"Oh my god…" Stevie moaned as she sank to the floor with her back still against the door. She literally looked like she had seen a ghost, and the irony of that phrase was not lost on Hollis.

Hollis walked to the door and slid down beside Stevie. "We were arguing."

"That's why I came in," Stevie mumbled. "I heard shouting."

Oh, no. "Did anyone else?"

She frowned. "I don't think so. Miranda's not in her office."

"What did it sound like?"

"Really weird." Stevie shuddered. "Your voice was clear. But the other voice was muffled. I couldn't understand the words."

Hollis closed her eyes, feeling drained in the aftermath of their unresolved argument's adrenaline. "He was really mad."

"What did you fight about?"

"Matt."

Stevie shuddered again. "Yeah. That was so, so weird."

Hollis opened her eyes. "Could you see him clearly?"

"Yes—but he wasn't solid. I could see through him." Stevie turned her face to Hollis's. "But when I looked into his eyes? Oh my god, Hollis. I can't even explain what that felt like."

Hollis's brow twitched. "Good or bad?"

Stevie hesitated. "Both, I think."

Hollis found that answer a little disturbing. "Why bad?"

Her friend's features twisted. "I could feel how upset he was."

Interesting. "And good?"

Stevie relaxed for the first time since she entered Hollis's office. One corner of her mouth lifted. "You couldn't tell on that camera on Monday, but damn, Hollis. He really is one good looking man."

*****

Hollis didn't see Sveyn for the rest of the afternoon. That was probably just as well, considering how angry they both were when he stormed off. While she understood how Sveyn's existence would be impacted if she renewed her relationship with Matt, she still thought the Viking was unnecessarily heavy-handed in his accusations.

And mean, to be honest. An apology was in order.

She wondered if she was beginning to see his original temperament forged in an ancient and violent time, before it was smoothed by constant contact with increasingly modern men.

Hollis's cell phone rang. The display said it was George Oswald.

Hi, George," Hollis greeted the lawyer. "What's up?"

"Hi, Hollis. I'm calling to let you know we have a court date for your civil suit against Everett sage."

Oh, no. Hollis already shredded emotions took another hit. "When?"

"January seventh."

"Will I have to testify?" *Do. Not. Cry.*

"Maybe," George admitted. "We have until the trial begins to reach a settlement. And even though he can easily afford it, one point eight million is a lot of dollars."

When George first mentioned the amount she should ask for, Hollis was shocked—until he explained that he set the number high enough to prompt Sage into negotiating a settlement, rather than risk losing that much in court.

"So no panic yet," she murmured.

"Right." George's tone was optimistic. "And if he agrees to half—nine hundred thousand—then after court fees and commissions you should end up with over half a million."

Hollis had to admit, "That's a lot of money."

"And—don't get your hopes up yet—but I'm trying to convince the firm to cut their fees in half. This is a high profile case and could be great advertising for us."

Wow. "What would that mean for me?"

"You'd be looking at about seven hundred and fifty thousand."

Hollis fell back in her chair. "Seriously?"

"Yep." She could practically hear the smile in his voice.

Reality poked her. "But I could lose the suit and get nothing."

"That's true," George admitted. "But nothing ventured, nothing gained."

Hollis smiled for the first time in hours. "What would Jane do?"

George laughed. "Exactly."

*****

Sveyn was waiting in her car when Hollis left work. She got inside and started the engine before he spoke.

"She saw me, Hollis. She looked right into my eyes."

"*That's* what you want to talk about?" Hollis turned and stared at him. "Really?"

Sveyn twisted in his seat. "You do not understand. No one, and I mean not one single person, has ever been able to see me outside of my twenty-two previous manifestations, going all the way back to when this first happened to me."

Hollis folded her arms. "No one."

"No."

"Not even the slightest glance in your direction."

"Never. I swear to you, Hollis."

She lifted her chin. "Have you ever been that angry before?"

That stopped him. Sveyn rubbed his forehead and stared at the floor of the car.

Then he began to slowly wag his head. "No."

"Really?" Hollis pressed. "Nothing made you that angry? Even the guy who didn't speak to you for twenty seven years?"

He met her gaze again. "I was irritated. And bored. But nothing like the sort of anger I which experienced today."

Hollis gave him an unconcerned shrug. "So that explains it, I guess."

His brow was puckered and his cheeks drawn. "Do you truly believe so?"

"How should I know?" she scoffed. "This is centuries newer to me than it is to you!"

Hollis shifted the car into reverse and hit the gas. The car shot backwards and she jammed on the brake before throwing it into drive.

"You are still upset with me," he said.

She shot him a look. "Ya think?"

"Please don't kill yourself over it," he said carefully. "I would miss you."

Hollis stilled.

She took a breath.

Then she drove to the end of the employee lot and parked.

"You were mean to me, Sveyn," she said without looking at him. "You hurt my feelings."

"I was not being mean, Hollis," he stated with authority. "I was being honest."

"Said every rude asshole ever." She slid her gaze sideways toward him. "There is a difference, you know."

Sveyn was quiet. He seemed puzzled by her statement, but didn't ask her to clarify it. Then he shifted in his seat to face her more squarely.

"I have three things to say about our situation." He held up one finger. "First if all, yes. I am jealous. I love you more intensely than I believed possible, and the simple idea of you being affectionate with another man is nearly intolerable to me." He paused, regaining his composure. "I must, however, tolerate this, because I have no choice."

"Sveyn—"

"Second." He held up another finger. "I will make no additional comments regarding Matt, and I will endeavor to stay out of your way and allow you to do what you must." He paused again. "I know you, Hollis. You will not ever be able to finally let go of that man unless you follow this path which you are so determinedly set upon."

In spite of the clearly negative outcome included in his promise, Hollis knew how hard this was for the Viking.

Apparently he was more advanced than she had given him

credit for earlier.

"Thank you."

"You are welcome." Sveyn dipped his chin, and then held up the third finger. "And lastly, when you reach that moment when Matt shows you his true character, and your heart is broken once more, I will do everything in my power to comfort you. And after that I will never mention his name, or this conversation, ever again."

•

•

•

Chapter
twenty four

Hollis shook her head. "You're very confident, aren't you?"
Sveyn's expression didn't change. "Yes."

Hollis was faced with an unexpected conundrum. If he was wrong—as she hoped he was—then she would be forced to choose Matt over Sveyn. Though that would be the obvious choice to make, the idea of doing it made her sad.

But if Sveyn was right, she was facing heartbreak even more hurtful than the first one. Having Matt crawl back to her, admitting he was wrong to leave her in the first place, satisfied that part of her that demanded justice. Having him fail her again, however, made her twice the fool.

"I honestly don't know if I want you to be right or wrong," she admitted.

His expression transformed from resolution to empathy. "If I am right, you will have certain misery ahead."

"But then our illogical love wins out," she countered. Her smile faded. "And if you're wrong…"

"You will marry Matt." Sveyn's gaze dropped his hands his lap. "And I will be forced to listen to you tell him how much you love him over and over. I cannot stop hearing."

Hollis gasped. "I hadn't thought of that. That's horrible."

"It is the hell to which I have been condemned." He returned her gaze to hers. "And yet, for you to live with *me* is to never fully live."

True.

Crap.

"This situation will have to play itself out, and what will be, will be." Hollis shifted the still-idling car into drive. "I think this night calls for a bag of garlic knots and a big bottle of red wine."

Sveyn's mood lightened a little. "I do like that. I can smell the garlic."

Hollis drove toward the pizza place without talking. Sveyn's words were sadly accurate—his current existence was a special sort of hell. And, although she would never tell Sveyn this, she didn't completely trust Matt. How could she? The man had a lot to prove.

Hollis pulled up in front of the pizza shop and went inside to order her food. Just like the last time, Sveyn wandered around the kitchen, watching and sniffing.

Stevie had called him a good-looking man. As Hollis watched him she wondered if Stevie held anything back in her appraisal, or if Sveyn was so achingly handsome in her own eyes because Hollis knew the man so well.

The ridiculous idea that she would choose to turn away the flesh-and-blood Matt in favor of an apparition with no certain longevity taunted her. Dream sex was fine for her body, but left her soul lacking.

Then there was inevitable of course: she was going to continue to age. If he stayed with her for the rest of her life, the time would come when the thirty-four-year-old Sveyn would be tethered to a seventy-year-old Hollis.

How pathetic would that be?

Hollis's number was called and she collected her food. Sveyn followed her to the car and they drove to her condo in

poured the wine and unwrapped the food,
spoke up. "Would you allow me to try and taste

Obviously, the Viking's thoughts had been focused on a
completely different subject than hers. *Typical man.* He clearly
thought their unprecedented and uncertain relationship quandary
was a completed discussion.

"Um, sure." Hollis held up one of the knots, the dripping
butter pooling in her palm.

Sveyn leaned over and stuck out his tongue. The tip of his
tongue passed through the knot.

I am so not eating that one now.

His brows pulled together. He did it again, more deeply this
time. Then his eyes jumped to hers. "It is a sharp taste. With salt.
Am I correct?"

Hollis stared at him. "When was the last time you tasted
anything?"

"Am I correct?" he repeated, his tone and his gaze growing
more urgent.

"Yes."

Sveyn sucked a huge gasp and staggered back. His
expression was so shocked it could be funny in another setting.
But not here. Not now.

"Never. Not since I—I need to sit down." Sveyn took the
three steps required for his long legs to move from the bar-height
counter to the dining table and he dropped into the nearest chair.

Hollis scooped up the food and followed him. "How are you
dizzy?"

"I do not know that I am." He looked up at her as she
dumped the fragrant load onto the table. "I just felt—weak."

Hollis turned around to retrieve her glass of wine. "That
doesn't make sense either."

"I know." He rubbed his forehead. "I am lost."

Hollis sat in the chair beside his. "Do you want to try it
again? Or maybe the pizza?"

His hand fell to the tabletop. "Yes."

Hollis held out the same knot he had licked before. Sveyn heaved an airless breath, then leaned toward the twist of garlic-butter-and-salt-coated bread. He closed his eyes and pushed his tongue through the knot, slowly and completely.

Watching him was oddly sexual, and her body responded very inappropriately for the occasion.

Later.

Sveyn paused, then opened his eyes. "I believe a little heaven has just entered my hell."

Hollis smiled softly. "Try the pizza."

She held up a slice—another piece of her dinner she definitely wasn't going to eat. "There's garlic in the pizza, too. And cheese. The red stuff is a sauce made from tomatoes, but you didn't have those back then."

Sveyn nodded his understanding and tasted the thickly piled slice. "Salt. And there is another flavor. Smoke."

"That could be the sauce or the sausage."

"And a spice of some kind." He shrugged. "I do not know it."

"Oregano, maybe. Do you taste the cheese?"

Sveyn shook his head. "No. And I do not believe I can taste the tomatoes. Those few flavors which I can discern are very distinct and separate."

Hollis set the slice down. "It's probably like smelling things—it's starting with strong scents and strong flavors."

Sveyn pointed at her glass. "May I try the wine?"

Hollis hesitated. "Let me pour some on a saucer."

Sveyn's lips quirked. "You do not want to have my tongue in your food."

She felt her cheeks tighten with embarrassment. "Well you have to admit it's a little weird."

The Viking's amusement lit up his face. "You cannot catch what I have, you know."

"I know." Hollis stood and went to the cabinet to get a saucer. "But this will be easier. I won't risk spilling it."

She poured a splash from her wine glass into the saucer and pushed it in front of Sveyn. "Do you want me to hold it?"

"No. This will do." He bent over and laid his tongue in the liquid.

Hollis wanted to laugh because the Viking looked so silly basically face-planting on the tabletop, and took a slow sip of her wine to keep from doing so. But when he looked up at her again, the look of bliss on his face made her want to cry.

"I have not tasted wine for nearly a thousand years," he said. "Now I know for certain that heaven has joined me at last."

"Do you want to try more things?" Hollis jumped up and went to her refrigerator. "Let me see what I have..."

Her meal forgotten, Hollis hauled out anything she could find that had strong flavor. Pickles, onions, orange juice, mustard, salad dressing, strawberry jam, maple syrup, sharp cheddar cheese, salsa, dark chocolate.

Sveyn tasted item after item, some with success and others without.

"Acid seems to be a key ingredient," Hollis decided, looking over the tabletop strewn with more than a dozen saucers of food. "And sugar is a no-go at this point."

Sveyn grinned and patted his flat belly. "It is a blessing that I do not feel hunger, or my inability to eat any of this would reinstate my hell with a torturous vengeance."

At his mention of hunger, Hollis's stomach rumbled. "I never ate my dinner!"

Sveyn waved an arm over the messy table. "Please eat it, if you can find it. I would gladly clean all of this away for you if I was able."

Hollis laughed. "Maybe that'll come next."

Sveyn's expression sobered. "I do not see how."

Too late, Hollis realized her joke was thoughtless. "I'm sorry, Sveyn."

He gave her a polite smile. "Have no worries. Please eat."

Hollis cleared a space and helped herself to a fresh slice of the cooled pizza. It was still delicious.

"So now you can smell and taste. And sometimes be seen or heard. What do you think that means?" she asked between bites.

"I have no idea, Hollis. I truly do not." He gave a small

shrug. "Perhaps it is because I am with you."

As much as she liked hearing that, logic still pushed her to ask, "Why would that have anything to do with it?"

The Viking looked into her eyes. "Love perhaps? Intense emotion?"

That was possible. "Intense emotional feelings prompt physical feelings of a sort?"

He nodded, his fingers drumming silently on the table. "It is the only connection that I have been able to discern."

An unhappy possibility dawned on her. "So when you manifest forward, or you fall out of love with me, you might lose these abilities?"

Judging by his expression, Sveyn had not considered that. "I suppose that could be true."

Hollis hated that she had to press the point, but she couldn't let this opportunity slip away. She had to know what might happen and now was the time to ask—or lose her mind obsessing over possibilities.

"And if I marry Matt. What then?"

His gaze cut to hers. "Will I stop loving you?"

"Yes."

Sveyn looked at his fingers, now tapping at half their speed. "I would have to believe that it was *possible* for me to stop loving you to ponder that question."

Hollis clenched her hands under the table. "If I do marry Matt, could that make you manifest forward?"

Sveyn's fingers stilled. His eyes didn't move.

"Do you know the answer?"

He shook his head slowly, his eyes still fixed on his lifeless hand. "I do not."

He looked at her then, his cheeks pale and drawn beneath the scruff of his beard. "But if God sees my situation, then it would be a great mercy if I moved. Then I would not have to watch and hear another man love you as I long to, but am not able to."

Hollis took another bite of the pizza, but it tasted like cardboard in her mouth now. She dropped it back in the box and started cleaning up the mess.

Sveyn stayed in his seat, staring at nothing, his clenched jaw muscles rippling his cheeks. When she finished removing the last traces of the tasting whirlwind, he rose and stood in front of her, so close that she had to tilt her head back to look up at him.

"What?" she whispered.

He ran a finger down her cheek, leaving a faintly tingling path. "I will love you tonight, Hollis. I will take you someplace very special, and love you until you cannot breathe."

•

•

•

Chapter
twenty five

Friday
December 18

"Vikings were dirty." Stevie looked up from her list. "True or false?"

Hollis looked at Sveyn, ready to repeat his answer for Stevie. He shook his head. "We bathed every week."

"Really?" Hollis blurted.

"What?" Stevie asked.

Hollis turned to her co-worker. "They took baths every week."

Stevie typed the answer into the children's book manuscript. "Are you kidding? That's so awesome!"

"The people whom we encountered on our raids thought us vain." Sveyn chuckled. "Or exceptionally foolish."

Hollis repeated his words.

Stevie nodded and kept typing. "Ask him why they were

they so—exceptional—for the era."

Hollis turned back to Sveyn. "Why were you so clean?"

He grinned. "Longhouses."

Hollis knew what those were, of course. "So because so many families shared the same living space, you all washed to keep it from stinking?"

"Can you think of a better reason?" Sveyn countered. "And once a man is accustomed to being clean, then he is more aware of the discomfort of filth."

Hollis wrinkled her nose. "Not to mention lice."

"What did he say?" Stevie prompted.

Hollis told her, then asked Sveyn, "After the Roman Empire collapsed, there were was a millennium where European societies descended into filth and ignorance. Why did your society thrive and grow?"

The Viking looked at her like that was a stupid question. "We traveled."

"Travel," Hollis repeated for Stevie. "You interacted with other cultures and their people and learned from them?"

"Yes. My people traveled to this continent, and to what is now called Europe and Asia."

"You went as far as Asia?"

"I did not," Sveyn clarified. "But others did."

Hollis looked at Stevie. "The sunstone allowed them to navigate on the sea, as well determine their direction on land and rivers."

Stevie smiled as she typed. "We have seen that before in our work. Cultures who are isolated don't progress like those who explore."

"This is very true," Sveyn said. "And cultures which welcome strangers, as opposed to attacking them, grow as well."

Hollis picked up on that. "Are you saying you didn't always attack and raid? That sometimes your arrival was peaceful?"

Sveyn shook his head. "We responded as we were met, and only dealt with resistance with our swords."

Hollis told Stevie what Sveyn said.

"I always wondered about that," she said. "I mean, for a

society with such beautifully crafted artifacts, such advanced sailing skills, and such obvious intelligence, they couldn't have been mindlessly barbaric."

Sveyn bowed in Stevie's direction. "Thank you."

Hollis smiled. "He bowed and said thank you."

Stevie fingered the holly-wreath brooch on her sweater. "So what about Christmas?"

"Christmas?" Hollis returned her regard to the apparition. "That's a timely question."

"Vikingers did not celebrate Christmas." Sveyn rubbed the bloodied gash in his vest, seemingly a reflex. "After the new religion came to us and began to spread, our king declared Norway a Christian country. We stopped viking at that time."

Hollis repeated his words and added, "So Vikings didn't technically celebrate Christmas, but Norwegians eventually did?"

"That is correct. And in their wisdom, the priests gave new Christian significance to our pagan rites, rather than demand that we forego our ancient traditions," he explained.

Hollis was surprised by his comment. "Some people say that practice bastardized Christianity."

Sveyn laughed. "The God we learned of was much stronger and less petty than our gods. I do not believe He saw it that way."

"What practice bastardized Christianity?" Stevie asked.

Hollis gave her Sveyn's explanation.

As she typed in his words, Stevie made a face. "What does he think of our modern celebrations? Talk about bastardizing…"

Sveyn frowned. "To what is she referring?"

"Do you mean the commercialization of the holiday?" Hollis asked Stevie.

"Well, yeah." Stevie looked up from her keyboard. "What does he think?"

Hollis gave her friend a guilty look. "I haven't taken him to the mall."

Stevie's jaw dropped. "You haven't? Why not?"

"What is a mall?" Sveyn asked.

"I'm an only child, and my parents are going on a cruise," Hollis explained to them both. "I paid for one of their excursions as my Christmas gift to them. There's no need for me to be part of that insanity."

"What is a mall?" he asked again. "And why is it insane?"

"Except that there is." Stevie waved her hand in the direction that Hollis was addressing her questions. "Sveyn needs to see it."

Hollis rolled her eyes. "This is the weekend before Christmas!"

Stevie shrugged. "All the better."

"What is an insane mall?" Sveyn barked.

Hollis whirled to face him. "A shopping mall is a huge enclosed version of the marketplace. Tons of different stores all opening into a center walkway."

The Viking frowned. "And insane people shop there?"

"An insane *amount* of people shop there," Hollis clarified. "Especially the weekend before Christmas."

Stevie giggled. "It's in important part of our culture, Hollis. He deserves to see it."

Hollis glared at her. "I hate you."

Stevie blew her a kiss.

*****

Hollis's phone intercom beeped. "Ms. McKenna?"

"Yes?"

"You have a package at the front desk."

"Okay. I'm on my way." Hollis crossed to her office door and spoke over her shoulder. "I'll be right back."

The package waiting for her had no postage, barcodes, or return address.

"How did this get here?" she asked the volunteer behind the desk. Her nametag said Eleanor.

"A young man came in and handed it to me. Then he left."

Hollis frowned. The corrugated cardboard box was heavier than it looked. "That's strange. Can I use your scissors?"

The woman pulled a pair from the jar holding her pens and

handed it to Hollis. Hollis cut the clear tape sealing the top and flipped it open. Then she folded back the tissue paper.

Hollis screamed and threw the box halfway across the lobby. Her heart banged against her ribs so hard she was afraid her bones would crack.

Sveyn was instantly beside her.

The box landed with a thick thud and slid a few feet across the polished floor. Bodies appeared from all sides, drawn by her shriek.

Eleanor's eyes were huge. "What is it?"

Hollis stared at the box, trembling. "Call the police."

"What? Why?"

Hollis rounded on the woman. "*I said call the police!*"

When she hesitated again, Hollis shouted, "Dammit, do what I say!" Then she reached over the counter, knocked the receiver out of its cradle, and dialed nine-one-one.

When an older gentleman approached the box, Hollis cried. "Don't touch it!"

He looked up at her, puzzled. "Is it a bomb?"

"No. At least I don't think so." Hollis shuddered. "It's a dead cat."

A tinny voice escaped the phone's speakers. "Nine-one-one, what is your emergency?"

"A suspicious package," Hollis called out before the woman at the desk interfered. "We need an officer as soon as possible."

"Could it be a bomb?" the voice asked. "Or hazardous materials?"

"Someone delivered a dead cat in a box." Hollis's voice shook and she met Sveyn's eyes. "Beyond that, I have no idea."

*****

The museum was emptied of attendees, all of whom were instructed not to speak to anyone about what had happened, and given two free passes each to return another day with a companion. Just to be safe, Miranda guided them all out the back door.

The police arrived within minutes. Two uniformed officers plus a two-man team in hazardous material suits who wrapped the box in heavy plastic and removed it from the museum.

One of the uniformed officers quizzed the front desk attendant and Hollis about how the box arrived—and why.

"This nice looking man walked in, set the box on the counter, and said it was a special delivery for Hollis McKenna…" Eleanor's hands held each other in a white-knuckled death grip. "So I buzzed her office and told her it was here."

Tom the intern was standing off to the side, looking like he desperately wanted something to do. "I'll have the security tapes pulled up and saved!" he offered, then hurried away before someone could stop him.

The officer's attention shifted to Hollis. "Were you expecting a package?"

She swallowed, her mouth uncomfortably sticky. "No."

His expression softened. "Forgive me, but it's Christmas next week. Are you sure?"

"I'm sure. Yes."

He made a note on his pad. "Did you recognize the cat?"

Hollis gasped. "No—but do you think he thought it was mine?" The idea that some unsuspecting family would need to get a new kitten this Christmas was heartbreaking.

The officer's gaze cut to hers. "He? Do you have an idea who sent this?"

"No, I just assumed it was the guy who delivered it."

"Hmm." He looked back at his notes. "Do you own a cat?"

Hollis shook her head. "No. Cats aren't a thing with me, so if it's meant to be significant it was a bad choice."

Stevie sidled up next to her. Hollis hadn't noticed she was there. "Could it have to do with the ghost hunter people?"

The officer's head jerked up from his pad. "Ghost hunter people?"

His partner turned around and crossed the lobby. "Are you the one from the news?"

"Yes. Possibly." Hollis scowled. "What does that have to do

with anything?"

"Witches. Druids. Ritual killings." The second officer looked at the one asking the questions. "Could be related to casting spells or whatever."

"Ghosts and witches aren't the same thing," Stevie pointed out.

He shrugged. "It's all occult, one way or another."

"None of that—or this—has to do with the ghost sighting here," Hollis stated firmly.

"But someone might *think* it does." Stevie pointed a finger at her. "Maybe it's a spell to protect you from the Blessing thing."

"Or cause me to succumb, more likely."

The officer in charge looked confused. "Blessing thing?"

"I'll explain in the car," the second one said.

"Relevant?"

"Doubtful."

The first one handed Hollis his card. "We'll have forensics inspect the cat and look at the security video." He turned to Miranda and held out a card to her as well. "Have everyone on staff watch the video, and call me if anyone recognizes the guy who brought the box."

"Yes, sir. We'll do it now, before anyone goes home." Miranda's enthusiastic attention dropped to the officer's left hand and her expression dimmed; the thick gold band was obvious.

He turned to Hollis. "Call me if you think of anything else."

*****

The security video viewing proved nothing. No one—neither paid staff nor volunteers—recognized the Cat Box Guy, as Hollis thought of him.

"It's an appropriate name," she whispered to Stevie. "The guy's a pile of crap to have done what he did."

Stevie pursed her lips. "I have to agree."

"Is there anything I can do?" Sveyn asked.

Hollis drew a deep breath. "Not that I can think of."

Stevie's head turned toward hers. "What?"

Hollis whispered in her friend's ear. "Sveyn wants to know what he can do."

"Oh."

Miranda looked over a list of people. "There are nine volunteers who weren't here today. I'll have them all watch the video the next time they work."

Hollis stood. "Good. Can we go home now?" She glanced at Stevie and lifted one eyebrow. "I have a big day of super-fun mall shopping planned for tomorrow and I need to carbo-load."

●

●

●

Chapter
Twenty Six

Saturday
December 19

Though she acted unfazed by the incident, Hollis found her thoughts going back to the odd and inexplicable delivery again last night as she washed her hands for the fifth time.

"What could possibly be the reason for killing a cat and sending it to someone?" she asked Sveyn. "It just doesn't make sense…"

The apparition sighed airlessly. "As I said before, I agree with the police officer. I do believe it has something to do with occult practices. Perhaps if you ask your visiting group on Monday, someone might be able to shed some light on its meaning."

"That makes sense. It does." Hollis pulled a sigh of her own. "I'll try to stop thinking about in the meantime."

Scottsdale Fashion Mall was as good a distraction as any.

Hollis pulled up to the valet. "So worth the money," she told Sveyn as she hooked the Bluetooth over her ear to disguise to whom she was actually speaking. "This place will be a zoo today."

And it was.

Sveyn was gob smacked. "This is all for Christmas?"

"Yep. And it started two months ago." She gave him a wry look. "Bet it wasn't like this during World War two, huh?"

Sveyn shook his head. "No. Not at all. Not even a small bit."

Hollis wove through the streaming crowd and thankfully Sveyn did the same, not allowing anyone to walk through him. He did peek into the shopping bags, however, when someone was standing still.

"This is unbelievable." He looked up at Hollis. "How much money are these people spending?"

"Hundreds. Easy." She headed toward the Nordstrom's. "Thousands, even."

As she led him past store after store, all displaying twinkling lights, silvery balls in a myriad of colors, and endless garlands of greenery, Sveyn didn't seem to be able to process what he was seeing.

Once inside the high-end department store, the Viking halted. "I need a moment."

Hollis faced him, concerned. "What's wrong?"

He shook his head. "There is too much."

She stepped closer. "Too much what?"

"Too much of everything." He sank to the floor. "Normally my surroundings have no impact on me. But today I feel... pressed."

"Pressed?" Hollis looked around for a chair; squatting beside Sveyn would draw unwanted attention.

"I cannot think of another word for it." He tipped his head up to face her. "It is as if the world is closing in on me."

This is weird. "You actually feel it?"

"No, not like anyone is touching me." His expression brightened. "More like wind."

Hollis looked around again. Store employees were beginning

to pay attention to her. "We can't stay here. Let's go to the food court. I'll get some lunch and you can taste it."

Sveyn climbed to his feet. "Yes. That will be good."

Hollis stood in line at a retro diner selling cheeseburgers and ordered onion rings and a chocolate malt to go with hers. When the food was served, she carried her tray into the center area searching for an empty table among the hundreds arrayed there.

"There!" She hurried over to a small table with only one chair. "Do you mind?"

Sveyn squatted beside her. "Not at all."

Hollis used a plastic knife to cut her cheeseburger into quarters and pushed one quarter to the edge of her plate. She also set aside an onion ring.

She picked up one quarter of the cheeseburger and bit into it, her gaze moving everywhere except the Viking licking the food she set out for him. As much as she understood his situation, the action was too undignified for her to feel comfortable watching.

Sveyn was a proud and intelligent man. Hollis wanted to preserve those qualities in the front of her thoughts.

"Hollis?"

She turned toward the voice.

"I told you it was her, Tony." Tony Samoa's wife Carmen was grinning at Hollis from the table behind her. "So you decided to brave the crowds as well."

Hollis glanced at a scowling Tony and the cluster of bags hanging from the third chair at their tiny table.

There's my other chair.

"Hi, guys. Yeah. I'm here against my better judgment."

Carmen turned in her chair to face Hollis more squarely. "Have you seen the commercial yet?"

Hollis hated when people asked questions with only half the necessary info. "Commercial?"

"For the new season of *Ghost Myths, Inc.* Your episode is the season opener!" Carmen was practically squirming with excitement. Tony was just squirming.

That's just craptastic news. "No, I haven't. When will it be on?"

"Wednesday, January sixth." Carmen leaned closer. "They showed a glimpse of the ghost. I had no idea!"

The bite of cheeseburger suddenly felt like a rock in Hollis's stomach. "Guess I better mark my calendar."

Carmen waved a hand toward her husband. "Tony says that the museum will be hosting a screening. I can hardly wait."

Hollis looked at her rival. "What else does Tony say?"

Tony straightened in his seat. "We've had our differences, Hollis, but I can admit when I'm wrong."

Carmen turned to her husband and pinned him with a negating gaze.

"Sometimes," he hedged.

Carmen flashed a satisfied look. "That's better."

Tony cleared his throat. "And in the case of the hoard and the wing, I have to admit I was wrong. Attendance is way up, and the guests are exploring the whole museum, not just the new stuff."

Hollis dipped her chin. "Apology accepted."

"I wasn't apol—never mind." Tony leaned forward the same way his wife had. "So you saw that ghost? The one on the camera?"

Keep it truthful. "I actually didn't see what was on the camera."

"What did you see?"

"Not much, I'm afraid." Hollis gave a one shoulder shrug. "But I saw the tape and how he was answering Justin's questions."

"He *spoke?*" the pair exclaimed in tandem.

She shook her head. "No—he raised one hand for yes, the other for no."

Carmen was clearly disappointed. "But they have that voice thing—didn't they use it?"

"They did. But it didn't pick up anything. Sorry." *Why am I apologizing?* "Anyway, I'm glad to know the date."

Sveyn stood. "Ask Tony about the cat."

Surely he didn't… Hollis made eye contact with Tony. "Did you hear what happened to me yesterday?"

"At the museum?"

"Yeah."

Tony shook his head. "I got back from Tucson after seven last night. What happened?"

Hollis kept her gaze locked on Tony's. "Somebody had a dead cat delivered to me."

Carmen recoiled. "What?"

Hollis shifted her regard to Carmen. "Yep. Wrapped in tissue paper in a cardboard box."

Tony's scowl deepened. "Why would someone send you a dead cat?"

Hollis cut her gaze back to his. "Maybe they thought it was funny."

"There's nothing funny about it!" Carmen declared.

"No, there isn't," Tony concurred. "It sounds more like someone is trying to scare you."

Interesting. *But why?* "Do you know of any Mexican or Native American legends involving dead cats?"

"Not off the top of my head. But I'll do some research this weekend."

"Thanks." Hollis gave the couple a skeptical expression. "The cop thought it might be some occult thing. Because of the ghost hunters."

"Hmm. Maybe." Tony motioned to Carmen. "You ready? I want to get home in time to catch the soccer game."

"All right. Don't rush me." Carmen stood. "See you at the party tomorrow, Hollis. Are you bringing a date?"

Hollis smiled politely. "He's out of town."

While the couple gathered up their bags and left, Hollis turned back to her cooled food. Her appetite had returned as she talked to the Samoas, encouraged by Tony's almost-apology.

"He didn't do it," Sveyn said.

"I don't think so either."

"What party?"

"The museum staff Christmas party." Hollis took another bite of her cheeseburger. It was still delicious. "What did you think of the food?" she asked with her mouth full.

"I tasted the meat." The Viking's eyes lit up. "I have missed roasted meat more than I can explain."

*****

Hollis gave the valet her ticket and waited in silence for her car to be brought around. She tipped the guy three bucks and climbed inside, probably the only customer he would have all day who was returning from the mall empty handed.

After their shared lunch, Sveyn suggested that they see a movie. Hollis welcomed the distraction. They sat in the back of a theater showing a seasonal romantic comedy and Hollis thoroughly enjoyed every minute of it. Sveyn even seemed to engage with the characters, laughing at the appropriate times.

When they got home, Hollis turned on the cable station that ran *Ghost Myths, Inc.* "I want to see the commercial that Carmen was talking about. I hope it doesn't take too long to show up."

Three minutes in, there it was.

"Wow." Hollis stared at the screen. "Is my butt really that big?"

Sveyn guffawed. "Is that what catches your attention?"

"Any woman would wonder the same thing." She threw a glance over her shoulder. "Don't judge me."

"It is my opinion that your butt, as you call it, is absolutely perfect." Sveyn approached the TV. "However, I believe you should be prepared for more attention, Hollis. This is a very compelling commercial."

She hated to admit it, but the Viking was right.

Monday
December 21

Last night's party was horrible.

Between questions about the dead cat and the ghost on the commercials, Hollis was bombarded the entire evening.

"I didn't know everyone had cable," she grumbled to Stevie

as they waited to be served at the free bar. "They've all seen the commercial dozens of times already."

"It's just basic cable," Stevie qualified. "That's been the new normal for a while now."

Hollis carried her glass of Chardonnay to the table where George and Stevie were sitting.

"Any word from Matt?" George asked when Hollis sat down.

"He texts me every couple of hours when he's on the road," she replied. "Tonight he's staying in Albuquerque."

"Almost here!" Stevie looked giddy. "Aren't you excited to see him again?"

There was another million dollar question.

Hollis looked at the clock in the tray of her computer screen. Two-thirty. Today's paying guests should arrive about three and they paid for the four-hour minimum. She should be getting out of work about the same time that Matt pulled into Phoenix, weather permitting.

I should check the weather report for northern Arizona.

"Hollis?"

Hollis smiled. "Hi, Miranda."

The statuesque brunette walked into the office. "Matt's coming today, right?"

"Yep."

"Do you have plans for Christmas?"

Nope. "Are you doing another one of your straggler gatherings?"

Miranda sat in the chair facing the desk. "Not exactly. I keep it more intimate for Christmas, and we do an elaborate white elephant exchange."

"That's sounds fun." It actually did. "I was going to wait for Matt and see if he had anything in mind, but if he doesn't I'd love to join you."

"Great." Miranda grinned.

Hollis screwed up her mouth. "Do I have to cook from scratch again?"

Miranda laughed. "No. Just show up."

The offer moved Hollis more than would have expected it to. "Thank you, Miranda. I'll let you know tomorrow."

Her desk phone beeped. "Hollis?"

"Yes?"

"Your group is starting to arrive."

Hollis looked at the clock. Two forty-five. She should have put in a stipulation for exact start times when they planned all this hoopla. "I'll be there in a minute."

Miranda stood. "Who is it today?"

"I have no idea." Hollis stood as well. "Makes it more interesting that way."

•

•

•

Chapter twenty seven

"The Exor-Clergy?" Hollis repeated to make sure she heard the man correctly. "What is that?"

He flashed a very handsome smile. "We are a small ecumenical group of pastors who perform exorcisms."

That explained the black suit and white collar. "What do you mean by small?" she asked and then clarified, "I mean how many of you are coming today?"

"We only act when there are three of us in attendance." He leaned a little closer and Hollis caught a warm whiff of his pleasantly spicy aftershave. "A cord of three strands is not easily broken."

"Ah. Ecclesiastes."

He looked impressed. "Not only beautiful, but educated as well."

Hollis frowned. "Are you flirting with me? Aren't you a priest?"

A rich baritone laugh rumbled from his chest and his eyes

twinkled. "Episcopal. We're allowed to marry."

Hollis swept the trim man with an evaluative gaze.

No wedding ring.

"Well, I'm currently spoken for." She lifted one teasing shoulder. "But you can leave your business card in case it doesn't work out."

Her gesture was rewarded with more enticing laughter. "I will."

Two clergymen walked through the front door together. One was carrying what looked like a leather shaving kit. "Fred! Good to see you!" one called out.

The three black-clad men, ranging in age from Fred's mid-thirties to a wizened eighties, greeted and embraced each other heartily. Fred introduced her then clasped his hands together.

"Shall we begin?"

*****

"This should prove interesting," Sveyn said as the group made their way to the collections storeroom. "I'm curious as to how exorcisms are performed in this time."

Good question.

"Gentleman, can I ask you something?" Hollis stopped at the door and held up her keycard. "Are you going to perform an exorcism today?"

"We plan to, yes," Fred answered. He seemed to be the spokesperson for the trio.

"Isn't that for demons?" Hollis swiped her card and the lock clicked.

"Yes."

Hollis shot him a confused look before she opened the door. "And you think that's what's happening here?"

"Yes. We believe that what passes as the spirits of dead people are actually demons taking on those personae."

"I believe he is right," Sveyn opined. "I have never encountered another soul in my realm—whatever my realm is."

"It's an interesting take," Hollis answered both men.

"The Bible says that to be absent from the body is to be present with Christ," Fred explained. "There is nothing about anyone's soul remaining earthbound for any reason."

Hollis cut a quick glance toward Sveyn. "Come on in gentleman, but please don't touch anything."

The middle-aged pastor set his little satchel on the plastic table Hollis had prepared and pulled out what must be the tools necessary for the rite: a silver cross, a white candle, and a crystal bottle with a cork.

"Holy water, I assume?" Hollis asked as she took her seat at the table.

"Very good." Fred sat across from her. "Now, as we proceed, we ask you to please remain a silent observer."

"No matter what you hear or see, young lady," the elder priest warned as he lit the candle. "Can you do that?"

Hollis nodded. A knife blade of fear sent a shiver up her back. Sveyn knelt beside her. His presence made her feel a little safer.

Her phone vibrated and she pulled it from her pocket.

Heading into snow in Flagstaff. Hope it's not too bad.

She texted Matt back: *Keep me posted.*

Fred gave her a stern look. "Let's all turn our phones off."

*****

Hollis watched in fascination as the Exor-Clergy guys moved through the ritual. First the men each prayed for protection against evil. Then the priest asked God to free the subject—in this case the museum—from the devil and his demons.

The pastor prayed next, demanding in the name of God that the devil and his demons leave the museum. Fred walked around sprinkling holy water throughout the storeroom, assuring Hollis that it landed on nothing but the concrete floor.

"Is that all?" Sveyn looked surprised. "I have been exorcised with whips, hammers, and handcuffs. This is so uneventful."

"Have we finished?" she ventured.

"We finished in here." Fred corked the crystal cruet.

Hollis looked at the three men. "What do you mean?"

"We would like to perform the same rite on the Blessing of the Gods," the pastor explained. He waved a hand around the storeroom. "There doesn't seem to be any more demonic activity in here, and our actions have sealed the space against further manifestations."

"You didn't mention that before," Hollis hedged. After her own experience with the damned thing, as Sveyn called it, she was leery of touching it again.

"Let them do it, Hollis," the Viking urged. "Perhaps that will stop the curse."

Hollis looked at her watch. "We can go look at it know. But we can't start until the museum closes in another twenty minutes and all the guests are gone."

Fred smiled his dazzling smile. "Understood."

While she led the clergymen out of the administrative office area and into the museum proper, Hollis retrieved her phone. She turned it on and was greeted with seven texts from Matt.

Snow is starting. Tiny pellets at this point.

Not too heavy, but still an hour outside Flagstaff.

Are you there?

Can't see the mountains anymore. Not a good sign.

Hello? Going to stop in Flagstaff for dinner.

Are you getting these messages?

Please text or call soon as you can.

Hollis huffed an irritated sigh. There was no way she could call him right now. Didn't Matt remember that Mondays were her 'extra duty' days?

She directed the men toward the Kensington wing, excusing herself to go to the ladies room. Once inside that sanctuary she texted: *Got your messages. At work with exorcism guys.*

As an afterthought she added: *Can't wait to see you. Drive safely.*

Matt's reply was immediate: ☺ *Can't wait to see you, too!*

*****

Hollis opened the pair of locks on the Blessing's case while Sveyn hovered beside her. She handed Fred and the middle-aged pastor each a pair of white gloves. "The two of you should hold one half. But don't get them too close to each other."

Fred looked at her oddly. "You sound like you believe the legend."

Hollis shrugged. "All I can say is that both men who possessed the halves went crazy."

The elder priest opened the little satchel again and set the silver cross on the lid of the opened case. Fred jumped and almost dropped his half of the icon.

"Careful!" Hollis blurted. "They're really old!"

Fred's eyes widened and he stared at his partner. "My God— is yours vibrating?"

"Yes." The pastor's face blanched and he swallowed audibly. "Let's pray."

As the trio bent their heads and fervently invoked God's presence in the room, Sveyn spoke in Hollis's ear. "Can you hear that? They're humming."

She nodded and looked up from under her brow to try and see the clergymen's faces.

Sveyn's tone hardened. "It's getting louder."

"Amen." Fred lifted his head and looked at Hollis. "Do you hear something?"

"You mean the buzzing?" Her pulse surged as the sound grew louder. "Yes."

The pastor's hands began to shake and his grip tightened on the icon. "Mine is pulling toward yours."

"Don't let them touch!" Hollis shouted over the angry noise. "Back away!"

Sveyn stepped between the men. "Use the holy water!" he bellowed.

"What did you say?" Fred looked at the pastor. "Holy water?"

Sveyn tried to push against the pieces but his hands slid uselessly through them. "Yes! Holy water! *Now!*"

The elderly priest nodded. "Yes. All right." He uncorked the cruet and wet his fingers.

"Don't just piddle on them!" Hollis cried. "Douse the damned things!"

She slapped her hands over her ears. The buzzing sound thrummed palpably through her veins. Her body felt like a hive of bees.

"Do it!" Sveyn roared. "Hurry, you old fool!"

The priest glared at Fred. "Don't call me an old fool!"

Fred looked confused. "I—just do it!"

The priest crossed himself and stepped forward, pouring the holy water over the two halves. "In the name of Jesus I command you to leave and never come back!"

When the water hit the Blessing a keening screech seared through the air.

Hollis dropped to her knees, her hands still pressed over her ears. It didn't help; the furious wail of pain slid through her palms and resonated against her eardrums.

Sveyn held his ground.

Fred's face was an angry mask of determination. He held his half of the icon in stiff, outstretched, and shaking arms.

Buoyed by his companion's display of fortitude, the elder pastor did the same. Eyes squeezed shut, he snarled his opposition to whatever forces were manifesting in the room.

Water dripped from the baptized pieces and puddled on the floor.

Hollis wasn't sure how much time had passed when the buzzing faded to silence. She looked at the four men in the room—three corporeal, and one not—trying to discern what they were thinking.

Sveyn leaned against the open case, panting airlessly.

Fred sank to the floor. He sat cross-legged with the wood and metal piece still clutched in his gloved hands. "Well that was unprecedented."

The pastor opened his eyes but otherwise remained rooted. "What in hell—and I do mean that literally—was that?"

The elderly priest stared at the empty cruet. "I've never seen anything like that. The curse on that Blessing was real."

Fred let go with one hand and gestured toward the pastor. "It's a good thing you mentioned the holy water when you did."

The other man frowned. "I didn't say anything."

"I know you were in the heat of it, Fred," the priest grumbled. "But you didn't need to call me an old fool."

"I didn't. I didn't say anything like that."

Hollis sat still and tried to remain inconspicuous. Even so, three pair of eyes fixed on her.

"Did you hear it?" the priest demanded.

Hollis glanced at Sveyn, wondering what he thought she should admit to. "Hear what?"

"Did you hear someone say to use the holy water?" Fred asked.

Hollis was trapped. Sveyn was no help—he looked as stunned and clueless as the clergymen. "Yes," she admitted.

The priest stepped forward. "And did you hear someone tell me to hurry and call me an old fool?"

She nodded.

The trio stared at each other, their shock obvious.

"They heard me, Hollis." Sveyn snorted his disbelief. "They heard my voice. All of them."

"Four of us witnessed a miracle." The priest crossed himself again. "We heard the voice of the Lord."

Sveyn recoiled, eyes as round as saucers.

Hollis's jaw dropped.

Though not the truth, of course, that was probably the best explanation anyone could offer. Better yet, it was one that would be unquestioned and accepted in this little crowd.

"What happens next?" Hollis ventured.

The trio considered each other again, pensively this time.

"We don't normally publicize our experiences," the pastor began.

"Oh, please don't!" Hollis interrupted. "Please! I beg you."

The priest faced her, skepticism slashed all over his expression. "Why? So you can continue to bamboozle the public?"

"No! Of course not!" Hollis climbed to her feet. "There is

more than enough interest in all this ghost craziness already. If you reveal what happened here this evening, you'll only add fuel to that unhealthy fire."

Fred nodded and regained his feet as well. "She has a point."

"Wouldn't it be better to allow the curious cats to keep coming," Hollis continued. "Knowing that the danger is gone now?"

"Good, Hollis," Sveyn said. "Keep going with that."

She smiled. *Thanks.* "Then after time passes and nothing notable happens, their interest will move on to the next sensation."

"I agree with Ms. McKenna." The pastor walked around the display case and set his half of the icon back in its place. "We don't want to encourage the wrong kind of interest."

Fred followed his friend's example and laid his half to rest as well. "We've never done this to bring attention to evil, but to banish it. Let's stick to our policy of silence."

The priest nodded. "Yes. My lips are sealed as well."

The men pulled off their cotton gloves and handed them to Hollis.

"Thank you for a most interesting evening, Ms. McKenna." Fred's eyes were starting to regain their spark. "I guarantee I won't forget it soon."

"My... pleasure?" she replied.

Fred smiled, reached into the pocket of his jacket, and retrieved a business card. "In case it doesn't work out."

Hollis's phone vibrated in her hip pocket. She grabbed the card and smiled.

"Thanks."

•

•

•

Chapter
Twenty Eight

•

Leaving Flagstaff. Braving the snow.

Hollis shoved her phone back in her pocket without answering Matt's text. It was only six-thirty, but she had just escorted the Exor-Clergy guys out the back door. Time to secure the building and head for home.

"Will Matt expect to see you tonight?" Sveyn asked as they walked to her car.

"Probably," she admitted. "But it's not going to happen."

"Why not?"

Good question. "Because I don't want him to think I'm just waiting here with nothing else going on."

"Why not?"

Hollis rounded on the Viking. "Because he needs to work on getting me back. I'm not a sure thing."

Sveyn smiled. "I am very glad to hear that."

"Oh, hush." Hollis unlocked her car. "What do you want to

taste for dinner?"

Sveyn thought a moment. "Fish?"

"Sushi?" Hollis's mood brightened at the thought.

"What sort of fish is a sushi?" the Viking asked.

"It's not *a* fish—it's how the fish are prepared." She grinned as she started her car. "It's mostly raw."

"Dried? Salted?" Sveyn nodded. "I know these methods."

"Sure." Hollis shifted in reverse. "Let's go with that."

*****

Hollis texted Matt back while waiting for her sushi to be made: *On my way home from work with takeout. Crazy day.*

She watched her screen and waited, hoping he wouldn't text back while he was driving. She smiled her relief when the auto-reply *I'm driving* pinged back.

Sveyn was wandering through the sushi bar's prep space, clearly fascinated by the variety of fish, shellfish, and flavor-enhancing additions.

"Let's go," she said quietly as she accepted her order.

Sveyn reached her car the same time that she did. "I have never seen fish prepared this way."

"It's Japanese. And it's only become popular in America in the last couple decades or so." Hollis smiled. "We tend to be overly cautious about our food preparation."

He nodded. "Yes, I have seen the words on the menus that warn about eating raw or undercooked food."

Hollis changed into her pajamas before eating her supper. She opened a bottle of pinot grigio and sat at the dining table, spreading the options out on a plate and pouring a saucer of wine.

"You can taste whatever you want," she offered.

Sveyn chuckled. "And then you will throw it away?"

She felt herself blushing. "No. I think I'm over that. I'll eat it after you taste it. I just won't watch."

Hollis focused on her meal, allowing Sveyn full rein with his experimentation. For the most part, his expression was pensive—

until he stuck his tongue into the spoonful of wasabi.

"Ahh!" He jerked back. "What sort of vile poison is this?"

Hollis laughed. "A taste-killing one. It's meant to be used in moderation."

"I can understand why!" Sveyn leaned over and laid his abused tongue in the saucer of chilled wine.

Hollis stared at the top of his head. "Does that help?"

"Uh-huh."

"Sveyn—do you feel temperature?"

He raised his head and looked at her. His pupils were dilated with shock, turning his eyes into black pools rimmed in light blue. "I—perhaps. Either that or the fermented wine has an effect on the poison."

"It's not poison, it's just strong. But that's beside the point." Hollis rested her fists on the tabletop. "You felt the sting and the wine took it away?"

The Viking sat up straight and wiped his mouth. "Yes."

"How?"

"I don't—"

The doorbell rang.

Sveyn's brow lowered. "Are you expecting someone?"

Hollis's shoulders drooped. "Oh, no."

"Matt?"

"Has to be."

Sveyn shrugged. "Will you answer it?"

Hollis stood, smoothing her cotton-knit pajamas and pulling the pony-tail tie from her hair. "I have to."

She walked to the door as the person on the other side backed up the doorbell with a sharp knock. Before she opened the door she peeked through the viewer.

Yep. It was Matt.

Hollis drew a breath, held it, then opened the door. "Hi!"

When a gust of cold air hit her, she curled her bare toes and wrapped one arm over her pajamas to hide her body's braless response. "I wasn't expecting you to come by. Obviously."

A tired-looking but still devastatingly handsome Matt grinned at her. "I couldn't wait to see you. Can I come in?"

"Oh! Yes." Hollis stepped out of the way and closed the door after he came through. "I was just finishing supper."

She followed him past the kitchen, dragging her fingers through her annoying curls in an attempt to pull her appearance together. "I have sushi and white wine. You want some?"

"Sure." Matt took off his jacket and laid it over Sveyn. "I had dinner in Flagstaff, but that was a couple hours ago. I could snack."

The Viking moved through the coat and stood. "I will wait over here." He walked to the sofa and sat, his face oddly blank and his hands clasped in his lap.

Hollis returned to the kitchen and grabbed a second wine glass and plate. "If you'd told me you were coming over, I'd be more presentable."

Matt picked up one sushi roll with his fingers. "If I'd told you I was coming over, you'd have said no." He popped the roll into his mouth.

Hollis poured the wine. "Do you want ice?"

Matt chuckled. "No. Are you still doing that?"

Hollis's cheeks heated and she handed him the iceless wine. "I live in a desert. Everyone does that."

Matt accepted the plate and served himself several rolls. "This is really good sushi."

"Have some wasabi," Sveyn suggested from the couch. "A lot of it."

Hollis barely stopped herself from telling the apparition to be quiet. She corked the wine instead.

"How far is it to your place?" she asked, sliding into her seat across from Matt.

Dang but his eyes were amazing. Bloodshot from three long days of driving, the redness only enhanced the gold streaks in his rusty brown irises.

"Five miles, I think."

Oh, right. *I asked a question.* "Do you already have the key?"

Matt reached into his pocket and pulled out a keychain. "I have two." He laid it on the table and slid it toward her. "This one is yours."

Hollis picked up the gaudy sparkly-heart-designed bauble. "Um, thanks."

"I bought that at a truck stop so I wouldn't lose the second key." Matt smiled. "You don't need to keep it."

She set it back on the table. "It's fine for now." *Whether I keep it depends on the next several weeks.*

"So… Christmas."

Hollis blinked. "What about it?"

Matt suddenly looked uncomfortable. "Do you have plans? With anyone?"

"Yes—I mean no." Hollis shook her head. "I do have plans but you're invited to join us."

Matt's features twisted. "The captain won't mind?"

Hollis startled. "Oh, no. Not with him." She glanced at Sveyn, then returned her determined gaze to Matt. "He's… out of town."

"So you and he are still together?"

"Yes," was the easiest answer.

Matt lifted another roll to his mouth. "Tell me about these plans, then." He bit into the sushi. Bits of rice tumbled to his plate.

"Miranda is hosting like she did at Thanksgiving, but with a smaller group." Hollis refilled his wine without him asking. "Of course, if you had something else in mind, she'll understand."

Matt shook his head. "I wasn't certain I'd be able to see you. I'd love to be your Christmas date at Miranda's."

"Great." Hollis poured the rest of the wine into her own glass. "There'll be a white elephant exchange there, but let's not do personal presents."

"Too late."

Hollis set the empty wine bottle down harder than she intended to. "Matt…"

He put both hands up in surrender. "I bought it two weeks ago. And you are under no obligation to retaliate."

Hollis was pleased, but refused to admit it. "I won't. I don't have any time to shop in the next three days."

"Understood." Matt rose to his feet. "And I need to go before I collapse."

"Dinner tomorrow?" Hollis suggested before he suggested lunch. Her heart was already warming to Matt much faster than was safe. She stood as well. "I can meet you somewhere."

"Great. I'll text you once I've explored my new surroundings." He walked to the door, then turned to face her.

Hollis tilted her face upward a little. At six feet, Matt was half-a-foot shorter than Sveyn, so her neck was less pinched when she looked into his eyes.

Her heart thumped with realization.

He's going to kiss me.

And he did.

Matt was always a good kisser, but when he had an agenda to achieve and a point to make, he was truly exceptional. Hollis grabbed his arms to keep her balance as his tongue tangled with hers. His warm breath tickled her cheek, contrasting with the scrape of his unshaven chin.

When he pulled away, her eyelids felt too heavy to open.

"Good night, Hollis," he whispered, his knuckle lifting her chin. "I talk to you tomorrow."

Hollis closed the door behind him and leaned her forehead against it. She was in deep already, and falling farther fast.

What the hell am I going to do?

•

•

•

Chapter
twenty nine

•

Tuesday
December 22

Hollis called Stevie into her office first thing the next morning and shut the door. "I need a huge favor."

"Good morning, Stevie. How are you today?" her friend huffed.

Sveyn chuckled.

Hollis winced. "I'm sorry. Good morning, Stevie. How are you this morning?"

"Fine, thanks. And good morning to you, Hollis." Stevie gave her a sly grin. "Did Matt make it to Phoenix last night?"

Hollis nodded. "He did."

"And did you sleep well?"

"No, no, no!" Hollis clarified. "He has his own apartment and he slept there."

Stevie tilted her head. "That's probably wise, considering Sveyn and all."

The Viking bowed. "Thank you, Stevie."

"And considering that he and I aren't a couple at this point!" Hollis reminded both of them. "It's *not* a foregone conclusion, Stevie."

"Hmm." Stevie perched on the arm of a chair. "So what do you need from me?"

Hollis folded her arms, preparing for Stevie's response. "Matt's asking about the retired special ops navy captain that I invented as my boyfriend."

She blinked. "Excuse me?"

"Very handsome. Over six feet tall. Dark blond hair. Blue eyes." Hollis wrinkled her nose. "I was inventing on the fly."

Stevie's jaw dropped. "You made an imaginary boyfriend out of Sveyn?"

Sveyn grinned. "Who else?"

Hush.

"I didn't want to look like a total loser when Matt showed up at the opening, so yeah." Hollis shrugged apologetically. "I used Sveyn as my inspiration. I said he sails a trade ship now."

Stevie giggled. "Does this particular navy-turned-trade-ship captain happen live in the desert?"

Hollis cheeks flamed. "Maybe. But that's not the point."

Stevie giggled harder. "The point is that he's conveniently out to sea, right?"

"Yes."

"But there needs to be some sort of proof of life."

Hollis nodded. "Exactly."

Stevie clapped her hands together. "Okay. Okay. I've got this. Easy peasy."

Hollis blew a sigh of relief. "Thank you!"

"First, we both download one of those free chat apps that uses Wi-Fi," Stevie began. "Then I'll create his profile so I can text you through it."

Hollis nodded. "And that's perfect if he's at sea!"

"Next, we find a picture or a graphic to use as his avatar—

because you know as well as I do that Matt will want to look over your shoulder when the captain texts you."

"And I need to let him, or it looks suspicious." Hollis walked around and sat at her desk to start the search. "We'll use a public domain photo or clipart."

Stevie followed her around the desk and stood behind her. "And of course he needs a user name, this captain of your heart."

"I think that is how I should be called from this day forward," Sveyn declared.

Hollis shot him a look. *Not helpful.* "Captain Hart—without the 'e' of course. It's perfect."

Stevie nodded. "That actually works. And his first name?"

"The easiest lie to remember is based in truth," Hollis said. "We'll use Sveyn."

"Speaking of which…" Stevie glanced around the room. Are we alone?"

Hollis sighed. "Never. He's here, harassing me."

"Oh!" Stevie smiled and gave a little wave. "Hi, Sveyn."

Another bow. "Good morning, Stevie. You look charming today."

"He says good morning and you look charming."

"Why, thank you!" Her cheeks pinkened.

Hollis turned her screen to face Stevie. "Which do you like?"

Stevie tapped the screen. "That one."

Sveyn leaned over the computer. "I approve."

Hollis downloaded a muscular fisherman standing on the deck of a boat and photographed attractively from behind. "Good choice. It doesn't show his face."

"As I think about it," Stevie said as she circled around to the front of Hollis's desk. "We should just use his first initial for his user name, or Matt might go searching for Captain Sveyn Hart."

Hollis nodded her agreement. "Good point. We'll use S. Hart."

Stevie started laughing. "Better put an underscore between the S and the H."

Hollis looked up at Stevie. "Why?"

Stevie laughed even harder. "If you don't, his screen name is *shart!*"

Hollis burst into laughter at that. "Well—he *is* a load of crap and hot air!" she whooped.

*****

Miranda interrupted their hilarity via intercom. "Hollis? Can you come to my office?"

"Yep." She wiped her eyes. "Be right there."

A uniformed police officer waited with Miranda and a loosely closed box rested on her desk.

Hollis's name was written on the top in black marker.

Sveyn peeked inside the box then met her eyes. "This is not good, Hollis."

Foreboding swamped Hollis making her knees wobble. "Not again…"

"I'm afraid so." Miranda glanced at the officer—a different one from three nights ago. "This is Detective Campbell. He's going to handle your case now."

"Case?" Hollis looked at the cop. "I have a case?"

"Yes, ma'am," he said. "The first dead cat might have been a prank. But the second one indicates something else is ongoing." He lifted a card from the desktop. Hollis noticed he was wearing gloves. "This was tied around the animal's neck."

Hollis stared at the card. "Life number two?" She shifted her gaze to the officer. "Like cats have nine?"

Sveyn startled. "They do?"

Hollis shot him a *shut up* glance.

"That's my interpretation." The detective lifted the edge of the lid and slipped that card inside.

"Are seven more cats going to die?" It was a horrifying idea.

"We hope not."

Hollis looked at Miranda. "Was this one delivered like the first one?"

Her boss shook her head. "The package was left by the front door before the museum opened this morning. I called the police to come open it before I bothered you." Miranda's eye dropped to the box then met hers again. "I assumed you'd forgive me if it turned out to be harmless."

Hollis nodded numbly. "Why is this happening?"

Detective Campbell straightened. "I intend to find out. Do you mind if I ask you a few questions?"

Hollis's gaze swept over the dark navy uniform replete with a variety of devices, cords, and weapons and her heartbeat stumbled. "Um. Sure."

His mouth quirked. "Would you rather I was in plain clothes?"

"No. No. It's okay." She glanced at Miranda. "Here or in my office?"

"Here's fine." Her boss gestured toward a chair. "Can I get you coffee?"

Hollis shook her head. "No. But thank you."

Detective Campbell took a chair as well. "The first question is obvious: who is angry with you?"

Hollis blinked. "Angry with me?"

"Anyone holding a grudge?"

"Well… there was Tony Samoa." Hollis looked at Sveyn, then Miranda "But I saw him Saturday at the mall and he apologized."

"Who is he?" Detective Campbell asked.

"The museum's permanent Lead Collector," Miranda said. "Hollis was brought in on a one-year contract to handle the Kensington bequest, but Tony felt like we were betraying the museum's integrity by accepting it in the first place."

The detective's lips quirked. "In spite of the twelve mil that came with it?"

Hollis was impressed. "You've done your homework."

"I try."

Miranda turned to Hollis. "You said he apologized?"

"Yep. He said it turned out to be a good decision after all and he was sorry for giving me such grief about everything."

"Everything?" Campbell asked. "What is everything?"

Hollis waved a hand. "Oh, the whole ghost business. He thinks it's dumb."

To me it obvious that it's Dregthat I can't [handwritten annotation]

The detective looked at his notes. "You were caught on camera with some sort of entity. And now the museum is encouraging spiritualists to investigate. Is that right?"

"They are paying for the opportunity," Hollis clarified. "But yes."

"Paying the museum? Hmm." Detective Campbell met Hollis's eyes. "What *was* on the camera?"

"He believes the image was fabricated in some way," Sveyn warned.

Hollis faced the detective squarely. "I swear I am telling you the truth, Detective. I can't explain what showed up then, any more than I can explain what the *Ghost Myth* guys caught on their cameras."

Sveyn shook his head. "You have said too much."

"What did they see?"

Hollis rolled her eyes. "Watch the commercials. You'll see."

Campbell looked at his notes again. "Is it possible that some religious groups are trying to warn you away from this shift toward the occult?"

Hollis coughed a laugh. "If they are, then last night's exorcism should appease them."

His gaze shot up to hers. "Is that public knowledge?"

"No. Not yet." Hollis looked at Miranda. "Maybe it should be?"

Miranda nodded. "We'll talk after this and issue a press release."

"All right." Campbell leaned back in his chair. "Anyone else who might resent you for any reason?"

Sveyn leaned over and spoke in Hollis's ear. "Matt's wife cannot be pleased."

Hollis's eyes widened. "Suzan Wallace!"

"Who is she?"

How do I make this short? "I dated, lived with, and was engaged to a man for ten years. He broke up with me two years ago, and married someone else soon afterwards."

Detective Campbell's bland expression didn't shift. "Go on."

"This guy—Matt Wallace—showed up at the opening of the

believe this section

new wing claiming his marriage was a wreck and he wanted to reunite with me." Hollis felt her cheeks getting tight. "I haven't agreed yet, but he filed for divorce and has moved to Phoenix for a few weeks to try and convince me."

"From where?"

"Milwaukee."

Detective Campbell raised his brows. "Not to discourage you, but I'm from Minnesota. Moving to Phoenix for the winter has more than one draw."

Rude. "That's on him," Hollis snapped. "I said I didn't agree to anything."

"Fair enough." Campbell scribbled something on his pad. "What does Suzan Wallace know about you?"

Hollis scowled. "Whatever Matt told her, plus whatever's on the internet."

"So basically everything."

She shrugged. "I guess."

"And sending a package to the museum—or having one delivered—would be easily done." Campbell turned to Miranda. "Are there security cameras by the front doors?"

"Yes, and the back door. I'll see that the files are sent to you."

"Neither delivery was to the back door, correct?"

"Right."

The detective returned his attention to Hollis. "Anyone else you can think of?"

Hollis shook her head. "No, sir."

"All right then." Detective Campbell closed his notepad and stood. He fished a business card from his shirt pocket. "Give me a call if you think of anything else, no matter how insignificant."

Hollis accepted the card. "I will."

*****

"Dead cats?" Matt asked over the phone. "That's creepy."

"Yeah. And cruel." Hollis shuddered. "But I have to ask you something."

"Shoot."

"How mad is Suzan at you? Or me?"

The question was met with silence.

"Matt?"

"Are you suggesting that Suzan is doing this horrible thing? *Really?*" His tone was hard as granite.

Hollis winced. "No. But the detective asked me who might have a grudge against me, and I did mention her name."

"Oh, Hollis…"

"I don't think it's her, Matt," Hollis repeated. "But I do want to know how upset she was when you told her why you filed for divorce."

More silence.

"Matt?"

"I didn't."

Hollis slumped in her chair. "Didn't what?"

"I didn't mention you."

"Does she know where you are?"

"Well, yes." He cleared his throat. "She needs to know where to mail things. Documents."

"So she knows you're in Phoenix." Hollis kept her voice level. "And when she Googles me, she'll know I'm in Phoenix. You don't think she'd put that together?"

"Why would she Google you?" The man sounded sincerely confused.

"You left *me* for *her*, Matt. Obviously I'm the first person she'd look for after you left her." Hollis sighed her impatience. "She'll want to know if you came back to me." *Duh.*

Matt was silent again.

"The truth is, Matt," Hollis said. "Men don't leave unless they have somewhere to go."

He drew a deep and audible breath. "Shit."

•

•

•

Chapter Thirty

•

Hollis met Matt for dinner after begging and pleading with Stevie to talk George into joining them.

"It's your first dinner together," Stevie objected. "Why do you want company?"

"We had dinner last night, in my condo, after he arrived." *If you can call leftover sushi licked by a Viking apparition dinner.* "And I really want to get your and George's takes on Matt. I don't trust myself to be objective."

Bless his heart, George was on board.

The quartet sat in a corner booth at a busy Mexican restaurant, crunching away on corn chips and salsa. Sveyn waited outside in the car. Or somewhere.

"I will still hear what you say," he reminded Hollis. "So I will know with some certainty what the conversation entails."

Though that uncomfortable reality colored her conversation, Hollis tried to be as natural as her nerves would let her.

Matt seemed to have regained his composure, following Hollis's obvious but previously unconsidered revelation about female behavior in the twenty-first century. He remembered meeting Stevie and George at the opening of the Kensington wing, so that helped.

Once they placed their orders, George turned to Hollis, his expression grim. "I understand there was another 'delivery' today."

Hollis nodded and avoided looking at Matt. "I now have an official case, and an official detective working it."

"He asked her if anyone held a grudge. She mentioned my soon-to-be ex-wife." Matt apparently had no more qualms about throwing Suzan under the police bus.

Stevie gave a little gasp. "Do you think it could be her?"

"I didn't at first," Matt hedged. "But as I thought about it, she can be pretty vindictive when she wants to be."

"What about you, Hollis?" George asked.

Hollis scooped a chip through the fresh but tame salsa. "I don't know the woman, to be honest. But I figured she's not happy with Matt, so she's not happy with me by extension."

Stevie faced Matt, her expression incredulous. "You *told* her you were going back to Hollis?"

"No." Matt's gold-streaked eyes jumped to Hollis's. "But I have been assured that she knows."

Stevie gave a little shrug. "That's probably true. She would have done her Google and Facebook due diligence."

Matt looked at George. "Does every woman know about this?"

"I guess so." George pulled his surprised gaze from his fiancée. "We are screwed, my friend."

"Oh, stop it." Hollis wrinkled her nose. "It's not like we are actual stalkers. But if the information is out there, then it's out there. Simple as that."

"And we'll find it." Stevie smiled sweetly at George.

The waitress arrived with their dinners. "Be careful, the plates are hot."

Said every waitress in every Mexican restaurant ever.

Hollis risked touching hers and then adjusted its position on the table. "Why do they heat the plates so much, do you think?"

Stevie giggled. "So they can say that."

Once everyone was situated, George turned another grim expression toward Hollis. "Did you give this detective the obvious name?"

"What obvious name?" Hollis asked, her mouth full of very hot enchiladas.

George's brow wrinkled. "Everett Sage."

Hollis coughed red sauce onto her plate.

Matt pounded her back. "Drink some water."

Hollis took a big gulp of the ice water and got immediate brain freeze. She winced, rubbed her forehead, and stared at George. "I thought he was in prison."

George nodded. "He is."

"So how?"

"He has money. Lots of it." George sipped his margarita. "With resources like that he can get things done, even from behind bars."

Hollis's shoulders slumped. "You think Everett Sage is doing this from prison?"

Sveyn appeared by her side. "I want to hear this."

She didn't argue with him.

"Let me talk to the detective," George said calmly. "If there is any chance it's Sage, he'll be able to put a stop to it. Solitary confinement, or whatever."

"Less than the miscreant deserves," Sveyn grumbled.

Hollis dug Detective Campbell's business card from her purse and handed it to George. George put the policeman's contact info in his phone and handed the card back to Hollis.

"I'll call him tomorrow." He patted Hollis's hand. "Let's talk about happier things."

"Yes." Stevie's eyes twinkled dangerously. "Like why you want Hollis back."

"Stevie!" Hollis's face burst into flames. "That's not—"

"Actually, I'd like to answer that," Matt interrupted.

"Really?" Stevie grinned. "Okay, spill."

Sveyn leaned against the next table. "I am interested as well."

"Ugh!" Hollis covered her face with fists gripping her bright green napkin. "Somebody just shoot me now."

Matt pulled her hands down. "Will you please listen like a grown-up for once?"

For once?

What did that mean?

Hollis forced a smile. "Sure. Let it rip."

Matt faced Stevie and George. "I first met Hollis at the University of Wisconsin—Milwaukee on an overly warm September afternoon. Between the unexpected heat and the normal humidity, she was an out-of-control cloud of wild red curls and the bluest eyes I have ever seen. It was over in that moment. My heart was claimed."

Hollis wagged her head. "You've always said it was love at first sight, but you didn't ask me out for six more weeks."

Matt turned his amazing eyes to hers and her heart lurched precariously. "One does not rush a goddess, my love. I couldn't risk scaring you away."

Sveyn crossed his arms. "He makes a point."

Shut up.

And go away.

Stevie rested her elbows on the table, and her chin in her hands. "Tell us about your first date."

Matt's expression brightened. "Ah! The art museum."

As Hollis squirmed inwardly, Matt outlined the progression of their relationship in a fair amount of embarrassing detail. With each life step forward—dating, going steady, graduating, moving in together, and getting career jobs—he sang Hollis's praises.

Listening to him tonight, it was impossible to believe that he ever walked out on her.

In the midst of Matt's romance-novel-worthy love story, Hollis experienced a jolting moment of clarity.

"And then," she said. "You met Suzan."

George, Stevie, and Matt all startled, the spell of his narration abruptly broken. Matt's cheeks flushed burgundy.

"Yes," he admitted after a pause. "Then I met Suzan. And made the worst string of decisions in my life."

*****

Matt kissed her goodnight for a solid fifteen minutes. It would have been longer if the night hadn't grown so cold and Hollis hadn't refused to make out in the car like teenagers.

"Will I see you tomorrow?" he whispered.

Hollis looked up into his eyes, black in the restaurant's dim parking lot light. "Sure. You can come with me when I shop for the white elephant gift for Miranda's Christmas party. Unless you don't want to play."

"Oh, no! I've heard her white elephant exchange is legendary." Matt grinned. "Send me the rules so I can start planning our strategy."

"I'll forward the email when I get home." Hollis planted one last kiss on Matt's lips then stepped away. "Goodnight."

Sveyn was in the car, waiting for her. Hollis started the engine and cranked up the heat. "Most people think Phoenix is warm all the time."

Sveyn tipped his head toward hers. "It is. From what I understand, it never snows and seldom freezes."

"Snow has fallen," she corrected.

"But it melts right away, does it not?"

"Unless the ground is frozen."

"Which it never is."

Hollis stuck out her tongue at him. "My point is, sometimes the nights do get below thirty-two. And with a breeze, fifty degrees is chilly."

Sveyn laughed. "Duly noted."

Hollis backed out of her spot and turned toward the street. "So what did you think of Matt tonight?"

"Do you mean what do I think about what he said?"

"Everything." She glanced at the Viking lounging in her passenger seat. "All of it."

Sveyn seemed to draw a breath. "I am still convinced he is here because he believes you to be a safe haven."

"I can understand that. We've known each other a long time," Hollis conceded. "But what'd you think about what he said *about* me?"

Sveyn leaned forward so he was in her peripheral vision. "I would not have waited six weeks."

"You said he had a point about not scaring me off."

Sveyn chuckled. "I would not have scared you. I would have taken time and gentled you into my arms. Two weeks and you would have been mine."

Two weeks and I was yours.

Stop it. This is about Matt. "Do you trust him?"

"That is an interesting question." Sveyn leaned back in his seat again. "I do believe he trusts himself."

Hollis frowned. "What does that mean?"

"It means, that if he is being untruthful to you, it is because he is being untruthful to himself first."

Hollis drove without speaking, trying to puzzle out what the Viking was actually saying. Just before she pulled into her condo complex, she said, "You don't think he loves me."

"That is not what I said."

"So explain it to me. Apparently I'm an idiot." She took the turn a little too fast.

Sveyn didn't answer until she shifted the car into park. "It is my opinion that Matt thinks he is in love with you."

Hollis turned her head toward him. "Isn't that the same as *being* in love with me?"

"No." Sveyn slid through the door, exiting the car.

Ugh.

Vikings.

Hollis opened her door, got out, slammed it shut and locked the car. Sveyn was halfway to her front door.

"How is it different?" she called to his back.

He turned around and watched her approach. "Someday, he will be required to act on his love for you. If he does what is asked of him, then his love for you is true."

"But if he doesn't, then he was lying to himself." Hollis stomped past Sveyn to unlock the door. "Is that it?"

"Yes."

She spun to face him. "And you think that if that time—"

"When," he interrupted. "When that time comes. Because it will."

"Fine. *When* that time comes, you think he's going to bail?"

Sveyn's brows pulled together. "Bail?"

"Jump out. Like an airplane. With a parachute." The double meaning of her analogy hit her in the gut.

With a parachute; another safe haven.

Sveyn nodded. "Ah, yes. I saw parachutes in the German war. Bail is what I mean. He will jump out of your relationship."

"And land safely somewhere else?" she snapped.

Sveyn gave her a sympathetic look. "That was your choice of words, Hollis. Not mine."

Wednesday
December 23

Hollis read through the list of requirements for Miranda's white elephant gift exchange while Matt looked over her shoulder. She smelled his aftershave, and the scent took her back over two years to when she thought they were happy together.

"There must be three components that relate to each other. Only one can be new. And the total value must be between twenty-five and forty dollars."

"Is there a size requirement?"

"Nope."

Matt's gaze swept the Goodwill. "The hunt begins. Let's find the weirdest thing we can, and build from there."

Hollis hurried back to the housewares. "Too bad we can't give away something from Ezra's hoard," she said to Sveyn who was helping in the search. "That stone dildo would be hilarious."

"Look at this." He pointed to a bright turquoise object lying on its side. "What is this used for?"

Hollis picked it up. "Oh my gosh! It's a ladle shaped like the Loch Ness Monster." She grinned at Sveyn. "When it is in a pot of soup, it'll look like there's a dinosaur in there."

She turned around and scanned across the racks for Matt.

"Matt! Come here!"

He wound his way over and she explained what she found. "That's hilarious," he agreed. "Now, let's choose our theme."

"Scotland? Hollis suggested. "Or dinosaurs? Turquoise? Soup?"

"I love Scotland. Let's see what we can find in a tartan—then include some whisky as our new item."

"And our saving grace. People will go for that."

"I would go for the monster in my soup," Sveyn said as he wandered off. "It is a fun joke."

Hollis flipped the ladle over. "Ninety-nine cents." She looked up at Matt. "If we find something plaid here, we can afford to get some good whisky."

"Over here." Sveyn waved his arms.

"No way!" Hollis scurried over to the Viking. "Look at this, Matt—a miniature Scotch cooler." She flipped it over. "Ten bucks!"

"Done!" Matt grinned at her. "Off to the grocery store and we are done in record time."

Hollis walked to the front of the store with Matt's arm casually draped over her shoulder. *This feels right.*

Her phone chimed a sound she didn't recognize. She pulled it from her pocket and swiped the lock screen. She sucked a quick breath when she saw the display.

New message from S_Hart.

•

•

•

Chapter Thirty One

•

Hi, babe!

Hollis bit her lips between her teeth to keep from laughing.

"Anybody I know?" Matt asked.

Hollis shook her head and kept her eyes on her phone. She had to hold it together if this ruse was going to work. "My captain."

Matt's eyebrows shot upward. "From out at sea?"

"Yeah. There are Wi-Fi apps you know—it doesn't have to be through a cell tower." Hollis texted back, holding her phone so Matt could watch if he wanted.

Hi, Sweetie. How's sailing?

She stuck her phone back in her pocket. "Let's pay for this stuff and go get the whisky."

Matt hesitated like he wanted to know more, but then stepped up to the cashier and paid for the two items they were buying. As they exited the store and walked to Matt's car, Hollis's phone chimed again.

"You going to get that?" he asked.

Her ruse was working—Matt was at least curious if not

outright jealous. Hollis decided to step up her game. "In the car. Do you know how to get to the Fry's?"

Matt unlocked the car. "Yeah."

Hollis opened the passenger door and got inside. She immediately retrieved her phone and opened the app. Sveyn leaned over the seat and she held the phone so he could see the screen.

We hit some rough waters off Baja. We're clear now.

She replied: *Glad you're safe. I do worry sometimes.*

That's nice to know.

Matt started the engine. "Everything all right?"

Hollis looked up. "Rough waters off Baja but he's fine."

"There was a pretty decent storm. I saw it on the news last night."

Stevie was doing her homework, apparently; Hollis would have to thank her for that. "I prefer not to know. It makes me crazy."

She returned her attention to her phone as Matt drove out of the Goodwill parking lot and texted: *I miss you so much.*

Me, too. I miss the way your hair smells after a shower.

Hollis's cheek warmed. She knew Stevie was writing the messages, but somehow they felt like they were from Sveyn.

And I miss the feel of your beard on my neck, she replied.

Just a few weeks, babe.

I know. Sail fast!

Back to my safe harbor. I will. Bye, babe.

Hollis sucked a breath. Why had Stevie chosen those words?

Bye, Captain.

She added a heart emoticon then turned off her phone.

Sveyn reached through the seat and laid his hand over hers. Hollis stared at it, wishing for the impossible so hard that her chest hurt.

*****

Hollis left her phone lying on Matt's coffee table when she went to use the bathroom at his apartment. When she returned, she noticed it had been moved, just like she expected it would. She wondered if he had always checked up on her and she hadn't noticed back then, or if her interest in another man had prompted his snooping today.

Either way, Hollis wasn't worried about it—the ruse with her captain was part of her plan to make Matt step up. They were both in their thirties now and time was wasting if they wanted to marry and have a family. As much as she cared about Sveyn, and she truly did, the Viking was a dead end.

Well, sort *of dead.*

The thought occurred to Hollis that if she had checked up on Matt two years ago, she might not have been blindsided. Should she check up on him now? Was there a chance he might be looking at reconciliation with Suzan?

So, she asked.

"Reconcile?" Matt shook his head. "You don't know what kind of woman she really is."

Hollis sat on the couch next to him. "Tell me."

"Rich women have a level of expectation that's hard to describe. Everyone's always trying to be the top of the pile—whatever pile they're on at that moment." Matt heaved a sigh. "It's exhausting. And it gets in the way of intimacy, if you catch my drift."

Hollis wanted answers, not drifts. "Sex?"

Matt cheeks reddened. "Well... yeah."

"So Suzan is frigid?" Hollis gave him an incredulous look. "Didn't you know that? I mean, didn't you guys…"

Matt's embarrassment became even more pronounced. "Yes. A couple times. But she said she really wanted to wait until we were married to do everything."

Now Hollis's cheeks flushed. "Everything?"

"You know. Besides just missionary-style penetration."

"Ah." Hollis knew very well that Matt really enjoyed oral options—especially on the receiving end. "So when you did get married, nothing changed?"

Matt shook his head.

"And sex is the reason you wouldn't go back?" Hollis

needed to be clear on what she might be up against, should she decide to fully engage.

"Not *just* sex," Matt stated. "But good sex would have made the rest tolerable. At least I think it would have."

Hollis highly doubted that, but didn't argue the point. She knew she had to ask the next question, and hoped Matt would be honest.

"How was our sex life? I mean, really."

Matt's mouth twisted and he stared at his hands, resting on his thighs. His fingers flexed and wrinkled his jeans. "I never told you, but I was a virgin when I met you."

Hollis sat up straight and smacked his arm hard with the back of her hand. "Matt Wallace! Are you kidding me?"

"Ow!" He rubbed his arm. "That hurt!"

Hollis didn't care. "We were both virgins? Why did you tell me you weren't?"

"Because I wanted you to think I knew what I was doing." Matt scowled at her. "My manhood was at stake."

Hollis flopped back against the couch and covered her face. "And all that time I wondered how I compared to your previous lovers." Her hands fell away and turned into fists. "I am so pissed at you right now!"

"Why? Because you were my first? " He looked genuinely confused. "That's messed up, Hollis."

"No! Because you lied to me for ten years, you idiot."

Sveyn reappeared after Hollis asked her sex life question and was now hovering in the apartment's short hallway. What she said next was intended for both sets of ears.

"Women want—no, *deserve*—respect above all else. And that means being honest about everything in the relationship." She glared at Matt. "Even if something is hard to say, hiding it only makes things worse."

Matt nodded. "I get it."

Hollis shot a glance in Sveyn's direction.

"I cannot lie to you, Hollis," he said.

"Hiding truths counts as lies, you know," she countered. "In case you are doing that."

Matt played with the UWM college ring on his right hand. "I get that, too."

Sveyn backed out of her sight and said nothing.

Hollis got off the couch and went to Matt's fridge. He had a six-pack of White Barrel beer with three bottles left. Hollis grabbed one, popped the top, and took a long sip. The microbrew was amazing

She looked at Matt and held up a second bottle. "You want one?"

"Yeah." He stood and walked toward her.

Hollis held her ground as Matt approached until they were standing face to face, close enough for her to feel the heat from his body. He accepted the beer with his left hand and set it on the counter beside her. With his right hand he reached for the bottle opener on her other side.

Hollis was surrounded.

She looked up into Matt's eyes. A flood of repressed memories swamped her. The man was gorgeous and sexy and damn but she wanted him back.

Matt leaned down and kissed her softly. He held back, waiting to see what she would do.

Hollis let him wonder for a moment.

He shifted his weight forward, so that their bodies were in full contact from chest to knees. His kiss deepened.

She crumbled.

Her brain was screaming *get out before it's too late*, but lower parts of her frame were telling it to shut up. While dream sex had its advantages, holding a flesh-and-blood man, especially one whose bulges and valleys were so familiar to her touch, was intoxicating. Overwhelming.

Dangerous.

Hollis put her palms against Matt's chest, pushing him away and leaning backwards over the counter.

"Not yet…" was all she could manage. Her lips were on fire and her groin ached. Her breath was infuriatingly uneven.

Matt stared at her. "Why not?"

"Because this is too fast." Hollis slid sideways to freedom.

"We are not back together yet."

Matt calmly opened his beer, then turned around and leaned on the same edge of the counter which she just abandoned. His eyelids were heavy and his lips curled in a sultry smile. "And why aren't we?"

"Because I don't trust you," Hollis declared before she chickened out. She pointed at the coffee table where her phone still lay. "And you don't trust me. You read my messages from Captain Hart."

Matt recoiled. "How did you—"

"I set my phone on a forty-five degree angle when I went to the bathroom."

"Seriously?"

"Yes." Hollis gripped her beer tightly enough to whiten her knuckles. "I expected you to snoop, so I paid attention."

Matt took a long pull on his beer, lowered the bottle, and began to worry the label with his thumbnail.

"Why did you expect me to snoop?" he asked after a long silence.

"Because you want to know what you're up against." Hollis squared her shoulders. "And you aren't used to losing."

"It's true. I don't want to lose you, Hollis. Not again."

Hollis couldn't let *that* comment slide by. "You never 'lost' me, Matt. You threw me away. When are you going to own up to that?"

He reached for her. "Hollis—"

She pushed his hand away. "Because if you don't stop trying to rewrite what happened between us, then none of this is going to work. Ever."

Matt looked defeated. "You're right."

Hollis took another draught from her bottle, wondering if he would say more.

His eyes narrowed. "You've changed."

"Yeah, well. Heartbreak does that to a person." Hollis finished her beer and set the empty on the counter. She took Matt's beer out of his hand. "Take me home."

Hollis was feeling much more generously toward Matt as she drove him to Miranda's house for Christmas dinner. Last night had helped.

Sveyn wanted to go to church. "I lost my life, as it was, defending the new religion. Christmas Eve is very important to me. And, I am curious to see what traditions have survived, other than the evergreen tree and Saint Nikolas."

So Hollis looked up churches online, and found one nearby that had a candlelight service at eleven o'clock. She excused herself from Matt's company at ten, sending him home after they wrapped the white elephant gift well enough to disguise what it contained.

Rather than freeze outside in the car for an hour, she slipped inside and sat in the back. Sveyn walked to the front. He knelt and crossed himself, then sat in a pew between an older couple and a single woman.

Hollis relaxed after the service began, knowing no one would try to talk to her at that point. She really didn't want anyone asking her why a stranger had joined them that night. Her truth was unbelievable, and she didn't feeling like lying in a church.

The scripture reading from the book of Luke was familiar to her because of the Peanuts cartoon she watched every year growing up. She found it unexpectedly soothing. The Christmas hymns lifted her mood as well, and she even sang along.

When the service was finished, she hurried out.

"I'm in the car when you're ready," she said softly, knowing Sveyn would hear her.

When he did get in the car, he was quiet. Hollis waited for him to say something, and when he didn't she asked him what he thought.

He looked at her, his expression an odd mix of peace and frustration. "I am glad that I went, Hollis. Thank you for taking me."

"You're welcome, Sveyn," she murmured.

At the next stoplight on the way to Miranda's, Hollis turned to look at Matt. She could see Sveyn in the rearview mirror. "Merry Christmas, by the way."

"Merry Christmas," the two men answered together.

Matt was looking at a weather app on his phone. "Sixty-five degrees, and a high of seventy-two is expected."

"Very nice!" Hollis grinned. "What's the temperature in Milwaukee?"

"Twenty-one. A high of twenty-eight is expected."

"Snow?"

"Eight inches on the ground."

Hollis laughed. "I was reluctant to give up my white Christmas, but I have to admit it's nicer not to freeze."

Matt reached over and squeezed her hand. "I'm just glad I'm with you."

Hollis smiled at him, glad he was with her. If nothing else, he was fine man-candy. When her phone-messaging app chimed, she asked Matt to read the message to her since she was driving.

Matt squinted at the screen and cleared his throat, obviously not thrilled with the task. "It says: merry Christmas, babe."

"Aww. He's so sweet." Hollis turned down Miranda's street. "I'll answer him after we get there."

•

•

•

Chapter Thirty Two

•

It was actually sweeter of Stevie to take the time out of her family's celebration to play their game. Hollis decided later that night to give her friend a nice gift card to shop the after-Christmas sales with as thanks for her help.

The company at Miranda's party was fine, the food was pretty good, and the white elephant gift exchange was hilarious. Hollis walked out with a cute set of mugs with saguaro cactuses on them, which she planned to regift to her mom in February.

"All in all, a good time," she said to Matt as they snuggled on his couch with glasses of wine and watched *A Christmas Story*. That movie was their traditional end to Christmas day back when they were together, and it felt good to watch it now.

Hollis yawned.

"None of that," Matt teased.

"Sorry. But all that food, and all that laughter; I'm worn out."

Matt tightened his arm around her. "And cuddling on the couch with wine doesn't help."

Hollis yawned again and heaved a happy sigh. "It's all

good."

She woke up long after the movie was over. Matt was watching some hunting show.

"Oh no, I slept through it." She pushed the lap blanket off of her and sat up. "I'm sorry."

Matt smiled and tucked a loose hank of hair behind her ear. "Don't be. It felt like old times."

Hollis stretched, trying to wake up, and looked around for her shoes. "I should go."

"Do you have to?"

She gave him the sternest look she could muster. "I am not sleeping with you."

And there's Sveyn.

Trust the Viking to appear whenever her conversation with Matt hinted at anything sexual.

"I'm not asking you to sleep with me," Matt said. "I asking if you want to spend the rest of the night here, instead of going out into the cold, and risk driving home when you're only half-awake."

"Oh." Hollis scratched her head and then tried to run her fingers through her hair. The offer was tempting. Very tempting. "In your bed?"

"Not necessarily. This is a sleeper sofa. We'll even keep our clothes on."

Hollis nodded. "That I can agree to."

"Good. Now get up and I'll make the bed."

Hollis stood. "I'm going to wash up while you do."

Sveyn followed her to the bathroom. "Do not have sexual congress with that man."

"I'm not," she whispered once the bathroom fan was on. She turned on the faucet, letting it run until the water got hot. "I'm just too tired to drive home."

She looked up at the Viking, his words having just sunk in. "Sexual *congress?*"

"What do you call it?"

"Just plain having sex." Hollis giggled silently. "You're funny."

She washed her face, and rinsed out her mouth. Then she removed her bra and folded it to fit in her purse. "I wish I had a comb… Oh, well."

Hollis padded barefoot back out to the living room. Matt had opened the sofa bed, brought a down comforter from his bed, and stacked every pillow in his apartment as a backrest. He went into his room to change, and returned in flannel pants and a t-shirt.

He handed her a set of flannel pajamas. "Unless you're comfortable in your jeans and sweater."

"Oh—thank you!" Hollis grabbed the flannels and changed in the bathroom. This time when she returned, Matt had opened another bottle of wine and was making a plate of cheese and crackers.

He waved a hand. "I know—I know. But I'm hungry."

Hollis climbed under the comforter, leaned back against the pillows, and waited to be served. It was a sort of test, considering that Matt was seldom so thoughtful in their previous relationship.

This time though, he passed.

Matt carried the cheese plate first, then poured her wine and brought it to her, before bringing his glass and the bottle to the sofa bed.

He picked up the remote. "What do you want to watch?"

"Do we have to be done with Christmas?"

Matt shook his head. "Not if you don't want to be."

Hollis smiled. "White Christmas?"

It was another test; Matt hated musicals in general. He huffed a little laugh. "Tonight, your wish is my command."

As he pulled the movie up on Netflix, Hollis stacked some cheese on a cracker, ate it, and sipped her wine. Things with Matt were going better than she expected, and she felt her walls start to come down.

"Do you mind if I watch?" Sveyn asked. He sat on the floor on the other side of the end table. "I will be quiet."

Hollis sighed.

And then there's the Viking.

Saturday
December 26

Hollis slept late, not opening her eyes until nearly nine thirty. Matt wasn't in the bed but the smell of bacon told her where he was. She sat up, stretched, and tossed the comforter aside.

Matt turned around when the bed squeaked. He smiled at her from the tiny kitchen. "Good morning."

"Morning." Hollis got out of bed. "I'll be right back."

"Take your time." He turned back to the stove. "Scrambled okay?"

"Sure." Hollis preferred over medium, but when someone else was cooking she was willing to flex. "Thanks!"

She hurried to the bathroom, wondering if Matt had a spare toothbrush. He did.

Hollis washed her face, brushed her teeth, and changed back into her jeans and sweater. She dug through her purse for a hair tie and, using her fingers as a comb, corralled her curls with the elastic.

"At least it's out of my face," she muttered.

Sveyn stood behind her and watched in the mirror. "I love how you look in the morning."

"You are a majority of one, then." She looked at the Viking's reflection. "Were you bored last night?"

He nodded. "I am afraid I have become accustomed to watching television while you sleep."

"I'll be at home tonight. Alone. I promise."

Hollis folded the flannels and left them on the bathroom counter, then went out to join Matt in the kitchen.

"Coffee?"

"Please. With cream."

He grinned at her as he popped a K-Cup into the machine. "I remember."

Breakfast was basic: crisp bacon, eggs scrambled in the fat, whole wheat toast with real butter, coffee. All-American comfort food.

"What do you have planned today?" Matt asked. "Since you don't have any gifts to return, that is."

Hollis laughed. "I'm not sure. Maybe clean my condo."

Matt lifted his coffee mug and winked at her. "I'm available for boredom removal. Just give me a call."

When she finished eating, Hollis didn't offer to stay and clean up the kitchen—yet another test. "I better get going."

Matt glanced at the dirty dishes but didn't say anything. "Okay. I'll call you later."

Hollis gave Matt a medium-depth kiss goodbye. More than a peck, but nothing like last night. He opened the door and she nearly tripped over the box on his doorstep.

Hollis cried out and stumbled backward.

Matt caught her. "What is it?"

Panic zinged through her veins. "Who is that addressed to?"

Matt started to pick it up, but Hollis stopped him. "Don't touch it! Just read the label."

Matt straightened. "There is no label."

Hollis turned around and retreated into the apartment. "I'm calling Detective Campbell."

*****

The detective donned latex gloves and cut open the corrugated cardboard box. He folded back the tissue paper. Hollis hid her face in Matt's shoulder.

"It has a tag," Campbell said. "Number three."

"A dead cat?" Matt's voice was strained. "So this is what you were talking about?"

"Yes," she said into his shirt. She heard the snap of a plastic bag and turned to look at the detective. "How did they know I was here? Are they following me?"

Campbell tied the bag shut. "At some point, maybe. But it's more likely that they know about your relationship with this gentleman." The detective stood as he addressed Matt. "I'm going to need to take a statement from you."

"Um, sure. Yeah." Matt's face was pale.

Campbell took the grisly package to his car, then returned with his notebook. He asked Matt all the basic questions while Hollis grew increasingly upset.

"How are the cats killed?" she interrupted.

Detective Campbell appeared appropriately concerned, yet calm. "The first two were asphyxiated. Probably a plastic bag over their heads."

"Is that a clue?" she demanded.

He smiled softly. "Everything's a clue."

"But did they know I was here? My car's outside."

"In a visitor spot, right?" Campbell shook his head. "This is a big complex. Experience tells me that Mr. Wallace was the targeted recipient, and your being here was coincidence."

Matt's eyes widened. "Why go after me?"

The detective made a show of looking through his notes. "I believe you recently filed for divorce. And you had a previous long-standing relationship with Ms. McKenna?"

"Yes…"

Campbell met Matt's eyes. "Her place of employment and your residence are both known to your wife?"

"Oh, god."

The detective stood and walked toward the door. "I'll have one of my colleagues in Milwaukee stop by and have a chat with her."

Hollis cringed. Suzan was going to go absolutely ballistic.

She gave Matt a sympathetic glance. He looked like he was being strapped into an electric chair, while his soon-to-be ex was at the switch.

Thursday
December 31

Hollis had to admit it; this last week had been magical.

Or Matt-gical.

She giggled happily and accepted another glass of New Year's champagne from a tray. Matt had bought tickets to a party

What about Captain Hart? wc who would she say sh

at the top of the tallest building in Phoenix, and while d'oeuvres were average, the view was spectacular. And champagne was flowing freely.

Matt pulled her into another dance, holding her close against his chest. "You are so beautiful, Hollis," he murmured into her hair. "It's like we were never apart."

Hollis shook her head. "No, Matt. You've changed."

He looked down at her. "Have I?"

"You seem to appreciate me more."

He huffed a laugh. "It's true I think. Now I realize how stupid I was to walk away from you."

Hollis smiled. *He finally said it.* He didn't lose her, he left her. "Well, don't make that mistake again."

He kissed her warmly. "I won't."

Hollis rested her cheek against Matt's shoulder and considered the Viking standing by the window, staring out at the city. Ever since Matt arrived ten days ago, Sveyn had kept his distance. He hadn't entered her dreams once—and after what she began to think of as regular conjugal visits, she missed him.

Of course she couldn't have simultaneous relationships with two men, even if one wasn't entirely real. Hollis was a one-man-at-a-time woman, and right now she needed to focus on Matt. She had to know if he was going to be her future, or only her past.

Future's looking good.

The urge to cry surprised her. Were these happy tears? Or tears of regret?

And if they were prompted by regret, what was she giving up?

Hollis wasn't a fool. She knew that answer.

Sveyn entered her life like no man ever had—and not because he was an apparition. The Viking had accepted her just as she was from the very first day.

He told her his story with complete honesty. He assured her she wasn't going insane. He observed her imperfect life twenty-four-seven and went along for the ride without complaint.

And then he fell in love with her, and he loved her

wholeheartedly.

On her side, she adored showing him her twenty-first century world. She enjoyed how quickly he learned. How deeply he embraced life, even in his odd state. The Viking was a very extraordinary man.

And she was absolutely in love with him.

Tears sprouted then. Hollis pulled her head away from Matt's shoulder to keep from leaving tear blotches on his jacket.

His brow furrowed. "What is it, darling?"

"I'm just emotional." She couldn't say she was happy and be truthful. "It's been a weird month."

"Yes it has. I can't argue with that." Matt kissed her forehead. "But tomorrow a new year begins, and there are so many possibilities ahead."

Sveyn turned around and looked at her. His expression was somber, his eyes full of love—and pain.

"Yes," Hollis whispered.

And so many impossibilities.

•

•

•

Chapter
thirty three

•

Friday
January 1

Except for Christmas night, Hollis had slept alone in her own bed since Matt arrived in Phoenix. Last night, however, she almost caved.

"Whatever you feel for the man, and whatever your shared past, you must not give too much of yourself too quickly," Sveyn warned. "Or you will not be able to discern his motive for returning to you."

"I know," Hollis grumbled as she tumbled into bed wearing her slip and strapless bra.

"Finish changing," Sveyn chastised. "Or you will not be comfortable."

Hollis groaned and sat up. "You're annoying."

"That is why you love me."

"No. It's in spite of that." Hollis stood, her head spinning from the champagne. She stripped the garments off and let them fall to the floor. "Happy?"

Sveyn's intense gaze traveled slowly over her skin making it pucker with pleasure. "Very."

With a groan of frustration, Hollis fell back into bed and covered herself to her armpits. Then she punched her pillow, plopped her head on it, and closed her eyes.

"Goodnight."

After a moment, she added. "Don't think about me."

Sveyn didn't respond, so she opened one eye. He was not in the room. Even so, Hollis knew he heard her.

This morning she awoke with a dull ache in the back of her head, and a sharper one in the front.

Damn champagne.

Gets me every time.

New Year's Day was dedicated to football in America, and Hollis couldn't care less. Matt was all excited because the University of Wisconsin Badgers were playing in the Fiesta Bowl and he scored a pair of tickets. Hollis declined to go, so he invited George Oswald to join him.

In retaliation, Stevie was coming over later to work on wedding stuff.

"Okay, she's not actually coming here to punish me," Hollis admitted after her shower. "But weddings aren't my favorite thing."

Sveyn sat on her bathroom counter and leaned against the mirror. "I have not attended a wedding for over a century. I admit I am curious."

"Well, this won't be typical by any stretch of the imagination." Hollis combed out her wet curls. "Being in costume and on a public stage is not normal."

"Will you wear the yellow dress again?"

Hollis paused. "Maybe. I'll ask."

Sveyn smiled. "You were exceptionally beautiful in that gown."

"Thank you." Hollis's mood lifted at the Viking's words. She put her comb in the drawer and looked at the man. "If Matt knew about you, what do you think he'd say?"

An airless laugh burst from Sveyn's chest. "He *will* know about me after the *Ghost Myth* program is shown on the television."

Hollis startled. "That's true. I hadn't thought about it."

Sveyn lifted one shoulder. "What you tell him after that is your decision."

"Like how you're with me all the time, even when I'm naked?" Hollis teased. "Or that you've made love to me all over Europe in my dreams?"

Sveyn's head fell back and he roared his laughter.

Hollis grinned. "Maybe I won't tell him that."

Sveyn wiped his eyes. "Perhaps not. But after Wednesday night, you will have to tell him something. Especially if you choose to remain with him."

"Yeah, you're right." Hollis walked to her closet. "I'll decide after he sees the show. No sense in stoking a fire too soon."

Stevie arrived at one, just as she said. When Hollis opened the door, her welcoming smile faded when she saw Stevie's stark expression.

"Call Detective Campbell, Hollis. There's a package on the hood of your car."

*****

"Haven't you found out anything yet?" Hollis asked the cop. "Anything at all?"

The detective nodded. "We know how the cats died. We know that they are feral—meaning they are roaming around various neighborhoods without owners."

At least there's that.

"We also know that each package is put together by different person, because none of the fingerprints are the same. And, none of those prints are in the system."

"What about the tags?" Stevie asked.

"Different handwriting and different pens."

Hollis blew a sigh of frustration. "So the mastermind, if you will, is somehow convincing random people to suffocate feral cats, wrap them in white tissue paper, tie a label around their necks, put them in a cardboard box, and leave them somewhere?"

Campbell shrugged. "That's about the size of it."

"And that Hollis is the focus of these weird—threats?" Stevie added. "Is that what they are?"

"With the numbered labels it does appear that, unless Ms. McKenna stops doing whatever it is that offends the perpetrator, she will eventually be the target."

Hollis folded her arms over her chest. "And what I'm doing is either reconnecting with Suzan Wallace's husband, or dabbling in the occult with the spiritualists at the museum?"

Campbell nodded. "Possibly."

Stevie elbowed Hollis. "Don't forget what George said."

The detective's attention focused on Stevie like a gunsight. "George Oswald?"

"Yes. My fiancé. And Hollis's lawyer."

"For the civil lawsuit against Everett Sage." His pinpoint gaze shifted to Hollis. "I spoke to Mr. Oswald. He seemed the believe Sage might be orchestrating this from prison."

Hollis's gaze jumped from the detective to Stevie and back. "And?"

"We have a trace on all of his communications."

Stevie leaned forward. "Is he in solitary confinement?"

Campbell closed his notebook. "He will be, starting today."

Hollis' pulse surged. "What should I do?"

The detective stood to leave. "You could send Mr. Wallace back to Wisconsin and you could cancel the séances at the museum."

Hollis's shoulders slumped. "Those aren't great options."

The corner of his mouth curved. "You didn't ask for great options."

"If you did, you would know if it's Sage," Stevie offered.

Hollis shook her head. "The civil trial is in six days. There's hardly time to stop that train."

"At least cancel Monday's séance," Stevie urged.

"All right." Hollis drew a deep breath and rose to her feet. "Should I ask Matt to tell Suzan he's coming back to her?"

Campbell walked to the front door. "If you think it's her, that might not be a bad idea."

*****

"It's not Suzan. Trust me." Matt's tone was hot enough to fry her phone. "And I'm not going to toy with her emotions by giving her false hope!"

Hollis clenched her free hand. "I respect that, Matt. I'm only telling you what the detective said."

"Well, he's wrong. I mean, come on. You know Suzan."

Hollis's jaw dropped. "I *know* Suzan?"

Hollis heard a whispered *shit*. "She was at Jon and Cyndi's wedding."

"At?" Hollis prodded. "Or in?"

"In," he admitted.

"Cyndi's cousin? The maid of honor? Dammit, Matt!" Hollis dragged a hand through her hair. "*Her?*"

His silence was his affirmation.

Hollis hung up.

"So you know his wife?" Sveyn asked as Hollis's phone rang.

"I'm acquainted with her," Hollis said and rejected Matt's call.

"Do you believe her to be capable of these abominations?"

"I don't know. You can't tell by looking at someone." Hollis rejected the next call and turned off the ringer. "But she was a skinny thing with big eyes and amazing cheekbones."

Bitch.

Sveyn pointed at Hollis's vibrating phone. "Are you going to speak with him?"

She rejected the call. "Not yet. I'm too angry."

"Might you tell him that?"

Good idea.

Hollis answered the next call. "Matt, I'm livid. I think it's best if we don't talk right now." She hung up.

Hollis and Sveyn stared at the phone, waiting.

Nothing.

Hollis looked at Sveyn. "What do you want for dinner?"

*****

Matt arrived at the door an hour later with garlic knots, wine, and roses in hand.

At least they aren't red. Hollis shivered at the memory of Everett Sage's ridiculously large delivery and what it sparked.

"I am so sorry, Hollis."

Hollis walked away from the door, neither inviting Matt in nor telling him to leave. She sat down at the dining table, staring blankly at the detritus of Sveyn's latest tasting binge.

Sveyn seemed to sniff the air. "Garlic knots. Our favorite."

Matt followed. He looked surprised when he saw the table. "Was Stevie hungry?"

"Let's go with that." Hollis started piling the paper plates. "What do you want?"

"To apologize. Again."

Hollis lifted the stack of plates and stood. "What else are you keeping from me, Matt?"

"Nothing."

"And why don't I believe you, do you think?" Hollis stomped into the kitchen and threw away Sveyn's dinner, for lack of a better word for it.

Matt followed her again, silently opening cabinets in some undefined search. "Ah. Here."

He pulled out a plastic pitcher and filled it with water. "Scissors?"

Hollis was too dumbfounded to say anything. She pointed at her junk drawer.

Matt grabbed the scissors, cut the bottoms off the rose stems, and stuck the yellow flowers in the pitcher of water. "There."

Hollis grunted and walked around the raised breakfast bar counter and back to the table, where Sveyn's head was inside the bag of garlic knots. "Really?"

The Viking lifted his head. "Sorry."

"Really, what?" Matt asked coming around to her side, wine and glasses in hand.

"Nothing." Hollis circled a finger next to her head. "Too many thoughts right now."

Matt set the glasses down. "You have every right to be angry at me. But in my defense, until these last few days there was no reason for me to mention it."

Hollis regarded him with narrowed eyes. "What's changed?"

"Everything!" Matt took hold of her arms. "We are back, Hollis. You and me. Like the old days, but better. Like you said last night."

Hollis opened the bag of garlic knots. She claimed one and chewed it slowly, considering her next move.

Sveyn caught her eye. "Hold steady, Hollis."

She nodded as the realization of what she needed to do sank in. She shifted her gaze to Matt. "How much do you know about my guardian angel?"

Sveyn stepped between them. "Are you certain you want to do this?"

Hollis tipped her head in a get-out-of-the-way motion.

Sveyn complied. He wasn't happy.

Matt was understandably thrown for a loop. "You mean the smudge on the videos?"

"Yeah." Hollis sank into a chair and pointed across the table with the remaining half of her garlic knot. "You better sit down."

Matt sat. He watched her with a comically puzzled expression. "Do you have a guardian angel?"

"No. That's just what everybody else called him." Hollis ate the other half of the knot and licked her fingers. "He's actually a Viking who's been caught between life and death since tenseventy."

Sveyn waited.

Matt didn't move. "Wh—what?"

Hollis shrugged. "He just showed up back in September, and has been with me ever since."

"What do you mean *with* you?" Matt's head swiveled as he glanced around the condo's kitchen, dining room, and living room. "Is he here now?"

"Yep."

Matt's hands gripped the edge of the table. "Do you think I'm an idiot?"

"No, Matt." Hollis shook her head. "That's actually one thing that I never thought about you."

"So what's this game?"

Hollis leaned forward. "It's not a game. And on Wednesday night, on *Ghost Myths, Inc.* you are going to see him for yourself."

Matt scoffed, "Those shows are all faked!"

Hollis drew a calming breath. "Well, mine wasn't."

"Come on, Hollis."

"And neither was the fact that this—apparition—set off the motion detectors that saved my life." Hollis shrugged. "That's how he got the nickname, by the way."

"He does not believe you, Hollis," Sveyn observed. "If you truly wish him to, then you must tell him that Stevie has seen me."

Hollis stopped herself from responding to Sveyn. One step at a time on this road veering towards crazytown.

"If you don't believe me—or the cameras—then ask Stevie. She's seen him."

•

•

•

Chapter
thirty four

•

Wednesday
January 6

Matt hadn't been around much the last few days, but he promised to come to the museum to watch the special public showing of Hollis's episode on *Ghost Myths, Inc.* at nine o'clock that night.

He did, however, call her on Monday night with the news that Suzan had been visited by one of Milwaukee's finest asking questions about the Dead Cat Threats.

Suzan went as ballistic, just as Hollis predicted.

And she took her fury out on Matt, who tried very hard not to torpedo his burgeoning reconnection with Hollis while asking her to please call off the dogs.

Hollis had no sympathy for the beautiful, rich, skinny man-stealer. "If she's innocent—"

"She is!" he barked.

"Then it's over, Matt. Let it go. I don't care how mad she is at me, or how much she hates me." Hollis said the next words slowly and deliberately. "We were never going to be friends. In case that was your hope."

"I know," Matt groused.

Dead cat number five was at Hollis's front door on Tuesday morning. She now had a beat officer assigned to protect her, thanks to both Detective Campbell's diligence in the case, and her hysterical barrage of tears that morning.

"This person knows where I w—work! And wh—where I live! And where my b—boyfriend lives!" she wailed. Her breath was coming in those uncontrollable gasps that happen when somebody cries too hard. "He's g—going to k—kill meeee!"

The detective actually called 9-1-1 because she was hyperventilating so bad and nearly passed out.

And though the paramedics were calendar-worthy, and her breathing was back under control, Hollis was still too shaken to drive. She called Stevie to come pick her up for work.

Sveyn offered what help he could. "I'll stand guard over you, Hollis. I promise to alert you if anyone suspicious approaches."

That actually made her feel better than the beat cop outside, because the perpetrator couldn't tell he was being watched or hear Sveyn if he shouted a warning.

Stevie carried a cup of hot chocolate into Hollis's office. "Are you ready for the show tonight?"

"As ready as I can be." Hollis accepted the steaming cup. "Has Matt talked to you this week?"

"No. Why?" Stevie sipped her drink.

"I want you to be prepared tonight."

The cup lowered. "For what?"

"I told him about Sveyn."

"What?" Stevie set her cup on Hollis's desk so quickly that some chocolate spilled over the rim. "Why would you do such a crazy thing?"

Hollis handed her tissues to wipe up the spill. "If—and it's a big if right now—we end up back together, and Sveyn doesn't manifest forward, then the three of us will have to find a way to coexist. At least for a while."

Stevie looked horrified. "He'll be there? Even if you get married?"

Hollis shuddered at the thought of having sex with Matt with Sveyn hearing her every orgasmic utterance. "It's possible."

Stevie finished cleaning the spill and tossed the tissues in the trash. "So what'd he say?"

"He didn't believe me, of course. He thought I was trying to play him." Hollis blew on her chocolate.

"As would any normal person."

"Right." Hollis flashed an awkward grin. "Which is why I told him you've seen Sveyn."

The horrified look was back. "You threw me under the Viking bus?"

"Um… yeah."

"Sveyn, do you hear this?" Stevie called over her shoulder.

"I do," he answered.

"And should I be mad?" she continued.

"Probably not."

Stevie leapt out of her chair.

"Oh my *god!*" She started walking in a tight circle, shaking her hands like she touched something hot. "Oh my god, Hollis."

"What?" Hollis stood. "What happened?"

Stevie stopped and faced Hollis. "I heard him. I heard him answer me."

Hollis glanced at Sveyn who looked as shocked as Stevie. "What did he say?"

"He said I do and probably not."

Sveyn stepped forward. "Can you hear me now?"

Stevie turned toward the apparition. "I can hear mumbling. Like you're under water."

Hollis dropped back into her chair. "What. The hell. Is going. On."

*****

Mr. Benton insisted that Hollis sit at one end of the front row. "So everyone can see you."

She made Matt sit at the actual end so she could have him on one side and Stevie on the other. "He's too tall," she said when Benton questioned her. "People can't see around him."

The general manager nodded. "Good thinking."

There were fifty chairs set up facing a huge screen. A projector would cast the cable show in glorious six-foot by ten-foot splendor.

In addition to Benton and Miranda, Tony Samoa and his wife Carmen were there, plus Tom and the two other interns who helped clear out the hoard. George Oswald sat on Stevie's far side, holding her hand.

"Don't be scared," he said. "I'm right here."

Stevie flashed a nervous smile.

The rest of the chairs were filled with museum employees and volunteers—plus the three ladies whose séance was cancelled on Monday at Detective Campbell's suggestion.

Hollis sat still staring straight forward. She had no idea what to expect from Jason and his crew, and hoped she didn't look like a crazy fool.

When the program started, the lights were lowered and all eyes were fixed on the screen or her. She thought she could actually feel the stares.

*****

When the show ended an hour later, no one moved. Or spoke. The stunned silence in that space was scarier than the image of the tall, bearded ghost answering Jason's questions by raising his hands.

Benton cleared his throat and stood. "Would anyone like to ask Ms. McKenna a question?"

Oh no no no, please not that.

Benton held out a hand and motioned for Hollis to join him.

Crap.

Hollis rose and walked to the front of the stunned crowd.

Tony Samoa stood up first.

"You said you couldn't see him. Is that true?"

"What I have seen didn't look like the image on that camera," she hedged.

Tony pinned her with a skeptical gaze. "So what have you seen?"

Crap crap crap.

How should she answer that? And why didn't she think this through earlier?

Here goes. "I think a better description is that I'm aware of his presence. I felt him in the storeroom with me when he set off the motion detectors."

"Is he an angel?" one woman called out.

"No."

"Is he a demon then?" another countered.

"If he was, why would he do good?" Hollis challenged. "We had an exorcism last week, and nothing—" She corrected herself, "No beings responded. So no. He's not a demon."

Tony sank back into his seat as other shouted out questions less politely.

"How do you know he's not an angel?"

Hollis looked in Sveyn's direction.

"Tell them I am."

Hollis dropped her gaze to the floor, then returned it to her audience. "I don't know for sure," she admitted. "I guess he could be an angel."

"Is he here now?" one of the séance ladies asked.

Hollis told a truth. "I'm afraid I can't answer that."

*****

Matt remained in his seat until everyone but Hollis, Stevie, and George were the only ones in the museum and the front doors to the museum were locked. His expression looked like he was seriously doubting his own sanity.

And hers, to be honest.

"If you were telling the truth, and that thing on the screen is

real" he murmured, "why didn't you tell everyone the same story
you told me?"

Stevie grabbed George's hand. "She's protecting him. The
Viking apparition."

Matt's gaze slice to hers. "Hollis said you've seen him."

George looked at Stevie, clearly surprised by that bit of
news. "You have?"

Hollis saw Stevie's grip on George's hand tighten. "I've
gotten glimpses."

George looked stricken. "Why didn't you tell me?"

Hollis thought her petite friend was going to cry. "I didn't
know how."

Clearly it was time to set the story straight. Hollis swung a
chair around to face Matt, and motioned for George and Stevie to
do the same.

"I'll tell you everything under strictest confidence," she
offered. "But you are all sworn to secrecy. And if any of you
speaks of this to anyone, at all, at any time, I'll swear you are a
liar and just making things up for monetary gain. Is that clear?"

Three heads nodded, with each facial expression displaying a
different position on the bullshit scale.

When Hollis finished her tale, however, Stevie was smiling
triumphantly. George was scratching his head, looking as if he
was replaying Hollis's testimony and not finding any loopholes.

Matt's expression was the hardest to read. Incredulous and
sorrowful seemed the best descriptors.

"Matt?" Hollis took one of his hands. "Say something."

"I didn't believe you."

"I know."

"I didn't trust you." His expression twisted. "You, Hollis.
The most honest person I've ever known. I didn't trust what you
were saying. I thought you were—I don't even know what."

"Seeking revenge?" Hollis posited. "Trying to make a fool
of you, like you made a fool of me?"

Matt looked like he was going to cry. "You would never do
something like that, though. Would you?"

Hollis wrinkled her nose. "I have to confess, I've had a lot of mean thoughts."

Matt squeezed her hand. "But you didn't act on them. That's not who you are."

"I have a question." George turned to Stevie. "You admit you've seen this Sveyn guy?"

"Yes." Stevie's gaze cut to Hollis and back to George. "And… I heard him."

"What?" Matt perked up. "When?"

"This afternoon." Stevie looked to Hollis for help. "It started with strong emotions on Sveyn's side…"

Hollis took the hint and explained their theory that emotion made Sveyn more present in the real world. "That's how he tripped the detectors."

She decided not to mention that he could also touch, smell, and taste with increasing intensity each day. That was a mystery neither she nor the Viking could explain.

"This is crazy." Matt threw up his hands. "I know it is. But I have to find a way to believe it."

Sveyn had been sitting sideways in a chair several feet away this whole time, leaning his elbow on the back of his chair. The initial fear on his face had turned to fascination as—for the first time since his transformation in ten-seventy—people he had not manifested to were accepting his presence.

"Hollis?" he said.

Hollis hesitated, then decided to answer him. *Go Viking or go home.*

She turned to face Sveyn. "What?"

Her three companions all straightened in their seats.

"I have been thinking about this, and I believe that once Stevie experienced my presence, that made it easier for her to do so again."

"Ooh…" Hollis nodded. "You might be right."

Matt touched her arm. "What? Who's right?"

Hollis repeated the Viking's words.

Stevie got very excited. "I hope so, Sveyn!"

He chuckled. "As I do, Stevie."

Stevie stood and turned in Sveyn's direction. She waved at

the seemingly empty chairs.

"Do you see him?" Hollis asked.

"Nope." Stevie sat back down grinning like a lizard in the sun. "But I heard my name."

Hollis's phone rang.

"Are you expecting a call?" Matt's brow lowered. "Is it the captain?"

Hollis shook her head and answered, "Hello?"

"Ms. McKenna, this is Officer Howard. Are you still inside the building?"

"Yes, I'm sorry, Officer." She jumped to her feet and motioned for the trio to stand up and follow her quickly. Stevie turned off lights as they hurried passed the switches. "We're on our way out now. Coming out through the back door."

"Great. I have good news when you get here."

"You do?"

"Yes, ma'am. We apprehended a young man with a suspicious package near your car. I want to see if you recognize him before we take him to the station."

•

•

•

Chapter
thirty five

•

Sadly, she didn't.

The man was in his mid-thirties. His thin brown hair was in a ponytail that reached halfway down his back. Officer Howard lifted the box and folded back the tissue paper to expose what they all expected: a dead cat with a tag tied around its neck.

Number six.

"Were you paid to do this?" Howard asked.

The man gave him a tight-lipped glare.

Howard shined his flashlight on Hollis. "Do you know this woman?"

A glimmer of surprise flicked over the man's expression. He shook his head.

"Then why did you kill a cat and deliver it to her?"

Any communication from the perpetrator, no matter how slight, had retreated once again behind the defiant glare.

"Put him in the car," Officer Howard barked to his partner.

He turned to Hollis. "At least we've caught one of them. Maybe he'll shed some light on this bizarre case."

Hollis smiled. "Thank you, Officer. I do appreciate your help."

Howard touched the brim of his hat. "To protect and serve, ma'am."

The quartet, plus Sveyn, waited in place until the squad car pulled out of the parking lot. Then George turned to Hollis.

"Sage's civil trial opens tomorrow at ten. Do you have any questions?"

"He didn't settle, so I have to face him. Right?" The idea twisted Hollis's gut.

George gave her a kind look, clearly visible in the parking lot lights. "A lot of trials go down to the wire before someone caves. I'll be at the courthouse by nine in case Sage's lawyer has talked sense into his client."

"Because settling makes sense?" Matt asked.

"It does," George answered. "Sage pled guilty in the criminal court, and the security footage shows the state in which he left Hollis. Her suffering is demonstrable."

"So why wouldn't he have settled already?" Matt continued.

George shrugged. "He's a tightwad who thinks he can win, I guess."

Matt scowled. "Or he's hoping Hollis backs out rather than face him?"

"There is that possibility," George admitted.

"I'm not going to back out." Hollis looked from George to Matt to Sveyn. "You all will protect me against that ass."

Stevie shivered. "I hate to break up a party, but I'm freezing."

"I'm sorry darling. We can go." George put his arm around Stevie and pulled her close. "Nice to see you again, Matt. See you tomorrow, Hollis."

Matt turned to Hollis. "Can I come over for a little bit?"

Hollis unlocked her car. "Sure."

*****

Hollis heated up leftover pizza while Matt poured an old vine red zinfandel. They took the snack to the coffee table.

Matt sat on the couch. "Is he here?"

"In the condo? Yeah. But not in this room." Hollis lifted a slice of pizza. "He's very good about giving us privacy."

"Hmm." Matt sipped his wine, then twisted to face Hollis more directly. "I have to tell you something."

Hollis froze mid-chew. "What?" she asked past the cheese and pepperoni.

"When I showed up at the opening, I expected so see the Hollis I knew two, three years ago. But I was surprised."

This wasn't good. "How?"

"The girl I knew back then never could have done what you've done here."

Hollis was so surprised she didn't know how to respond. She took a drink of wine to empty her mouth before she asked Matt, "Could you explain what you mean by that?

He nodded. "You moved halfway across the country, took on this massive project, and managed to create a fantastic display."

Hollis's brow lowered. "Matt. That's what my degree is in. That was my job in Milwaukee. And in Chicago."

"I know but—"

"So either you never understood my degree, or my job, or you didn't think I was capable?"

Matt squirmed. "No. That's not what I meant at all!"

"Then back that truck up and try again." Hollis took a big bite of pizza and glared at him.

Matt ran his fingers through his hair. "Hollis, you've changed. You seem to have come into yourself. Finally."

That was better. "Go on."

"When we were together, you always deferred to me. You were always so generous and sweet."

"And I'm not generous or sweet anymore?"

"No, you absolutely are!" Matt looked panicked. "But the other side of your personality has blossomed. The confident side. The side that tells the world to sit up and take notice."

When Hollis thought about it, she realized that she agreed with Matt. The transition has been so gradual she hadn't realized it was happening. She slid her gaze back to his.

"Why is that, do you think?" Hollis had a good idea and was curious to see if Matt came to the same conclusion.

"Because of me."

Yep. He did. "Explain."

"I was too strong of a personality. I steamrollered you."

That's not how Hollis would have defined it. "I disagree, Matt. I think you were a self-centered a person who considered me less important."

Matt flinched. "Suzan says I'm self-centered."

"We all are to some extent," Hollis admitted. "But I pushed my wants down and—what did you call it?—deferred to you." She leaned forward. "Because I was in love with you."

"But you aren't doing that now."

Hollis leaned back again. "Nope."

Matt's expression shifted. "I can't tell you how sexy that makes you."

That was unexpected. "You think I'm sexier now than when we were together?"

"I do."

Hollis finished her second slice of pizza without speaking. This conversation was very revealing, partly because she wasn't pulling any punches. If Matt wanted something between them to continue she couldn't hold back any more.

"Can I say something else?" he asked.

"Sure." *What now?*

"I'm going so far as to say that my leaving you was good for you."

Hollis set her wine glass down before she wasted the delicious zinfandel all over his face. "You're saying that you think that your running off with Suzan was *good* for me?"

"In a roundabout way, yes." Matt waved a hand from her head to her feet. "Look at what you've turned into, Holl. You're a smart, beautiful, and articulate media sensation who's captured the world's attention because of what you accomplished."

Hollis's ego really enjoyed that sentence in spite of the slam that led into it, but she didn't want to agree with Matt's contention that, in an admittedly oblique way, he left her for her own good.

Yet the resultant changes he described were accurate. She was much more herself now than she had ever been in her life.

"What about you, Matt?" Hollis pressed. "What have you learned?"

He thought about that for a minute. "I've learned that I was actually looking for the exact woman that I was stopping you from becoming."

Hollis stared at him. "And you thought Suzan was that woman?"

"I did. But she wasn't you. Obviously." Matt smiled sadly. "And then I saw you on YouTube, and realized that you really were right for me all along. I guess I had to loosen my grip so you could blossom."

"Why did you hold me so tight, Matt?" Hollis whispered.

"Because I was terrified I'd lose you." He snorted softly. "And then I gave you up for not being what I wanted, even though I was the one who held you back."

*****

Sex with Matt was still not an option at this point. In spite of his revelations about himself and her, Hollis couldn't sleep with him yet. She needed something more definite from him. A commitment of some sort. Filing for divorce from Suzan was a very good start, but it was still only a start.

That didn't stop her from enjoying his body.

Matt was always an amazing kisser, and he knew how to kiss her where it counted. She used her hands and her mouth on him as well, until both of them sprawled half-dressed on her couch, panting in post-pleasure bliss.

Hollis was stabbed with guilt, though, as images from her dreams with Sveyn popped annoyingly to mind. She made an effort to be quiet during her play with Matt, knowing that Sveyn would hear every utterance of her arousal.

And she was definitely aroused. Having a hot, three-dimensional, and solid man caressing and stimulating her most sensitive areas beat the snot out of dream sex. Her body quivered and flushed with her peak like it never did in her sleep.

"I love you, Hollis," Matt whispered into her tousled curls.

Hollis hesitated, wondering if her words were true but saying them anyway. "I love you, too, Matt."

Thursday
January 7

Hollis sent Matt home last night, using today's civil trial as her excuse. "I really need to focus, Matt, and prepare myself to see that man again."

"Do you want me to come with you?" he asked.

That was sweet. "No. Thank you, though. I really want to do this by myself."

With Sveyn.

Hollis faced the Viking as soon as Matt left. "Don't judge me."

Sveyn looked sad and resigned. "I cannot hold anything against you, Hollis. As much as I do love you, and ache to be with you, I cannot give you what a living man can."

Remembering the stricken look on his face brought tears to her eyes now and she wiped them away as she pulled into the parking garage for the court.

"Will you stay where I can see you?" she asked the Viking for the third time.

"Of course, Hollis." He moved into her line of sight. "Try to relax. This man cannot hurt you any longer."

Right.

She paused to take a calming breath and then got out of the car.

Her assigned courtroom was on the fifth floor. As she rode the elevator, she wondered why the people sharing the space with her were there. Were they the good guys or the bad guys?

The doors opened to a hallway. Marble floors and wood-trimmed doorways gave weight to her surroundings. She stepped out and looked to the left, and to the right, searching for George Oswald.

A man in a dark blue uniform approached her. He put out his hand to keep the elevator doors from closing behind her. "Hollis McKenna?"

"Yes," she answered.

He reached into his jacket and pulled out a dead cat. "You are running out of lives."

Hollis screamed.

The man dropped the cat and leapt past her into the elevator. The doors closed.

As everyone turned to look in her direction Hollis ran away from the carcass, not really thinking about where she was going; just that she needed to put distance between her and it. She ran straight into George.

He grabbed her arms. "Hollis!"

She jerked back. "He threw a dead cat at me!"

Officers were already talking on walkie-talkies, gathering up the body, and shooing people away.

A police officer—a real one judging by the equipment strapped to his uniform—stepped between her and the brief crime scene. "Come with me, please."

George let go of one of her arms, but steered her with the other. It was a good thing. Her knees were threatening to drop her.

The two men hurried her into a small room, presumably used for lawyer-client discussions, and closed the door. Someone had the forethought to stock the room with water and cups.

The policeman poured Hollis a drink while she sat down. "Tell me what happened."

Hollis gulped the water, the cup shaking in her hand.

Sveyn sat in the chair beside hers. "I will tell you if you leave anything out," he said.

Thank you. "I got off the elevator. A man in a navy blue

uniform came up to me, and he asked if I was Hollis McKenna."

"And he stopped the doors from closing," Sveyn prompted.

Right. "He stuck out his arm so the elevator wouldn't close. Then he pulled the dead cat from inside his jacket."

"Did he say anything else?" The policeman was writing quickly and didn't look at her.

"Yes. He said I was running out of lives." She glanced at Sveyn. He nodded. "Then he dropped the cat on the floor and jumped in the elevator."

"Was there a tag tied around the cat's neck?" George asked.

Hollis couldn't remember seeing one. "I…"

"Yes," Sveyn said. "It had the number seven on it."

Hollis looked at the attorney. "I think it had the number seven on it."

George turned to the officer and gave him a brief explanation of the Dead Cat Threats. Then he spoke to Hollis. "Detective Campbell called me half an hour ago. He should be here now. I'm going to call him and tell him where we are."

"Okay."

George walked to a corner of the room to make the call while the officer taking her statement laid a piece of paper in front of her. "Do you have anything to add to this account?"

Hollis read the handwritten transcript. "Just that I ran away."

"Is it important that you screamed?" Sveyn asked.

"I did scream when he pulled the cat from his jacket." She looked up at the cop. "Does that matter?"

"Probably not, but I'll add it. Could you sign at the bottom?"

Chapter Thirty Six

George got off the phone and walked to the door. He opened it and stepped halfway out. "In here."

When he re-entered the room Detective Campbell was right behind him. Campbell introduced himself to the responding police officer and read over his account of Hollis's statement.

"Did he get away?" Hollis asked when the detective looked up from the paper. "Do you know?"

"I do know." Campbell flashed a grin. "And no, he did not."

"Thank goodness." Hollis shuddered. "Hopefully you can put a stop to this crap."

The responding officer excused himself to file his report, promising the detective he would get a copy.

George motioned for Campbell to sit down. "What do you have for us?"

The detective pulled out his trusty notebook. "The man arrested at the museum last night turned out to have an outstanding warrant for theft. He was quite happy to trade information for a plea deal."

"How much information?" George asked.

"Enough for us to trace other activity from the instigator." Campbell looked at Hollis. "He was very clever, as it turns out. And he had the cash to make things happen."

"Everett Sage," she whispered.

"Yes."

George looked at his watch. "It's nine-thirty. Our case is scheduled for ten. If you can give me a quick rundown, I'll talk to his lawyer once more before we convene."

"Sure thing. Long story short, he used Gypsies. Hired one man at a time to kill and wrap a cat. Hired different men to drive them to the drops, and others to pick them up after the boxes were delivered. Payment was in cash, handed over by the drop-off driver."

Hollis shook her head in disbelief. "Gypsies? Really? Those two guys I saw were dressed normally."

Campbell gave her a stern look. "There is a large Gypsy population in Maricopa County, and they dress like the rest of us. They just don't live like the rest of us."

"How do you mean?" George asked.

"They live outside society. No documentation, no permanent residences, no jobs."

"Then how—oh!" Hollis realized the answer was right in front of her. "So a cash job, no matter how odd, would be gladly accepted."

Campbell nodded. "And he paid a thousand dollars for each person involved in each drop."

"Three thousand dollars, times seven drops?" Hollis stared at George. "That's twenty-one thousand dollars as of today!"

George addressed the detective. "Has Sage been charged?"

"Yes. Filed this morning." Campbell referred back to his notebook. "Harrassment. Animal cruelty—though that might not stick, since he didn't kill the cats himself—and threats on Ms. McKenna's life."

George's brow pinched. "Those charges are admittedly weak, since Sage was one step removed from actually committing the acts, but the fact that they have been filed should give me what I need." He stood. "Wish me luck."

"What should I do?" Hollis asked.

"Wait here." George winked. "Hopefully the next thing that happens is we'll go out to lunch and celebrate."

*****

"I still can't believe it." Hollis stared at her margarita. "He settled for what you said he would, George."

"Nine hundred thousand." He lifted his glass, drawing Hollis's gaze. "And you, my dear, will have seven hundred thousand dollars delivered in a cashier's check by tomorrow at five."

"And I didn't have to face the pompous ass." Hollis grinned. "Even better."

Matt appeared at the restaurant's door with Stevie. George waved them over. At eleven in the morning, the restaurant wasn't crowded yet.

"Oh my gosh, Hollis!" Stevie gave George a quick kiss on the cheek, then slid next to her in the booth. "The museum has gone *crazy* this morning!"

With an apologetic glance at Sveyn, Hollis patted the seat on her other side. The Viking moved to make room for Matt. "What's going on?" she asked.

"That *Ghost Myths* show last night was covered on all four local news casts, and the line at the door this morning was longer than when the tapes of Sveyn were posted."

"Really?" Hollis looked at Matt. "I had no idea so many people watched that show."

He shrugged. "Maybe not much happens in Phoenix."

Though the city wasn't her official home, that comment stung. Before she could think of an appropriately caustic remark, Stevie spoke again.

"So spill. All George would say was that Sage settled."

With George's prompting, Hollis told Stevie and Matt about the morning's Dead Cat Threat, the Gypsies, and the settlement.

"Your life is definitely not boring." Stevie lifted her drink.

"Cheers to the end of a bunch of *ick*."

"I'll drink to that!" Hollis clunked her heavy glass against Stevie's.

"You'll want to invest that money, Hollis," George warned. "Let me connect you with my broker."

Hollis laughed for the first time that day. "I'm going to buy a new car, first. The broker can have the rest."

"You could buy a house," Stevie suggested. "That's good investment."

Hollis nodded and sipped her margarita. *If I knew where I was going to live it would be.*

Matt smiled at her. "I'm so proud of you."

"Thanks."

Hollis looked at Sveyn. He was beaming at her.

*****

Matt insisted on a candlelight dinner for the two of them that night. He even managed a private corner in an exclusive boutique restaurant, tucked away from people who were occasionally recognizing her that afternoon.

He held her chair, and Hollis sat at the beautifully appointed table. "Thank you."

"I took the liberty of ordering the food and wine pairings," he said as he took his seat at her side. "Pretend we're at my house and I cooked."

"You always were a better cook than me," Hollis admitted. "I'm afraid I haven't gotten any better."

Mann grinned. "I figured that when I looked in your fridge and saw nothing but condiments and beverages."

Hollis put up her hands in surrender. "If we're going to do this, then full disclosure is required. Don't you agree?"

"I do."

Hollis smiled. "I like the sound of that."

A waiter came and poured their first wine. "Please enjoy. Your hors d'oeuvres will be out shortly."

Matt lifted his glass. "To the most beautiful girlfriend a man could imagine."

Hollis blinked slowly. "Is that what I am?"

"I hope so." He clinked his glass against hers. "If you'll have me."

Hollis tasted the wine instead of answering. Her eyes widened. "Matt, this is amazing."

"I'm glad you like it. An amazing woman deserves an amazing experience."

She considered Matt across the table. His incredible gold-streaked eyes, trim six-foot frame, perfectly tailored shirt and pants, spicy aftershave. He made her heart ache with love.

This is what I always wanted.

And now, he was here.

Friday
January 8

Hollis let herself into the museum offices early. She wanted to avoid being seen, planning to hide out in her office for the majority of the day.

Tomorrow was the opening of the Renaissance Faire east of Phoenix, and all she needed to do was make it through today without too much drama. Tomorrow she would use the mindless and distracting event with friends as a cushion, before she dealt with the trauma and the money which Everett Sage's invasion of her life brought with it.

Things could be worse.

Hollis smiled.

Matt had been so nice to her, that she told Stevie to hold off on the text messages from Captain Hart. Based on Matt's occasional references to her imaginary lover, the ruse had done its job. Plus Matt was working hard on winning her back to his side.

Maybe I'll break up with the captain.

"Not yet," she murmured. "Let him squirm."

"Matt?" Sveyn asked. "How is he squirming?"

"Because of the captain. My imaginary boyfriend," Hollis answered. Someday she might remember not to talk out loud to herself.

Sveyn smiled. "The captain of your heart."

Hollis opened her email, and began putting out fires and deflecting offers to speak. Her mood plunged when she saw that the requests by various mediums, ghost hunters, and spiritualists had quadrupled overnight.

"Crap." She looked at Sveyn. "Now that we know the Dead Cat Threats had nothing to do with the occult, we don't have a reason to say no."

"But you do not need the extra money any longer," Sveyn pointed out. "You are a rich woman now."

Hollis chuckled. "Not really. You'd be surprised how fast that could be gone."

Miranda appeared in her office doorway. "I saw your car in the parking lot." She looked around. "Who are you talking to?"

Hollis shrugged. "Myself."

"Why?"

"I'm hiding from everyone else."

Miranda laughed. "So Sage settled."

"Yep."

"And you still showed up for work."

"It wasn't the lottery, Miranda. I still *need* to work, and there's plenty of work to be done." Hollis motioned Miranda closer. "Take a look at this."

Hollis leaned back and turned the monitor so Miranda could see all the requests to visit their resident ghost.

"Holy guacamole!" Miranda straightened. "The lines to get in yesterday were crazy."

"Stevie told me." Hollis put the monitor back in place. "I wonder what Benton's going to want to do with all this attention."

Miranda laughed again. "Make money. What else?"

*****

At one o'clock that afternoon, Hollis got her answer.

She sat in front of the General Manager's desk, sipping a diet cola, and bracing for whatever he was about to throw at her.

"When the Arizona History and Cultural Museum first received word of Ezra Kensington's bequest, we were overwhelmed to be honest." Benton spread his hands. "We were a museum whose mission statement focused exclusively on these lands and these territories."

"Yes, sir." Hollis supposed that was the expected response to the old news.

"But the Board took a look at the money, and the possibilities in the man's collection, and we rewrote our mission statement so that we could accept his most generous donation."

Again, none of this was new. "That was very forward thinking of you, sir."

Compliments never hurt.

He accepted the words as his due and continued, "Then we embarked on a search for the right Lead Collector to handle the massive amount of things that needed to be sorted, attributed, and catalogued."

"Stevie Phillips has been indispensable, Mr. Benton."

The GM looked surprised. "I was talking about you."

Hollis gave a little nod. "I know. But I don't work alone."

She had obviously thrown Benton off script. "No, of course not…"

"And I saw the position posted when I was working in Chicago," Hollis prompted.

"Yes. Yes! And while your references were impressive, your interview was unmatched." Benton smiled. "I hate to use a cliché, especially one so appropriate to our business, but…"

The rest is history.

"…the rest is history."

Hollis smiled. "Yes, it is sir."

Benton shifted in his chair and his expression grew more serious. "The question which faces us now is, what does the future hold?"

"For the museum?"

"Yes." Benton steepled his fingers. "And for you."

"I don't have any plans that go beyond February twenty-eighth," Hollis admitted. "That's the end of my contract here."

"I believe we need to make some plans," Benton said smoothly. "Don't you?"

"I am very open to that, sir," Hollis replied. "As long as my compensation reflects my permanent status."

One of Benton's brows lifted. "How much are we talking about?"

Now Hollis shifted in her seat. "I don't know if you've had a chance to check the requests for ghost visits, sir, but they had quadrupled by this morning."

"That's good news." He paused. "Isn't it?"

"It is, if we continue to charge what we have been." Now Hollis steepled her fingers. "The problem arises because there are only forty hours in my work week, so in order to fulfill all the requests, I would have to work an additional four hours a day."

Benton's face smoothed with understanding, then twisted in question. "What do you propose, Ms. McKenna?"

"I propose to work forty hours a week as a salaried employee, and those specific hours will flex depending on how many paying visitors we book and how many hours they buy of the museum's time."

"So we still charge them, but the museum keeps the money?" Benton clarified.

"Yes."

Benton was confused. "But you lose the extra one hundred dollars per hour that way."

"I received a substantial judgment yesterday from my civil suit against Everett Sage." Hollis gave the GM a patient smile. "Mr. Benton, I don't need that extra money anymore."

"Oh." Benton looked pleased. "Excellent."

Hollis shrugged. "And of course, with my time in such high demand, I'll need additional help to manage the Kensington collection."

His smile faded. "What sort of help?"

"I want you use the extra money to hire Tom the intern as my full-time assistant Collector." Hollis kept talking, not giving Benton a chance to argue. "He's capable, smart, and knows a ton about European history. I can trust him to take some of my load and perform well."

Benton gave a non-committal nod. "I'll take that suggestion under advisement, Ms. McKenna."

Hollis flashed her most dazzling smile. "I'm glad sir. Because I do like working for you."

As she rose from the chair, she let her happy smile morph to a tentative one. "I'd hate to have to move again so soon. I was really feeling settled in Phoenix."

Benton's email agreeing to her terms arrived in her inbox at five-forty-five that afternoon.

Contract attached.

•

•

•

Chapter
Thirty Seven

•

Saturday
January 9

Though Hollis got exactly what she wanted, she didn't sign the contract just yet. There was still her future with Matt to consider.

If he agreed to move to Phoenix, then she had her dream job nailed down.

And if things went south with him, she still had her dream job nailed down.

But he might want her to move back to Milwaukee with him. Until they talked seriously about their future, Hollis couldn't sign the contract and commit her services to the museum.

Matt had been so kind, so attentive, and so encouraging lately that Hollis was hopeful about their relationship. So hopeful, that she came very close to caving in to his request for full-fledged sex last night.

Until Sveyn reminded her of his presence in the condo. The effect was akin to being dumped with ice water.

"That wasn't an accident," she snipped at him later. "You interrupted us on purpose."

The Viking didn't even look contrite. "Yes. I admit that I did."

"Why?" Hollis glared at him. "Jealous?"

Sveyn glared back. "Of course I am jealous. He is able to give you everything that I deeply desire to, but cannot!"

"And never will be!" she shouted. "Don't you understand that?"

Hollis groaned and spun in a circle of frustration until she faced him again. "Do you really expect me to give up all hope of marriage and children because of you?"

"No!" Sveyn scuttled his hands through his hair, leaving it in unprecedented disarray. Hollis could feel his intense anger like a static charge raising the hairs on her arms. "But as I have said before, this man is not right for you!"

Hollis threw up her hands. "How do you know that?"

"I can feel this." He thumped his chest with a fist, his eyes dark with fury. "In here."

"Feelings? That's it?" Hollis shook her head. "No. You don't know what went on between us before."

"It does not matter."

"Yes it does!" Hollis stomped her foot, a sadly unsatisfying gesture on carpet. "Matt has changed."

"Men don't change," Sveyn growled.

"Yes they do! In today's world they can, and they do!" she cried. "So leave us alone!"

Hollis stormed into her bedroom and slammed the door. She didn't turn on the television either, leaving Sveyn alone with his thoughts and hoping he came to his senses.

When she started to dream about him, her subconscious had the good sense to remember their argument and she rebuffed the Viking's sly advances.

This morning, when she emerged from her bedroom already

dressed for the day, Sveyn waited on the couch. His hands were folded in his lap and he regarded her from beneath a lowered brow.

"I apologize, Hollis." His deep voice was quiet but it vibrated through her chest nonetheless. "Though my intention was to save you from further heartbreak, I perhaps acted inappropriately."

Hollis pinned him with her own gaze. "Perhaps?"

Sveyn gave her a sullen shrug. "I will not interfere again."

Hollis crossed the space between them. "I accept your apology, Sveyn. And I do understand your frustration."

He stood and looked down at her. "I love you, Hollis. More than I can say with words."

She gazed up into his beautiful blue eyes, noting the web of fine lines extending from their corners, the scruff of his beard with a few white hairs sprouting on his chin, and the thick sun-streaked hair resting on his shoulders.

Damn, he's sexy.

Hollis fervently wished he was real. This cosmic prank they had both fallen victim of wasn't amusing in any way.

"You look pretty good for a man born in ten-thirty-six, you know that?" She tried to touch his hair, but her hand moved through it. She let her arm drop to her side. "I don't like fighting with you."

"I do not like it either." He smiled softly. "I promise that I will strive to not provoke you again."

"Thank you." Hollis turned around to pick up her purse and make sure she had the tickets for the Renaissance Fair—and the backstage tour passes.

Sveyn looked over her shoulder. "Tell me about this Faire."

"I've never been there, but it's my understanding that the idea is to present what life might have been like back then." She looked at Sveyn. "Without the filth and the stench, of course."

"Interesting." The Viking looked skeptical. "May I tell you the errors I spot?"

Hollis laughed. "Sure. There will be plenty, I imagine."

A knock on the door prompted her to grab her jacket. She

walked to the condo's front door and paused with her hand on the doorknob and looked back at Sveyn.

"Just remember, this isn't a museum. The point is to have fun. So it's more like a theme park."

"What is a theme park?"

Hollis smiled. "You'll see."

*****

"How far is this place?" Matt asked as the density of the Phoenix area gave way to hilly desert and cactus.

Hollis looked at the map on her phone. "Almost there. It'll be on the right."

Sveyn pointed over her shoulder from the back seat. "There is a sign."

"Oh, there's a sign," Matt echoed the Viking's words.

Matt turned the car onto a dirt road and followed a line of cars into the huge parking lot. It was already more than half full. "Where are we meeting George and Stevie?"

Hollis closed the app and put her phone in her purse. "By the first aid building. She thought the information booth might be too crowded."

Matt steered the car in the direction that the parking attendant directed them. "Sun glasses, do you think?" he asked after he shut off the engine.

Hollis considered the cloudy sky that in any other climate might signal rain. "Probably. Want me to put them in my purse?"

Matt handed her his glasses case and the three of them exited the vehicle. As they approached the courtyard-like entry to the Faire, Sveyn's expression shifted into a broad grin.

Curious as to why, Hollis didn't want to speak to the apparition in front of Matt because it would remind him that they had constant company.

Plus she would look like a crazy woman. There was that.

And while the Bluetooth ruse was would keep others from doubting her sanity, she couldn't claim to have phone calls without Matt wondering who she was talking to all day.

Her only recourse for communicating with the Viking was to give him meaningful looks and hope he understood their point.

She turned away from Matt to look at Sveyn and lifted her brows in question.

"Do you see how the people here are dressed?" he asked.

Hollis nodded as she scanned the costumed actors and attendees.

"There's a costume shop over there." She pointed to one of the stores in the courtyard outside the turnstile-controlled entry points.

Matt shot her a surprised look. "You didn't want to dress up. Did you?"

"No. I was just making an observation." Hollis smiled at him. "But a lot of people get into this, apparently."

She handed the grinning King Henry the Eighth look-alike at the gate her tickets and he welcomed her and Matt with a flourish of his pewter wine cup. "Enter and be jolly, my lord and lady!"

Once inside, Sveyn repeated his question in her ear. "These people are wearing clothes that look like many centuries ago. Do you see this?"

Hollis nodded.

Sveyn strode ahead of her and Matt, then turned to face them, his grin as wide as his arms. "For today, my clothes fit the occasion!"

Hollis smiled. He was right.

The people strolling through the Faire were dressed in fashions from Sveyn's middle-ages through the sixteen hundreds. And leather pants, vest, and a linen shirt fit pretty much all those time periods.

"Looks like anything goes," she said to Matt. "The term 'Renaissance' is apparently fluid."

"Uh, huh." Matt was focused on the map. "Here's the First Aid building." He looked up and pointed. "Right there. Oh, dear."

Stevie and George waited outside the door. And they were both dressed in elaborate costumes. Matt slid his *what the hell* gaze to Hollis.

She elbowed him the ribs.

"Well those certainly aren't Jane Austin Society outfits," Hollis said to the beaming couple for Matt's benefit.

"No, but when we saw the costume shop we couldn't resist renting them for the day," George explained.

"We both just love dressing up in historical clothing." A giggling Stevie did a complete turn and faced them again. "And then—we appreciate our modern conveniences that much more when we take it off."

Hollis didn't look at Matt, afraid his expression might irritate her. "Did you ask anyone about the tour?"

Stevie nodded. "Yes. They said we should meet them at the gate beside the main arena at one."

"Great." Matt seemed to have gotten over his costume-induced shock. "That gives us time to explore. And eat. Who's hungry?"

*****

The grounds of the Renaissance Faire were actually fascinating. All the buildings were permanent structures, built by the shop owners at their own expense.

"We all had to have our products juried in and submit our building plans for approval," explained a woman selling tapestries that were obviously machine-made. "Everything has to look period appropriate."

As a museum's lead collector, Hollis found the idea intriguing. "So historical accuracy is second to convenience and pricing."

"Yep." She winked. "Hey—a gal has to make a living."

Hollis wandered back outside where George and Matt were sipping beers in the shade. "Where's Stevie?"

"Restroom." George flashed a rueful smile. "It'll take a while with that dress."

Sveyn appeared at her side. "Did you know that people live in these little houses?" He pointed to the second story that most of the stores had. "There are apartments on top."

Hollis looked around, noticing for the first time that Sveyn was right—most had viable second levels. "So the shop owners live above their stores, apparently."

"They'd have to. There's nothing else way out here." Matt stood and turned to George. "I want to show Hollis that jewelry store. We'll meet you for the tour."

As he led Hollis away from George, Matt whispered in her ear. "I just wanted some time alone with you."

Hollis smiled. "I wanted time alone with you too, to be honest."

Sveyn stepped back, out of sight. *Thank you.*

"George and Stevie are perfect for each other."

Hollis looked to see if Matt was making a snarky comment. "They are, actually."

Matt nodded, his expression sincere. "Like you and me."

A jolt of joy zinged through her. "You think we're perfect for each other?"

"I always did. And then I wasn't sure," he admitted. "But now I know I was right in the first place."

Though the sentence was awkward, Hollis understood what Matt was trying to say. "I always thought we were right for each other."

He nodded. "I know you did. That's why I was pretty confident when I showed up at the opening."

Hollis stopped walking.

Matt swung around to face her. "What?"

"What were you so confident of?"

Matt stepped closer. "I was confident of what you felt for me two years ago. And you're not a fickle woman, Hollis. When you love, you love with your whole heart."

That answer was more than acceptable. It was perfect. "I love you."

"And I love you." Matt kissed her with enough intent to punctuate his statement. Then he pulled away and stared into her eyes. "I'm so glad I came to Phoenix."

Hollis sighed. "Me, too."

*****

The backstage tour was even more fascinating that the grounds. Behind the historical façade of quaint shops, turkey-legs-and-ale food vendors, and costumed proprietors was a modern world of RVs, laundromats, showers, and trucks.

"Most of the apartments don't have plumbing because of the cost," their guide explained. "So we have facilities back here for our vendors who live here for the two months that the Faire's operating."

Matt pointed to a group of men in modern dress who were throwing a variety of ancient-look implements. "What're they doing?"

"Learning. Practicing." The guide smiled. "Not much opportunity to toss a hammer in our modern world."

"Not one that looks like that, anyway," Matt observed.

Hollis shifted into historian mode. "It was called casting the barre back in King Henry the Eighth's day. The handle is made of a hardwood like oak, and then the stone is strapped onto it. Or in Henry's case, he actually designed cast iron heads for his."

The guide looked surprised. "Right."

Matt leaned in with a smile. "She works at a museum, remember."

"Okay, well." The guide held out one arm. "Let's go this way. We don't want to get too close. Some of those guys are new."

*****

When the tour ended an hour later, George and Stevie headed back inside the Faire. Hollis, however, had made a decision.

"Go on without us. Matt and I need a minute."

"Is everything all right?" Stevie looked worried.

"Everything's fine, Stevie." Hollis took Matt's hand to add weight to her words. "We just need to talk about some plans, and sitting on these benches out here is quieter than inside."

"Oh." Stevie's expression shifted to happily conspiratorial. "You go ahead and talk about those plans."

"And if we don't see you later, I'll see you Monday."

"Don't worry about us. You enjoy your weekend, Hollis." George took his fiancée's arm and winked. "Maybe go car shopping."

Hollis laughed at the joke and walked to a bench under a desert tree that didn't lose its leaves. Matt followed and sat beside her.

"What's up, Hollis?"

"Well..." Her heart was pounding so hard she wondered if Matt could see it beating through her sweater. "I had a meeting with Mr. Benton yesterday." When Matt didn't react, she added, "The general manager of the museum."

He nodded. "Yeah."

Hollis cleared her throat. "We talked about what will happen when my contract expires at the end of February. Turns out, he's pretty impressed with what I've done there."

Matt made a *duh* face. "Of course. And with good reason."

"Thanks. Anyway, I was able to negotiate a pretty sweet deal which caps me at forty hours a week—even with the ghost people."

"Cool."

Hollis hoped for more of a response, but powered on in spite of Matt's lack of enthusiasm. "He's also hiring Tom, the intern, as my full-time assistant."

"Awesome."

Hollis waited to see if Matt would figure out what was on her mind.

When she didn't say anything, he asked, "Is that what you wanted to tell me?"

"Yes. And then I wanted to ask what you thought I should do." *Be more specific, Hollis.* "What we should do, I mean."

He looked confused. "We? It's your job. Your decision."

"What I mean is..." Hollis pulled a steadying breath. "I'll sign the contract if you're willing to relocate to Phoenix. But not if you want me to move back to Milwaukee with you."

•

•

•

Chapter
Thirty Eight

•

Matt looked like she had just hit him with one of those stone hammers. "Hold on, Hollis. Let's back this train up a minute."

Her brow plunged. "Why? What's wrong?"

"I'm—we—aren't ready to make a decision like that."

Hollis shook her head in disbelief. "You're getting a divorce—"

"Which will take months," he interrupted.

She ignored him. "And you came to Phoenix specifically to ask me to get back together with you."

"That's all true," Matt admitted. Beads of sweat formed on his upper lip in spite of the cool and still cloudy day. "But we haven't talked about anything beyond that."

Dread wound its claws around Hollis's heart. "We are now."

"It—it's too soon," he stammered.

"You said you loved me!"

"And I do." Matt jumped to his feet. "But that's a *huge* leap from I love you to who's going to relocate their career halfway across the country!"

Hollis stood as well. "So what *was* your endgame, Matt? Why did you come after me?"

"I wanted things to be like they were before." His tone turned pleading. "Like when we were happy."

"You were happy, Matt," Hollis clarified. "I was waiting."

How could he look confused—was he a complete idiot? "For what?"

"For you to marry me, you ass!" Her hands turned to fists which she ached to use. "To buy a house! To raise a family!"

Matt's mouth flapped but no words came out.

"Say something!"

He looked frantic. "In—in time—"

"Time! *Time?* Are you freaking *kidding* me?" Hollis leapt forward and punched Matt, hitting the arms he threw in front of his face. Then she punched him in the stomach, with all the power of her anger and pain pushing her fist deep into his belly.

He fell to his knees, gasping.

Hollis leaned over and screamed in his ear. "I *never* want to see you again! Ever!"

As she walked away, he called after her. "Do you think the *captain* is gonna marry you?"

Hollis whirled around. "The 'captain' is Sveyn! And you, Matt, are a damned fool!"

*****

Hollis spun back around. "Not a single word out of you Viking—do you understand?"

"I am proud of you."

"I said not a single word and I mean it, damn you." Tears flooded her eyes.

"I am trying to compliment you."

"Well, stop!"

Hollis tried to walk away from Sveyn, but he was always in front of her, blocking her way. She zigged to her left, then to her right. "Get out of my way!"

"No." Sveyn matched her path. "You need to calm down."

"Calm down?" Hollis swiped the gush of tears without clearing her view. "What you *really* want is for me to tell you you're right!"

"No, Hollis."

She tried again to get away from the Viking, zigging and zagging forward, but he was proving as stubborn as Norsemen were reputed to be. No matter her direction or her speed, she couldn't get past him.

"All right! I give up. I'll say it." She stopped and glared at him. "You were right. Matt was an ass before, and he's still an ass. Happy now?"

Sveyn tried to grasp her arms, but his hands passed through her flesh with a tingling shock. "Hollis, wait."

"Men don't change," she cried. "I get it!"

A chorus of urgent shouts erupted behind Sveyn pulling both of their attention. The Viking turned on one furred boot to look behind him.

The last thing Hollis saw was the hammer.

*****

She was surrounded by a pale gray fog. It didn't feel like a fog, though. It felt like nothing.

"Hollis?"

She knew that voice. She slowly turned toward it.

"Sveyn? What are you doing here?" *No, that's not the right question.* "Where am I?"

The Viking stepped forward. "You appear to be in my realm."

"Your realm? Did I die?" *That's not right.*
Sveyn didn't die.

"No, you are not dead. But at the moment you are not alive either."

"What happened to me?"

"You were hit in the chest buy one of those stone hammers.

It stopped your heart."

Hollis stared at Sveyn. "Am I going to die?"

He looked stricken. "I do not know."

A pure white light began to glow off to her side.

"What's that light?"

Sveyn stepped in front of her. "Do you see a light?"

She looked up at him. "Don't you?"

He shook his head. "I am still in your world. I see you lying on the ground with people trying to help you."

Hollis looked to her side again. The fog was growing darker, and the light brighter. "I wish you could see it. The light is so beautiful."

Sveyn tried again to block her view. "If you go the light you will die, Hollis." His voice cracked and drew her attention back to him. "And if you die, we will never see each other again."

I couldn't bear that. "How do you know?"

"I know."

Hollis watched in disbelief as tears rolled down the Viking's cheeks. She reached up to wipe them away. "I can feel you Sveyn."

He laid his hand over hers. "And I can feel you."

She looked at the approaching light again. It was warm and enticing and she longed to go it.

But she didn't want to leave Sveyn. Ever.

Why was this happening to her?

"What should I do?" she mumbled.

"Hollis, listen to me," he urged. "There is not much time."

She reluctantly refocused her attention on Sveyn. "What?"

He stared into her eyes, his gaze holding hers hostage. "I believe that the reason that I began to smell, and taste, and to be heard, and be seen, is the exact reason I manifested to you."

She struggled to ignore the pulsating brightness beside her. "Because I'm a woman?"

"Yes." He lowered his face closer to hers. "Women bring forth life, Hollis."

His words jolted through her with palpable realization. "But how? How can I bring forth *your* life?"

"I think you need to go back." Sveyn lifted his hands in front of her face. "And I think you need to take me with you."

Hollis grabbed Sveyn's hands. His long fingers wound tightly through hers as a fierce, suffocating agony convulsed her chest.

*****

Chaos. Pain. Gasping for breath.

Shouts. "Where did he come from?"

Fog clearing.

Eyes blinking.

Faces hovering over hers. "Can you hear me?"

Yes.

"Can you say something?"

"Yes." Was that really her voice?

Faces moving away from her and to her side.

Bellows of pain like she had never heard before. But they weren't coming from her.

Hollis turned her head toward the horrific sounds.

A bleeding Viking was writhing on the ground beside her.

An excerpt from:

A Modern

VIKING

Sveyn & Hollis: Book Three

A Paranormal
Romantic Suspense Trilogy
in The Hansen Series

Chapter One

Saturday
January 9

First time in Sveyn's head.

Absolute agony with touch. Readjusting to the physical world.

Blood work is odd. No vaccinations. No documentation.

Hollis is asked if she knows him… Awkward answers.

Says his mother was a gypsy, does not know his father.

How does someone become "real"?

THE HANSEN FAMILY TREE

Sveyn Hansen* (b. 1035 ~ Arendal, Norway)

***

Rydar Hansen (b. 1324 ~ Arendal, Norway)
Grier MacInnes (b. 1328 ~ Durness, Scotland)

Eryndal Bell Hansen (b. 1327 ~ Bedford, England)
Andrew Drummond (b. 1325 ~ Falkirk, Scotland)

***

Jakob Petter Hansen (b. 1485 ~ Arendal, Norway)
Avery Galaviz de Mendoza (b. 1483 ~ Madrid, Spain)

***

Brander Hansen (b. 1689 ~ Arendal, Norway)
Regin Kildahl (b. 1693 ~ Hamar, Norway)

***

Martin Hansen (b. 1721 ~ Arendal, Norway)
Dagne Sivertsen (b. 1725 ~ Ljan, Norway)

Reidar Hansen (b. 1750 ~ Boston, Massachusetts)
Kristen Sven (b. 1754 ~ Philadelphia, Pennsylvania)

Nicolas Hansen (b. 1787 ~ Cheltenham, Missouri Territory)
Siobhan Sydney Bell (b. 1789 ~ Shelbyville, Kentucky)

Stefan Hansen (b. 1813 ~ Cheltenham, Missouri)
Kirsten Hansen (b. 1820 ~ Cheltenham, Missouri)
Leif Fredericksen Hansen (b. 1809 ~ Christiania, Norway)

***

*Hollis McKenna Hansen (b. Sparta, Wisconsin)

Kris Tualla is a dynamic, award-winning, and internationally published author of historical romance and suspense. She started in 2006 with nothing but a nugget of a character in mind, and has created a dynasty with The Hansen Series, and its spin-off, The Discreet Gentleman Series. Find out more at: www.KrisTualla.com

Kris is an active PAN member of Romance Writers of America, the Historical Novel Society, and Sisters in Crime, and was invited to be a guest instructor at the Piper Writing Center at Arizona State University. An enthusiastic speaker and teacher, Kris co-created **The Dreams Convention**—combining Arizona's only romance reader event: ArizonaDreaminEvent.com and its author-focused companions: BuildintheDream.com and Realizing Your Dreams.

*"In the Historical Romance genre, there have been countless kilted warrior stories told. I say it's time for a new breed of heroes. Come along with me and find out why: **Norway IS the new Scotland!**"*

Proof

Made in the USA
Charleston, SC
22 October 2015